Morgana, My Queen

and other stories

By Fleur Blüm

This is for everyone who has ever had dreams that went horribly astray. I hope you sleep better.

Reader discretion is advised. This book contains content not suitable for children.

It also contains content that may be distressing for some readers, including explicit sex scenes, coercive control, discussion of self-harm, supernatural themes, and violence.

Fleur Blüm is a Melbourne-based writer, performer and musician.

Her blog can be found at https://fleurblum.com/blog

Also by Fleur Blüm
Novels:
Sophie's Path: A choose your own romance adventure
Discovering the Franklins
My Mother's Secret
The Sins of the Father: a Barrett Women novel
The Mother's Fault: a Barrett Women novel
Singular Focus
Singular Purpose

Poetry Collections:
My Body. No Apology
Consider the Watchmaker
Smells Like Teen Angst

First edition 2024

Copyright © 2024 Fleur Blüm
ISBN: 978-0-6483654-7-1

Editor: Annie Seaton
Cover Design: Get Covers

Published by Fleur Blüm, Melbourne, Australia

Contents

Morgana, My Queen

1.

'What time do you call this?' my boss Eli says.

'Uh…' I stutter in reply. I work in advertising, it's not very interesting but there are some great parties. I arrived at the beer garden a little late but given it wasn't my account I thought no one would notice.

'I'm kidding, you're only here for the free booze anyway, right?' Eli thumps my shoulder playfully. 'This is Brad's show.'

'Right.' I laugh, I'd been sure I was busted. The client is launching a new small-batch beer brand, and everyone in the agency was invited, including people like me who deal with the fruit and veg accounts. I almost always show up to a party with a tab.

The beer garden is in St Kilda Road, close to the city, where all the fancy corporates are—the ones who don't have budget for actual Melbourne CBD offices. It's not bad though; there's a bit of greenery and the Botanical Gardens aren't far if I want to go for a run at lunchtime.

The venue has arranged beer barrels on their ends, I assume empty, as tables, and bar stools around them, one long table near the kitchen is half-covered with nibbles and *amuse-bouches*, and roaming wait staff are carrying trays as well. The other half of the long table is the bar; cans of the new boutique beer sit in enormous steel tubs on beds of ice. I nod to a couple of colleagues as I make my way to the food and drinks.

The beer is all a blonde IPA, not really to my taste, I prefer a fuller body, but when it's free I'll drink it. I reach for one, the waiter behind the table swoops in to grab it and opens it before handing it to me.

'Thanks,' I say. I guess they want me to drink the beer instead of stashing it for later. I swipe a couple of the spring rolls from the nibbles table and shove one in my mouth; turns out I'm starving.

'Ricky, you made it,' a voice says from behind me as a heavy hand slaps my shoulder.

'Hey, Brad.' I half-turn to look at him, knowing he'll be wearing a smug smile and the deep flush after a couple of beers. I'm right. 'I came for the freebies.'

'Of course, you did, always looking for a bargain.' He doesn't mean that as a compliment. Brad advertises his wealth all over his body—Armani suit, Cartier watch, Paul Smith shoes. He thinks anything that's not the most expensive version is crappy by definition. No doubt he's never had a savings account because he spends all his money on trinkets and status indicators. He drives a brand-new Audi; the most expensive model the company's car plan will allow.

'I'm a tightarse and proud,' I say. Not that I would describe myself as such to most people but I'd admit to being anything to avoid being lumped in the same category as Brad.

'I know you're single, so I've taken the liberty of scoping out a couple of choice fillies for you.'

I shudder at the words "choice fillies".

'My girlfriend, Steffi, brought a couple of her work colleagues.' His girlfriend is as status obsessed as he is, and works in an organic cosmetics company, we haven't met but I know because he's told me repeatedly. 'Come over and I'll introduce you.'

'Thanks, you're a good mate.' I don't mean it. Why he thinks I want to be set up with people I can't understand; as soon as he heard I'd split up with my last girlfriend he's been on a mission to get me fixed up. Maybe it's another one of his status things; girlfriends are accessories to demonstrate how good a catch you are. I dunno, but if I'm getting a warm introduction to some available women, I won't say no.

We walk towards a group of women standing by one of the barrel-tables. I recognise Steffi by her long, loosely curled strawberry-blonde hair and model-thin body; Brad had shown me photos. So many photos. She's wearing an exquisite tailored grey power-suit with towering beige stilettoes. From the red soles I gather they're Louboutins. Next to her, the other women are beautiful but appear shorter and plumper by comparison. One immediately draws my gaze from the others, medium height, slim, but curvy in all the right places, her skin is so pale it seems to glow in the twilight of the early evening. Her nails are long, pointed and a red so dark it looks black in the dim lighting. Her ash-blonde hair, natural compared to Steffi's highly coloured blonde, wafts around her head in the slight breeze like a halo. Her lips match her nails though the rest of her face seems naked of makeup. Finally, I notice her outfit; a wraparound dress in a deep forest-green crepe, professional with a hint of untouchable sexuality, her heels and stockings are black, professional and understated. Something in me wants to touch her, to see if she's real.

'Babe, you know Ricky?' Brad says to Steffi as we broke into the group.

'Of course.' She smiles, but her eyes remain cold. No doubt she thinks I'm a slob, with my pudgy cheeks, feminine hips, glasses and thinning black hair. I have nothing on Brad with his gym-rat body, chiselled jaw and thick dark brown hair. 'I'd like you to meet my girls.'

The group of women titter a little at being called her girls, I have no idea why it's funny, but if I ask nicely, I might get the story.

'This is Stacey, she's in my team,' Steffi says, pointing to the woman on her left, 'Tina, Alissa and Morgana.'

Morgana, the woman who looks like a fallen angel; the woman whose deep grey eyes have been on me since the moment I walked up and haven't even flickered to Brad. Perhaps there is a woman who doesn't like his flashy brand of masculinity after all.

Morgana, My Queen

'Delighted to meet you all,' I say, shaking each woman's hand as they are introduced. When my hand touches Morgana's I gasp, her skin is cool and smooth to the touch; more like silk than skin. She trails her nails across my palm as she withdraws her hand sending electric thrills up my arm. I try to remain cool, but my neck and cheeks heat; the curse of my family's pale skin is to flush and blotch. I bet Morgana's skin never blotches. I glance back at her, her lips curve up in a tiny smirk, and then she winks at me. A conspiracy of attraction between us, or is she mocking me?

'What do you do, Ricky?' Her voice is deep, throaty, and tinged with a musical quality.

'I work with Brad, advertising, but nothing like this. He's good with the big accounts.'

'Does he get all the global brands? The soulless corporations?' Her voice drops as though she wants only me to hear.

I smile and lean closer. 'I would never say that … but I work with smaller, more grassroots organisations.'

'I see.' She sips the glass of white wine in her hand and the smile on her face broadens. I can see she isn't like Steffi or the other women from her agency. It's hard to pinpoint Morgana's age—I wouldn't have been surprised if she was twenty-five or forty-five—but her eyes speak of experience, she's seen some stuff. Glancing at my beer, she looks back at me.

'Do you need a refill?' she asks. Her glass is nearly empty, and I follow her gaze to the drinks' table.

'I'd love to.' My beer is still mostly full, but if Morgana wants to get away from the group, with me, I'm not going to turn that down. I have no chance with her, but I'm going to soak up every moment. She slips her hand into my elbow and spins me away from the group.

'What would you like?' I ask as we approach the drinks table.

'I don't think they have what I want on the menu.'

'I'm happy to ask, what are you after?'

She smiles, a slow unfolding of a grin. 'I would love to go someplace more intimate, where we can … talk.' She winks at me.

I'm silent. It sounds like a proposition, but she couldn't mean it the way it came out. This goddess, a perfect, petite beauty couldn't seriously be asking me to sleep with her.

'I'm sorry I must have misunderstood, I thought you found me attractive,' she says, looking away, her pale skin turning pink.

'No, no. It's not that.' I can't seem to speak properly. 'I thought you were, uh, making an indecent proposal but I thought I must have heard wrong.'

She raises her eyes, those deep grey pools which seem black in the low light of the beer garden. 'You weren't wrong.'

My throat grows hotter, I reach up to loosen my tie and pop open my top button.

'Oh,' is all I manage to say.

'Want to come somewhere else with me?'

I nod. This is like something in a dream, or a porno film. Gorgeous women don't ask me to take them away, it was some sort of joke, surely.

'Did Brad put you up to this?'

'Why would you ask that?'

'I … you're very beautiful and I'm, well, nothing special. I'm surprised, obviously ecstatic, but I never expected my night to go this way.'

'You're too hard on yourself, Ricky. I think you're hot, and I would like to explore that. Will you join me?'

'Yes, I'd love to.'

She nods, putting her empty wine glass on the drinks table. 'Finish your drink, and I'll get us a taxi.'

*

Sitting beside her in the taxi I can't catch my breath, it seems surreal. My cock hardened in my pants as soon as she took my hand to pull me behind her, now it's straining, and I have to sit awkwardly cross-legged in the back of the cab so she won't see.

I try to keep my eyes on the road in front of us, checking the driver was going the right way to my place, but a little way out from the beer garden Morgana's hand slides over the leather seats and spiders its way onto my thigh. I shudder involuntarily.

'Do you want me to stop?' she whispers.

'No.'

Her hand is cool resting on my heated thigh. Slowly, she runs her hand up towards my groin. I should stop her. We're in a cab, the driver can see me, but somehow, I don't say anything. When her hand finds my engorged, throbbing cock she giggles softly.

'You're a very bad boy.' Her breath is hot against my neck as she leans into me.

'Mm…hmm.' I catch sight of a building slipping past outside, a noticeable little house on the corner near my building. 'It's up here,' I say to the driver, my voice high pitched and strangled.

'This do?' the driver asks. Morgana withdraws her hand.

'Yes, thanks.' I fish my wallet out of my back pocket, uncrossing my legs temporarily and my hard-on creates a tent in the front of my pants. I hope he doesn't see. I thrust a handful of cash into his hand and exit the taxi as gracefully as I can, adjusting myself to make my arousal less obvious to passersby.

'Where to, handsome?' Morgana asks.

'Follow me,' I say, putting out my elbow as though to escort her. I don't know why; it seems like a good idea. I don't know how her hands are still cold when my whole body is hot with desire for her.

My apartment is a modest affair; one-bedroom, small kitchen and dining area, and ensuite bathroom. Clean, perhaps minimalist would be a good descriptor. At least I don't have to worry about my guest seeing a mess.

'Your home is very neat,' she says.

'Thank you. I don't have much in the way of decoration, I've never had the time to get it looking homey.'

'I like it. Simple, elegant, like you.'

'Don't tease.'

'I'm not.' Her eyes dance with an emotion I can't quite make out, perhaps amusement or something else.

'So, uh … can I offer you a drink? Maybe a tea?'

Instead of answering, Morgana presses her body against mine, her arms reaching around under my suit jacket, and kisses me. Her lips are as cool as her hands, but she smells intoxicating, lavender maybe, and cinnamon. My senses are overwhelmed, the hard-on I've been trying to tame returns with full force; there's no way she can't feel it against her.

Morgana pushes my jacket off my shoulders and discards it, then does the same with my tie. I have no idea how to get into her dress, it looks like it ties at the waist but I'd been tricked before by dresses that were faux wraps. I run my hands up her back and feel a zipper, I pulled it down and put my hands on the bare skin of her shoulders. She's hypnotic.

She pushes me away, and the smile on my face slips. Then she glides the shoulders of her dress off, and lets it fall to the floor. She's wearing stockings and suspenders and no other undergarments. Plain black stockings turn into erotic enticements in a moment. I lean forward to touch her and she takes a teasing step back.

'Where is the bedroom?'

I point behind her; she takes my hand and leads me to the bed. She pulls open the buttons on my shirt roughly, a brief worry that the buttons will pop off floats across my mind but I'm drawn back to her goddess-like body standing almost nude in front of me.

I lean down to kiss her again, she half turns away, before pushing me back onto the bed. In moments my pants and boxers are pulled down and she's straddling me, her body rubbing against mine, I'm sure she's going to slide onto me.

'Don't we need a condom?'

She put her hand over my mouth. 'I'm clean, I know you are, there's no need.' She kisses me hard, sinks onto my cock, and my mind is addled. Any thought that isn't her pale, flawless body next to mine, on mine, around mine, is gone.

*

I don't recall the exact sequence of events, but what I do remember is the best sex I've ever had. Totally enthralled by her, it's as though her cunt is hypnotic, and if it is then I'm not complaining. She had her way with me, used my body as her pleasure toy until she was spent, three orgasms at least, and then she let me come. I don't think I've ever had that much pressure, or that strong a release. I saw stars and went deaf for a moment.

'Thanks,' she says, stroking my chest with her long, blood-red nails. Every now and again she presses a little too hard, and I consider telling her to stop, but she always backs off and I stayed silent.

'What happens now?'

'Do we have to talk about that?' She pulls away.

'Sorry. I mean, do you need to shower? Should I get you something to sleep in, or will you head off?'

She laughs, the sound is like bells ringing and my mind wanders back to the feeling of being consumed by her. 'I don't sleep well in other people's beds, but I'll stay for a little longer.'

I only met Morgana that evening, and already the thought of her being away from me is more than I can bear. I want to weep at the thought of not having her cool, lithe body pressed against mine. I had tasted her, and I was intoxicated, but I can't say so aloud. It's too weird, too needy. 'Okay.'

I must have fallen asleep because I wake up in the grey early morning light alone. The space next to me that had been filled by her last night is empty. How could she have gone without saying goodbye?

The floor next to the bed where her dress had fallen was back to boring beige carpet. Her sensible black heels were not in the doorway where she had kicked them off. I get out of bed, naked still and covered in the fluids we'd generated the last night and walk into the kitchen. There's no evidence of her anywhere. My throat tightens, I can't swallow. I want to cry but no tears come.

Then I see the tiny piece of paper pinned to the fridge with a magnet advertising a local plumber.

'I had a nice time. Call me, Morgana.' She had left her number. The despair building at her absence is replaced with elation that she wants to see me again. I put out my hand and stroke the note. Her handwriting is spidery, old fashioned. She wants to see me again. I need her too.

I wait until that evening to text her. Nothing exciting: **Hi, it's Ricky. Thanks for last night. I hope you got home okay. Did you have a good day?**

I put my phone down and try not to hover over it until she replies. No doubt she's busy with any number of things. As I'm considering what she would be doing right now I realise I know almost nothing about her, except for her job, of which I know the barest essentials.

What does Morgana do for fun? To relax? To keep her body in such amazing shape. I sit on the couch daydreaming about her life, colouring in details about her house, her pets—in my mind she had two cats, one cream, one tabby. Her decorative style would be as exquisite as her taste in clothing; deep green, maroon, amethyst, sapphire blue. Perhaps she has velvet curtains.

*

After that first night, Morgana and I see each other a lot. For the first few weeks she visits me and we fuck like we did the first time, without many words. After a month or so, she invites me to her place, it seems like a new world of opportunities opening up. Since we'd started dating, or whatever this was, we hadn't had "The Talk". I had tried to eat better and do more exercise. Not that it's hard, I did exactly none before I met her. My body started to feel trimmer and more deserving of her attention with each week that went by, though if she wanted to see me and I had scheduled a workout or walk I would drop everything to be available.

I drive to her apartment in a converted mansion in Elsternwick, it oozes wealth and sophistication. If she rents, she must be earning more than I do to live there, and if she's bought it, her salary must have been at least three times mine.

I buzz her doorbell.

'Hello?' her deep husky voice sounds tinny through the tiny speaker.

'It's me.'

'Come up to the second floor.' The door crackles and beeps before a snick tells me it's open. Even the building foyer is lush; Italian marble flooring, greys and browns flecked with gold, flocked bronze-coloured wallpaper, and the staircase straight in front of me is carpeted in deep burgundy plush, complementing the mahogany bannisters. I can't see a lift, so I walk up, the stairs only creak a couple of times, and find her smiling down at me from the top of the stairs.

'Thanks for coming,' she says, wrapping her arms around my shoulders and planting a kiss on my lips.

'Of course. It's gorgeous, just like you.'

'Stop it,' she says batting my chest. 'Wait till you see inside.'

My visions of her apartment hadn't done it any justice; the colour scheme is accurate, but the quality and curation of the elements surpasses anything I could have imagined. The entryway is all burgundy, the same tones as the carpet outside, further into the apartment the living room is all forest-green—more flocked wallpaper, the couch, the armchair—the coffee table is dark walnut, the dining table and chairs match them.

'My god, it's…' I struggle with the right words, 'amazing.'

'I'm glad you like it. I've been able to perfect it over the years, a piece added here or there to make the effect pop.' Her grin belies her pride. I wonder how long she's been there, but it wasn't the time to ask.

'Can I offer you a drink? A beer maybe, or a cup of tea?' she continues.

'I'll have whatever you're having, I don't want you to go out of your way.' I'm still reeling taking in her home. She walks into the kitchen, it's whiter than the rest of the house, at least what I'd seen so far, and has a little bit of the farmhouse aesthetic. It isn't exactly in keeping with the drama of the other rooms, but perhaps even Morgana doesn't want to cook in a gothic castle.

We have our tea in the lounge on the enormous, lush velvet couch. I try to keep my eyes on her, she looks resplendent as always, but there are so many fascinating things to look at around the room. On one wall she has snake skeletons, of various sizes, in dark wood frames, set behind glass. The effect is somehow not as creepy as taxidermy, yet also creepier.

'Those are interesting,' I say, pointing to the bones.

'Ah, yes, my babies.' She flicks her eyes to the cases and then back to me. 'What I mean to say, is those are some pets I've had over the years, and to honour their memory I had them mounted. I was never a fan of stuffed animals, especially not reptiles, they don't hold up well, but I couldn't let them go either.'

I nod. I've never had a pet, unless you count the guinea pigs when I was eight. 'It's nice you can remember them.'

I don't mean it, they're giving me the willies, but Morgana is a particular sort of woman, and if that means she has dead snakes on her walls, then so be it. I can push down my squeamishness in favour of spending time with her. The sex alone more than makes up for it.

There are five or six skeletons on the wall, I wondered how young she must have been when she started to have so many past pets. Though I have no idea how long snakes live, or how hard they might be to keep alive.

'Do you have any pets now?' I ask.

'Yes, I always have at least one snake living with me. I also keep a few mice, to feed him.'

I swallow my tea with a gulp, reminding myself that it isn't that unusual. The fact I'd never met a herpetologist is not her fault and highlights the sheltered existence I live.

The apartment is very quiet, except for the ticking of a large mantel clock sitting on a shelf above the faux fireplace, something that had been updated to a gas fire that looks like burning wood. A little tacky compared to the rest of the apartment, but perhaps having a real fire is against the body corporate rules and would have needed much more maintenance.

'How's work?' I ask, at a loss for anything more interesting to say.

'It's going well. The usual array of stupid clients who insist on having things their way even if it means they won't get the optimal outcome.'

'Yeah, clients are the worst part of any job.' I finish my tea and want to kiss her. Even after weeks together I'm shy to initiate physical contact, as though she's too reified to touch. I stare at her lips, they're a deep burgundy, a little less intense on the inner lip, closer to her mouth, that wet, warm, welcoming hole I want to touch so badly. Morgana leans forward, her breath hot and sweet.

'Do you want me?'

'Always.' It come out like a sigh. She cups my cheek, her long fingers reach up into my thinning hair, and pulls me to her. The first moment our lips touch is like an electric shock. It's always like this, and it surprises me every time. I can't think about anything except her; wanting to be closer to her, skin against skin, wanting her to consume me.

After a while we move to the bedroom, my cock hard inside my pants, curving painfully in the fabric cage, but I don't move it. There's a deliciousness in that pain. Her bedroom is stunning, I almost forget about my physical desire as I try to take in the dark beauty around her— ebony four-poster bed, matching vanity with three mirrors, a deep purple Queen Anne armchair. The walls are papered in flocked dark grey damask wallpaper, I stumble forward, my arm out as though to touch it, my mind somehow blank, and Morgana grabs my hand, dragging my mind back to her body, and the pressure in my pants.

The spell, or whatever has come over me, breaks and I can't wait to push her back onto the high, plush bed covers and take her. She walks backwards to the bed, pulling me between her legs, I push up the folds of her skirt and find she's wearing stockings and suspenders, no underwear, maybe she never wears underwear, I think absently. My cock pulses, she wraps her legs around me, leans back on the bed and sighs. It's an invitation I don't need to be given twice, I unzip my trousers, push down my boxers and press into her.

It doesn't last long, she can make me orgasm whenever she likes, and this time she wants quick and dirty. Who am I to suggest otherwise? As I lie beside her, mostly clothed and only partially on the bed, she strokes my temples.

'You're a very good lover, you know. I'm sure you could have anyone you wanted, but I'm so glad you want me,' she says.

'You say that to all the boys.' I joke, uncomfortable with the idea that a woman as gorgeous and captivating and experienced as she thinks I'm good in bed.

'I mean it. I don't always feel such a deep, easy connection.'

I don't say anything, what can I say that won't sound flippant?

'You need to get used to accepting compliments,' she says. Morgana pushes down her skirts, arranging herself as though I haven't just spilt my seed inside her, and heads to the bathroom. I'm suddenly aware how sticky I am, letting my limp dick lie on her beautiful bedspread, probably leaving a little bit of cum with it. My cheeks feel hot, and shame washes over me.

What a disgusting creature I am. I come into her home, this delicately curated world, and spend the whole time thinking about what it would feel like to fuck her. With the clarity of post-sex shame, I want to crawl away and never return.

'Do you want to get something to eat?' Morgana asks from the bathroom doorway.

'Sure.' I still don't know why she wants to be there with me, but I guess I have to trust her judgement. 'Do you know anywhere good?'

Morgana takes me out to a quaint little Italian place around the corner. We walk there, the cool evening air, Morgana's hand slips into my elbow, and her calm voice telling me about some drama with one of her friends put out the fire of shame inside me.

Theres something about sex with her that makes me spin out in my head, as though all the bad thoughts I ever had were happening all at once. But that's probably my insecurity at being with such an awesome person. And it always wears off.

2.

With all my working out, and the athletic sex Morgana usually wants, I have more energy, but the day after seeing her I always feel like I'd been out clubbing all night with no sleep or something. It's like I have a hangover from her, but that's stupid, we don't drink that much. More likely, I spend a lot of nervous energy around her because she was so much cooler than me. If we lived together, it would go away, no doubt it's an unfamiliarity effect. We don't talk much on the phone, and she only texts a couple of times a day. She's old fashioned like that, wanting to spend time with me in person, and not through a device, she says.

She wants to go to a forest the following weekend, I don't know any good forests in Melbourne but she says she knows a good spot in the Dandenongs, Sherbrooke Forest. The name reminds me of Robin Hood and his merry men but that's Sherwood. Come to think of it, Morgana's name reminds me of some old English legend, but I can't remember which one.

So, I pick her up in my car, she doesn't like to drive, and we go up to the forest together. She packed a lot of crap for what's supposed to be a picnic and a short hike, but I know better than to question it.

Hell, I might be in for a little surprise if I'm lucky.

We park in a little square of asphalt off a winding road part-way up a small mountain. I guess it could be called a carpark, though there are no other vehicles, and it only looked big enough for four cars if they all squish together.

'Grab the stuff, would you baby?' Morgana says.

'Of course.' I don't want to carry all that crap up a hiking trail. I sigh and sling the giant backpack on. Morgana takes a folded blanket and an awkward-looking box.

The backpack is really heavy and clanks like metal-on-metal. The path is steep, slippery and muddy after the recent rain.

'Are we going far?' I ask, trying to keep the whine out of my voice. She's hot and I like walking behind her, but I'm starting to get tired after twenty minutes or so of schlepping up the hill.

'Nearly there. The clearing is beautiful, I promise it's worth it.' She doesn't turn around. I sigh again and search deep for a well of athleticism I don't believe I have. I feel tired and hungover, kind of like I do when I leave Morgana's place after a visit but we've only been together for a few hours. Maybe I'm coming down with something.

The path flattens out and widens up ahead. My thighs and calves are screaming and glad for the break of level ground.

'It's just ahead.'

I pant and don't reply. We round a bend and on the left of the track is a smaller trail, as though animals use it.

'We'll go through there. It's only a dozen metres or so, just out of sight of the main trail.' Morgana turns and winks at me.

My cock twitches, and I'm aware of the tightness of my boxers in a way I wasn't before, even while the rest of my body wants to lie down and sleep.

Morgana stops dead in front of me, and I almost walk into the back of her. I don't notice at first, but we entered a circular glade. It's cool, but not uncomfortable. There's a faint sound of dripping, the occasional call of a bellbird, the air is still, humid and heavy. She puts down the weird-shaped box, and deftly unwraps the blanket, flicking it down onto the ground with ease.

'Put that down and come sit with me,' she says, patting the blanket.

I kneel on the rug, trying to keep my muddy boots off the end of it. It's green and navy tartan, very plain, with a black plastic protective layer on the bottom so we won't get too wet sitting on the damp leaf litter.

It's surprisingly soft underneath me as I arrange myself next to my gorgeous companion. She reaches out to me, stroking my cheek. I want to pull away, sure I'm all sweaty and gross.

'It's okay, you look very rugged.'

I don't feel rugged, I feel drenched and bedraggled. 'Thanks. You look amazing, as always.' My cheeks burn and my cock starts to swell with her touch, her smell in my nostrils.

'I don't usually invite people up here. This is a very special place.'

'It's beautiful.'

'I don't know if you remember, I've always felt a connection to the land. To mother earth. She feeds and protects us, she nurtures us, she takes us back when we die.'

I nod.

'This place is special to me, and to a few people I worship with.'

I frown. 'Worship?' This is new.

'I'm a witch.'

'Huh?'

'I mean that in a religious sense, I practice Wicca. We're a coven, and now that you and I starting to get serious, I want you to know about that part of me. Surely, you've noticed all the bits and pieces in my house? The snakes and the herbs?'

'I have, yeah. I thought you were going for an aesthetic, but I should have known there would be more to it than that.'

'It is partly about the look, the Victoriana shop of horrors thing is quite appealing, but those objects hold power. I have some crystals, and I've dabbled with tarot, but the thing that really works for me is nature. Being outside in beautiful places like this and communing with mother earth.'

'Right.' I'm not sure what to think; it's both a surprising confession and not surprising at all. It makes perfect sense that she would be a Wiccan. Apart from all the cool accessories, everything I've read about it in passing suggests women are more revered, sacred feminine and female sexuality are given special focus, and for someone like Morgana, the restrictions and prudishness of Christianity make no sense.

'Is that all you have to say?'

'I … what am I doing here though?'

'I wanted you to do a ritual with me. It's something that we do on the equinox, a few ingredients, a few special words, and then we consummate the ceremony and give our sexual energy into the spell.'

'Right,' I say again. 'What is the spell for?'

'It's a prosperity thing, that we have a good winter, that the spring brings new growth, good health, that our relationship grows deeper and stronger.'

'Sounds okay.' I hear myself agree without really meaning to. It sounds fine but I don't know what she wants to do, although it would end in sex, which is alright with me.

The awkward shaped box folds out into a small wooden table, the top carved with symbols—the pentagram with crescent moons on two sides, a sort of three-pointed curvy star, three swirls coming from a central point, one circular image that looks like a maze, and many other patterns, curves, points and stars. From the backpack, she pulls out two short, stumpy metal candle holders, and places a candle on each, one white, one black, both with carved images on them like the table. It must be a portable altar. She also has a range of herbs and dried bits of plant, some animal bones and teeth, a few red ribbons, and a long, shiny, double-edged knife.

She sets up the altar without saying anything, I watch her quietly. Part of me thinks she might forget I'm there and I could join in the sex part. My tummy bubbles with anxiety about doing a magic spell, I was raised in a Catholic household and despite calling myself an atheist I still believe in hell.

'Come kneel here next to me.' Morgana points to a space on the rug by her lefthand side. I do as I'm told. She grabs my hand and holds it up, her other hand turned toward the sky.

'I call upon my ancestors, the women who have come before me, to guide and protect me in this work.' Morgana takes some salt from a small bowl on the tabletop and scatters some at four points forming a circle around us.

'I call upon the spirits of the north, keeper of the earth, watch over us. I call upon the spirits of the east, guardians of the air, watch over us. I call upon the spirits of the south, tenders of the fire, watch over us. I call upon the spirits of the west, masters of the water, watch over us. Spirits, and ancestors, allow us to prosper, give us your power.'

Morgana, My Queen

She lights the two candles, and repeats the words over them, her voice low and husky. Then she picks up the long dagger and holds it up.

'We offer you our devotion, and we beg you will bestow your gifts upon us. We offer you this blood—' Morgana runs the dagger across her arm, and mine where it is beside hers. It's so sharp I barely feel anything until the hot blood starts to well up through the cut. 'This blood to feed and maintain you, that you will show us favour in the coming year.'

I try to pull my hand away, but Morgana holds me firm. I feel as though I can't move, paralysed, or somehow outside of my body.

Into the small bowl which holds the salt, she starts to add the other items, herbs, a couple of teeth, and blood from our arms. The wound is bleeding slowly, perhaps it's not as deep as I first feared.

She wraps one of the red ribbons around our arms, binding them together, over the cut, stemming the bleeding a little. She drops the other ribbon into the metal bowl and sets the contents alight with the black candle.

'I pray to you, ancestors, keepers of the knowledge and power, to you, the spirits of the north, east, south, and west, give to us what we need. Give to us what we deserve.'

Thin grey smoke rises from the bowl, some of the herbs burn with a blueish flame, but maybe I'm imagining it. In another moment it's over, the flame dies out.

'Thank you, Ancestors, I release you from my working.' She blows out the black candle.

'Thank you, spirits of the north, east, south and west, I release you from my working.' Morgana blows out the white candle, and a shiver of coldness runs all the way down my spine. The sensation of not being able to move is lifted, and I slump back onto the rug, my butt hitting the ground with a thud and jolting me. Of course, my arm is still tied to Morgana's and she's pulled around and back with me.

'Are you okay?' she asks, her eyes turning to me full of concern.

'I don't know. I feel a bit weird.'

'That's natural. I used to feel very strange after rituals. I guess I'm used to it now. Lie back, get into a more comfortable position.' She unties the ribbon and I lie back on the rug. The ground feels very cold and hard underneath me. I let my eyes drift closed, though I can hear Morgana packing things away.

'Ricky?'

I open my eyes a slit, and Morgana had reached up under her skirt.

'We're not done yet.' There is a wicked gleam in her eyes, and through my exhaustion I rally. I know she is naked under her skirts. Ready, waiting, asking to be taken. The stirring in my groin that all but disappeared was back, even stronger than before. Morgana kneels over me, straddling, her hot groin hovering above mine. I try to move my hands to help her but they seem to be very sluggish.

'Let me,' she says, reaching down to my trousers, unbuckling and unzipping me. My cock, now free, stands ready for action.

It was unlike any sex we'd had before. I'm delirious, as though it's a dream and not real life. I float through the sensations, lying like a starfish beneath my gorgeous Wiccan Goddess, as she rides me and takes from me what she wants. After several of her own orgasms, my orgasm washes over me, but dulled and far away like the rest of the experience.

Morgana slides down beside me, her leg drapes over my still exposed groin. It takes several minutes for my brain to return enough that I remember to zip up my trousers. Not that anyone is going to find us, here deep in the wilderness but I'm not one for exhibitionism.

I close my eyes for a moment, Morgana moves from her place beside me and there is a rush of cold where her body used to be.

'Here, this will help.' She holds out an enamel covered mug, with steam rising from it. 'Tea.'

I sit up. 'Thank you.' I take it, almost dropping it when my fingers touched the scalding metal.

'I'm sorry I didn't warn you about the… blood.' Her cheeks are flushed, maybe embarrassed for not telling me.

'That's okay, I'm not sure if I would have been into it if you had, but it wasn't so bad.'

She smiles; she looks so beautiful in that moment.

I am exhausted.

'We'll rest here for a moment, there isn't long until it will start to get dark. We don't want to be on the path when that happens.'

'And we have to drive home,' I say.

'I'll drive this time. I find these rituals energising, I can't sleep for a while afterwards, but you look like you might fall asleep right here.'

She's smiling, perhaps trying to be empathetic, but it sounds patronising. I'm not a child, I certainly hope she doesn't do secret forest-blood-sex rituals with children. I sit to sip the tea, still surprisingly hot from whatever thermos she had produced after the drive up here and all the time in the ceremony. Morgana was right, the tea helps. We sit quietly, I'm not thinking of much, trying to stay upright, she looks flushed and pensive.

Once I finish my tea, Morgana was done with hers in about five minutes—apparently not bothered by the temperature—she stands and looks down at me. 'Come along then.'

I nod, heaving myself off the ground to help her. I carry the backpack down the mountain, it's still heavy and awkward, though perhaps a little lighter than on the way up. Morgana carries the altar and rug. It takes less time to get down than it did to get up, of which I am glad. I sling everything into the car, and we drive off without much conversation.

I fall asleep in the passenger seat almost immediately; Morgana shakes me awake when we arrive at her place in the dark.

'Do you want to come up and have some dinner with me? Or maybe it would be better for you to go home and get some sleep. You seem spent, poor love.' She touches my cheek, her hands hot against my skin.

'I…' My throat is dry, I swallow and start again. 'I should go home. I feel like I might be getting sick.'

'That's no good. You need to take care of yourself, I'll call you tomorrow and check in, okay?' Her hand on my thigh gives a little squeeze and she steps out of the car. I follow, waiting as she grabs the bags from the back, and give her a kiss. It's a chaste kiss, as though she's in a hurry to get away from me. I sit behind the wheel of the car for a few minutes as she walks into her building, trying to get up the energy to drive home. I've been tired before, but nothing like this. I wonder if I'll ever feel energetic again.

*

The next morning, I can't get out of bed, my limbs are heavy, and everything hurts. I wonder if it could be that new flu going around but I don't know anyone who has been sick. Morgana seems to have avoided it, she's perkier than ever when she calls me on Monday evening to check on me. I don't stay on the line long, I'm delirious in my sickness, imagining shadows hanging on the ceiling, sucking me dry. *I must have a fever*, I tell myself.

Morgana calls to check on me each evening, usually only a few minutes, but I'm glad to know someone cares about me. I order some groceries to be delivered from one of the food delivery apps. At least that way I don't risk giving anyone in the supermarket whatever I have. The boss is concerned at first but seems to forget about me towards the end of the week.

The next Monday when I show up for work, Brad seems surprised to see me.

'Ricky, I thought you'd died.' He grins.

'No, I'm still here.' I sniffle, still a little unwell, but determined to go into the office. Plus, I'm almost out of sick leave.

'We missed you.' The grin plastered on his dumb face suggests the exact opposite is true, but I'm not going to argue.

'I'm back, so you need not worry.'

He nods, slaps me hard on the shoulder and walks off. One pleasant side effect of being more physically fit was that those slaps no longer put me off balance, but they still bloody hurt. I frown at Brad's retreating back, wishing I was still infectious so he could have a few days flat on his back for a change. I shake my head, not a charitable thought I admit, but he's such a snake, he could do with taking down a peg.

Morgana is away this weekend, up in Sydney for a Wiccan conference or something, so it will be nearly three weeks before I see her again. My strength has almost totally returned and all I can think about is her white, creamy skin, her lush lips, and the feel of her body against mine. She's like a drug I can't quit, even when the come down is so harsh.

I don't know what to do with myself this weekend. I have been so consumed with spending time with Morgana my other friends have been neglected.

'Come out for a drink with us, Ricky,' Brad calls to me on his way past my desk on Friday afternoon.

'I dunno…'

'You never come out with us anymore. We used to have fun, didn't we?'

'Yeah.' I've had some good times out with Brad, though he often uses me as a comparison so he could pick up women. On the other hand, I was thinner and more muscular nowadays, so maybe it wouldn't be such a clear pick.

'Are you still seeing that hottie, Megan, was it?'

'Morgana. And yes, I'm still seeing her.' I can't betray her with someone else, even if I manage to attract some interest, but it can't hurt to flirt, drink, and have a good time. 'Alright, I can come out for a while.'

'Fuckin' oath.' Brad beams and slaps me hard on the shoulder again. I wish he wouldn't do that; no doubt telling him to stop would make it more of a game. Bullies use any perceived weakness against you.

'Anyone else coming?' I ask, hoping there would be at least one other person to keep Brad in check.

'I'm still making the rounds. Maybe Eli. I'll see who I can rustle up.' Brad swaggers off in the direction of the boss's office. Eli and Brad are the same kind of person, I heard one of the women in Finance refer to them as *Chads*, and while I didn't know exactly what it means, it seems fitting. The woman's scorn was clear. Strutting around the office if they close a deal or have good news, and I avoid asking them what had happened in those instances, lest I hear about the deal in excruciating detail. If I keep my head down, and do my work, they usually ignore me.

Technically, Brad reports to Eli, as the head of the department, but they're more like mates than boss and employee. It probably doesn't help they go out most Fridays and get shit-faced together, bonding in their drinking and womanising.

'Eli's in,' Brad says in a stage whisper as he walks back past me about twenty minutes later. With the two of them, I might appear like a sane option to any woman interested in conversation over chest-beating and other masculine mating displays.

The spreadsheet in front of me needs to be completed by the end of the day, but with my mind filled with thoughts of Morgana, and it being late Friday, it may as well have been in another language. My concentration has been terrible since the trip to the forest, and the following flu, and I wonder if Eli has noticed. If he says anything I'll tell him I must be still a little sick, but part of me is itching to get out of this job, to what I don't know, but like missing Morgana, this restlessness is increasing over time.

If she were a texter, I would send her a message, but I know she barely checks it.

At five minutes to five, my desk phone rings. 'Ricky speaking.'

'Hello, lover,' Morgana's deep, throaty, mezzo soprano voice purrs down the line.

'Morgana?' I'm surprised, she's never called me at work. 'What's wrong?'

'Nothing, I wanted to hear your voice. I've arrived at my hotel, and something told me I needed to speak to you. Right now.'

I swallow. All the thoughts I had of flirting and getting tipsy suddenly seem like betrayal. 'I'm glad you called,' I lie.

'Are you doing anything fun this weekend without me?'

'Brad wants me to go out for a drink, but I'll only stay an hour or so.'

'That sounds good. Don't do anything I wouldn't do,' she says. The words are light, but her tone loses all the laughter it had held.

'Of course. You know I'm devoted to you. I'll be on my best behaviour.'

'I know you will. I hope you remember the ritual we did; we're tied together now, the equinox is a powerful time for working spells, and I didn't take you there lightly.'

'I know.'

'I didn't want to go into this weekend without touching base. I know you want me to be more communicative when we're not together, and despite being an old fogy about some things, I should make an effort to meet your needs. A relationship needs compromise on both sides.'

'You're right. I'll stay home this weekend. Maybe go visit Mum for a coffee or something.'

'That sounds like a nice idea. You're a good man, Ricky. I don't know what I did to deserve someone like you in my life.'

My stomach does a flip. She's beautiful and out of my league—and I had been considering flirting with other women. If I wasn't in the office, I might have slapped myself. What do I say to that? 'You're amazing.'

'I've gotta go, I love you.' Her voice is like honey, soothing some of my itching need to see her.

'I love you too,' I say in a low voice, not wanting anyone to overhear. I hang up and sigh. My cock is pushing against my zipper again, stupid thing is ready for action at just the sound of her voice. Ignoring the sensation, I turned back to my screen and finish off a couple of last-minute things before logging off.

'Pub?' Brad's head pops up over the partition, surprising me.

'Jeez, way to sneak up on a guy. Yeah, but I can only stay for a bit.'

'You got a hot date to run off to, Ricky?' His mouth turns down at the corners as though he doesn't believe it.

'Something like that.'

Brad's eyebrows climb up. 'Really? Good for you. We're leaving in a minute.'

'Yep, be right there.'

Across the road in the beer garden, it's much less convivial than the summer months. The venue has tall gas space heaters spread around but it's still chilly. I shove my hands into my armpits and put my ice-cold beer on the top of a beer barrel.

'So, you hooked up with Morgana?' Brad returns from the bar holding a whisky cocktail.

'Um, yeah, I've seen her a few times.' I don't want to lie, but I also want to keep her to myself.

'You dog. I tried to get a date with her once, and she shot me down in flames. What the fuck did you do to get her attention?' Brad asks.

'Nothing really. I must be more her type.'

'She probably doesn't like show-boats like you, Tanner,' Eli says, giving Brad a nudge with his elbow. It isn't something I would ever have the guts to say to him, but he had a point. Brad has been described as all sizzle and no steak. A peacock, parading around, only interested in what you can do to make him look good. No doubt he's a selfish lover, only interested in getting his jollies and not willing to experiment or explore. A woman like Morgana, with her experience, desires, and refinement would get sick of him in short order. If she didn't eat him alive; I stifle a grin at the idea.

Brad slams back his drink and glares at Eli and I, not keen on being the butt of the joke.

'Ricky has nerd charms some women find irresistible. Those bookish types are catnip to the right woman, eh? Eh?' Eli is now nudging me. I take half a step away.

'I couldn't possibly comment, except to say she has been back for more than one date, so I must be doing something right.' As soon as it leaves my mouth, I know I sound far too cocky. What Morgana and I do outside of work is between us and should not be the topic of juvenile measuring contests, but if it is, I'm not going to let them off without fighting back a little.

I take a long pull from my beer, hoping to avoid dropping any further comments. Brad's cheeks are pinker than usual, and he looks away into the crowd. After a moment to collect himself, he turns back to us and tells me about a client he recently wooed over from a competitor. He really does relish being the centre of attention and since I'm no longer the topic, I'm happy to let his words roll over me as though they're waves on a beach. If I loosen my concentration his voice is almost soothing, though the nasal twang stops me entering a completely meditative state. Eli interjects every so often with his own proud moments, and I get away with muttering appreciative comments ever so often.

My mind is filled with Morgana. Does she know I'd been thinking about seeing her less often? Or is her desire to be more of what I need simply the natural progression of our relationship? And what's causing my tiredness? It's getting worse and seems to always be when I spend time with her. Yes, we spend a lot of time making love, and not much time sleeping, but the fatigue is deeper than that. I tell myself I'll make an appointment to see the doctor, perhaps tomorrow, if I can find a Saturday appointment. Maybe I have low iron or sleep apnoea. I hope it's the first—wearing one of those face masks at night would definitely reduce my sexiness to Morgana, although perhaps we've moved beyond mere physical connection. She took me to the forest with her after all.

My beer is finished, and Brad is telling Eli a story about a client meeting he had during the week. I've heard the story and I'm sure Eli has too, but perhaps they're both too drunk to remember.

'See you on Monday,' I say, keeping my voice low, hoping to slip away without their notice.

'Are you leaving? Weak. It's Friday night drinks,' Eli says.

'I told you I could only stay for one. I've got to get on. Have a good evening.' I start to back away from the knot of people even while Brad protests. I'm not interested in hearing any more from either of them. Now I've decided to keep my eyes to myself while Morgana is away there's nothing to keep me here. They're unpleasant drunks, and while I tolerate them at work because I'm being paid to be there, this is my time.

Fleur Blüm

I walk through the chill air towards the tram stop, hunching my shoulders trying to keep off the soft drizzle falling. In the last few weeks, I've become angry, irritable. Things that used to pass me by without so much as raising a hackle, are lingering in my mind. I work my jaw to unclench my teeth and roll my shoulders back. The tension and exhaustion have been so much worse since the ritual that Morgana did. It must be a coincidence, but the gnawing feeling in my gut, and in my jaw, make me wonder if I should take more care about being pulled into her witchy activities.

3.

When I wake the next morning, I feel terrible. My throat is dry and scratchy, my eyes heavy and glued shut at the edges. I hope I'm not coming down with something else but then again, lately I've been waking up feeling terrible most days. I remember the promise I made myself to go to the doctor. Maybe there is something wrong with me and all I need is an iron infusion or quick course of antibiotics.

The clinic I regularly attend has an online booking system; I manage to find one half an hour away. I'll have to move my arse to get there.

I step into the waiting room only two minutes after my appointment is supposed to start.

'I'm here for doctor … uh, I'm Ricky Osterman, here for my appointment,' I say, the doctor's name eludes my still sleep-addled brain.

'Thanks, have a seat, you're next on Doctor Sharma's list.'

I nod and sit down in one of the clear moulded plastic seats spread around the waiting room. Most of the other patients at this time on a Saturday are children with sniffles, and I wish I'd made a different time for my consult.

'Ricky?' a young man calls me. I wave my hand and stand.

'I'm Doctor Sharma, follow me.' He's short, with dark skin and lustrous short black hair. I go with him into a nondescript consulting room and sit down. Now I have to work out how to tell him what was wrong.

'What's brought you in today, Ricky?'

I try not to wince as he used my name again. It's a pet peeve of mine when medical types use your name a lot. It probably helps their memory, or builds rapport, but it's like fingernails on a blackboard.

'I've been feeling pretty run down lately. It's hard to describe, I feel like the life is being sucked out of me.' I spread my hands in front of me, before flopping them down on my knees. I sound like an idiot.

'What does feeling run down feel like? Can you be specific?'

'I've been sick more than usual. When I sleep don't feel refreshed.'

The doctor nods and makes a note. 'Anything else?'

'I have been working out, watching my diet and losing weight but … when I get home from seeing my girlfriend, I sometimes feel like my limbs are made of lead. It's hard to move.'

'I see.' More note taking.

'Any dizziness?'

I pause. 'I don't think so.'

'Ever feel like your heart is beating in your chest but you haven't been doing anything strenuous?'

'Not really.' My heart is racing now though.

'Headaches?'

'Yeah, sometimes.'

'Anything that makes them worse?'

'They seem to be a night thing, rather than a day thing, but otherwise no.'

'And when you say you're watching what you eat, what does that mean?'

'Nothing extreme, smaller portions, less saturated fat, more vegetables.'

'You haven't gone vegetarian suddenly? Or cut out a whole group of foods?'

'No, all the same stuff, but not quite so much,' I say.

'Any hair loss?'

'No.'

'And your sex drive, is that the same or different since you noticed the run-down feeling?'

My cheeks colour a little. 'No that's … very active. I wondered if that might be contributing, I didn't used to be quite so … active.'

'I see,' he says, pausing for more notes. 'Any nausea with the sex act?'

'No.' I frown. 'I don't really think it's the sex.'

'We're just gathering information. And your sleep, is it disturbed? Do you wake a lot?'

'No, I sleep through.'

'Intense dreams?'

'Not more than usual.'

'I see. There are a few things that can cause fatigue, but your symptoms don't seem to neatly fit with anything common. I think we should take some fasting blood samples and see what the tests say. Have you eaten today?'

'I thought you might ask that, so when I got such an early appointment, I didn't have breakfast.'

'Excellent. The blood nurse is on duty this morning, if you go to the front, they will take some samples and when the results are back, we can have another chat, alright?'

'Yes, that sounds good.' I nod, it's all much as I expected. Nothing obvious, have some blood tests.

The doctor prints out some instructions for the tests, and I take them with me. I settle up with the receptionist, then sit back in the waiting room, this time on the other side but in the same hard plastic chairs.

The blood nurse, a portly older man, calls my number and not long after I'm out of there. The whole thing took a little under an hour, and I reward myself with coffee and a raspberry muffin from the café next door.

What is Morgana doing now? I think to myself as I stroll back to my car. Probably listening to some puffed up presenter talk about something witchy I wouldn't understand. She told me about the conference in some detail, but it had fallen straight out of my head.

Morgana, My Queen

Saturday is usually my day to see Morgana, so I find it hard to settle without the anticipation of a date with her. I go home, vacuum my small apartment, and do a load of laundry and it's only mid-afternoon. Time is crawling by without her. The call yesterday was an anomaly, so there's no way she'll call me twice in a weekend.

I sit on my couch, holding a cup of tea that has long since gone cold, wondering what to do with my evening. A bar or club are out of the question, far too many women there, and I don't want the temptation of looking at other women. Not that I have any hope of attracting one of course, before Morgana there had been long droughts in my relationship history. Even thinking about it makes the pit of my stomach roil with guilt. I don't think my constitution would cope, what with the fatigue and irritation I've been feeling lately.

Maybe a movie. I'd be able to get out of the house, and feel like I'm participating in society, but won't be required to interact with any hot women, and therefore can't do anything that would approach cheating. I'm sure a Freudian would have a great time poring over how much of my mind is filled with avoiding other women; a sign I'm already tempted.

I look up the local cinema on my phone and start flicking through the session times; a comic book action movie, an unnecessary reboot of a classic 80s film, and a rom com with a dog. Not inspiring. Then I see a late showing of a new horror film, the promotional poster features a blood-spattered woman, probably a slasher. Horror isn't usually my genre, but it's intriguing nonetheless, given the other films on offer. I book a ticket and put my phone down. Now I've decided what to do with my evening I feel lighter, I close my eyes, maybe I'll have a nap.

When I open my eyes again, it's fully dark outside, I'm cold, and my belly growls in hunger. I haven't eaten lunch after all those chores this morning. The clock shows a little after seven thirty, still plenty of time for the ten o'clock showing. Maybe I'll treat myself to dinner out since I have nothing in the house and no time to shop and cook anything.

The cinema is a short drive away, surrounded by restaurants and coffee shops. The pizza place is half full at eight when I arrive. Glancing at the menu as I step inside the place is on the expensive side, but then I'm not paying for Morgana this time, so I can afford to splurge. She never expects me to pay, but I always feel I should when we go on dates.

Once inside I'm seated at a table for two by the window, I watch pedestrians and cars flowing past with a detached calm. I order a spaghetti carbonara, a cheeky treat given Morgana is away and I won't feel guilty for carb-loading in front of her. It's been months since I've eaten at a restaurant alone, the feeling is oddly soothing. When I'm with Morgana, I feel like I have to be on my best behaviour, as though I'll lose her if I make one wrong move. Of course, that's nonsense, she's been by my side for a long time now and I'm sure if I do something she doesn't like she would tell me, but it's hard to control the irrational thoughts when you're with someone you love.

My meal is very slow to arrive, a full thirty-five minutes after I order it. During my wait I snack on the *grissini* on the table and have almost lost my appetite until the smell of the freshly cooked garlic reaches my nostrils as the waiter lays my plate in front of me. My stomach gurgles in anticipation and I find myself gorging on the pasta like a child. It's so good—the sort of food I might wait in line for, something to fantasise about.

I haven't fantasised about anything other than Morgana since I met her. She is all my senses want and yet now we're supposed to be the closest we've ever been I find myself thinking again and again of other things. Remembering other little pleasures, I had before her. Not that there were many, I'm a loser by most definitions, but I lost touch with the things I did for fun before.

After scoffing all the pasta, and a nice glass of chilled white wine I ordered halfway through in a pause in my gluttony, I feel satiated and sleepy. I have half an hour until the movie starts, plenty of time for a second glass of wine.

I close my eyes and listen to the conversations around me, there were fewer people now, the dinner crowd has thinned out, and the drinks crowd hasn't started to arrive. To my left a family are having drawn-out birthday celebrations—the youngest member, I guess late teens, is scrolling through his phone and ignoring the others, two older sisters, and the parents. It must be the mother's birthday, since she's getting through the red wines at a pace, and the cake is placed in front of her. She's loud and loose, telling stories about her husband when they first met. The young man seems to be trying not to listen, and the sisters are both flushed in the cheeks, perhaps with embarrassment, or excitement, though they have also had a couple of glasses of wine by this time.

'He was so handsome when we were young. I thought he was out of my league but he's still here,' the older woman said. 'And adventurous—'

'You're beautiful, as always, darling, but perhaps we could use our inside voices?' the older man interrupts her.

I smile to myself, drinking the last of my wine to cover my mouth. She's probably about to spill a sexy secret about her youth, something the kids don't need to hear, though I'm a little curious. She starts giggling and mumbles something inaudible before filling her mouth with the dark chocolate cake in front of her.

Behind me, are a younger couple on a date, though it doesn't seem to be going very well. Their conversation is stilted, unnatural and there are long pauses where neither of them say anything at all. When I'm out with Morgana she dominates the conversation, though she's always careful to make sure she asks me about my day, or week. I've never been one for idle chat and am happy to listen most of the time, especially to her; she has so many interesting things to say. Perhaps other diners have been listening to my conversations with her on our dates and wondered what she sees in me. After all our time together, I don't really know but whatever she's getting out of it, it must be worth her while.

I pay for my meal, more than I expected, but that doesn't matter, and walk over to the cinema. After all that pasta I don't need any movie snacks, but I buy a soft drink, deciding against more wine.

The cinema is quite full, common for a late session on a Saturday night. I settle into my seat, and slouch down to look up at the screen. As the film starts, the hairs on my forearms stand up in goosebumps, the soundtrack puts me on edge, or perhaps it's the pervasive whistling wind.

The story is about a man tricked by a beautiful witch into giving up his soul, then she slices his throat open to drink his blood. It isn't what I expected, instead it's a lot of walking around in the woods and not much dialogue. My eyes droop a couple of times, but the eerie wind and rustling of the trees keep bringing me back from the edge of sleep.

I leave the cinema with an uneasy sense of foreboding and vague dissatisfaction. The story seemed to have gone off the rails somewhere in the middle and the characters were all making stupid decisions. Maybe it's a Stephen King adaptation, they always have unsatisfying endings.

4.

Morgana returns from her conference on Tuesday, I don't expect to hear from her straight away though I hope for it. She'll be busy with work and everything else.

My phone rings on Wednesday evening; it's her.

'Hey, how was your trip?' I ask.

'Hello, lover. It's so nice to hear your voice.'

Warmth starts in my belly and spreads around my body at the sound of her husky tones, sometimes I worry that she had such an effect on me, but then I remember the fun we have together, and I let it go.

'I've missed you.'

'I've missed you too, my darling.' She's honey in my ears. 'Have you been good while I was gone?'

'Always.' I grin, glad I'd fought the urge to do something stupid on Friday night. I can't fuck this up, she's my soulmate and I'm lucky to have her in my life.

'Are you feeling better? You were a bit sick last week?'

'Yes, much improved. Must have picked something up at work. With the weather getting colder it's bound to happen.'

'You're right. It's important to keep on top of your health. I'll make you something, an herbal remedy, that should help.'

'Thank you.' I have no idea whether her Wiccan background includes medicinal herbs but it may. Or, no doubt she knows someone who has the appropriate skills and materials.

'I wondered if you wanted to see me on Saturday? I'm having dinner with a friend, a member of my circle, it would be nice for you to meet her.'

'Wow, that's a big step.' I don't think I've met any of her friends before, only a couple of colleagues. 'I'd love to.'

'I'm so glad. We're going to a vegan place in South Yarra, it's all the rage apparently though you know my opinions on vegan food.'

'Sounds good, and I'm happy to go vegan for a holiday.'

Morgana has made it quite clear that she considers vegans weak—nutrition from eating animal flesh is how we evolved into the dominant species and, according to her, refusing the bounty of Mother Earth is sacrilege.

'Was it your friend's suggestion?' I ask.

'Sort of. She's dating one of the waiters and likes to show him off to her friends by taking them to eat there. It's all a bit performative for my tastes but one must try to accommodate a sister's eccentricities. We've been friends for aeons.' She laughs, deep in her throat, perhaps it's a running joke between them, showing off their boy toys.

'I guess vegans deserve love too.' I keep my tone light, to match her mood.

'I thought of you while I was away.' She pauses. 'Alone in my hotel room, I imagined all the things I would do to you when I returned.'

My throat is hot, my heart beats harder in my chest. 'Really? What did you do while you were thinking of me?'

'I lay in my big, empty bed. I took off my clothes and ran my fingers all over my body, pretending they were yours. I pleasured myself.'

'I wish I could have been a fly on the wall.'

'Maybe I'll show you on Saturday.'

'I'd like that.'

We continue to talk in promises for a little while longer, Morgana breathing heavily in my ear, and my cock pulsing in anticipation. In the end she leaves me hanging, she's very good knowing when to stop so I want her more. I have to wank immediately to relieve my straining hard-on, and I have a feeling this dinner with her friend will be a very drawn-out form of foreplay. I'm not sure whether to be excited or scared. Or both.

*

The restaurant is not at all what I expect for vegan or South Yarra; the interior is very over decorated, walls covered in multiple prints of classic impressionist artworks, the bar furniture tends toward overstuffed and is all plush velvet, a mistake for a restaurant in my opinion. The colours are muted; dusty pink, mint green, and tan, all very tasteful. When we arrive, we're seated in a waiting area until Arcadia joins us on a sectional beige vinyl couch encircling a central fire pit, which instead of an actual heat source, has been replaced with neon lights in the shape of flames.

Whoever is in charge of the décor needs a strong speaking to, I think.

'I hate this,' Morgana waves her hand in the direction of the fireplace.

'I agree. Dreadful.' I smile, it's nice to have a comrade in my distaste. 'I hope the waiter is worth being stuck here with it.'

Morgana's nose wrinkles in disgust as one of the waitresses comes over to take our drink order. 'Let's have a bottle of this, please,' she says, pointing to a mid-range red wine on the drinks' menu. I would have gone with white with vegan food.

'And for you?' the waitress asks.

'I'll share the bottle, thanks.' They don't usually ask me when Morgana orders for both of us. In her presence I blend into the background, which I'm happy with; I don't need adoration.

'Arcadia is always late.' Morgana taps her watch. Lateness is one of her many pet peeves. She's quite stuck in her ways for someone so young.

'It's alright, we'll have a glass of wine while we wait. I'm not super hungry anyway.'

She turns to me, and her eyes glint in the low light, it might have been the stupid neon lights, but she looks as though she wants to eat me. 'I'm waiting for what comes after dinner. It's been a while since we've been alone.'

'I'm looking forward to that too,' I say, shifting closer and putting my hand on her knee. Her dress is navy blue, almost black, with very little adornment. It clings to her gorgeous figure in a way that borders on indecent and having been apart for two weeks, my desire to touch her is heightened. Under her dress, Morgana's skin feels chilled.

'Are you warm enough?' I ask, though it was heated inside, the wind outside was brisk.

'I'm fine, darling. Don't worry about me.'

I nod. 'Tell me about the conference then?'

Morgana regales me with anecdotes from her trip to Sydney without further prompting from me. It sounds very specialised, and she uses a lot of words I barely understand, but I make sounds of approval every so often. She doesn't need much input to have a conversation, it's one of the things I enjoy about her company, that I don't need to be entertaining.

At the end of our first glass of wine, half an hour later than the scheduled time, Arcadia walks in.

'We're over here.' Morgana stands and waves over another ethereally beautiful woman. Where Morgana is ash-blonde, Arcadia is brunette, but they share the same pale, luminous, flawless skin. Arcadia's face is pointed, her chin, nose and cheekbones are sharp and prominent, they made her seem otherworldly, unattainable rather than ugly. Her long wavy hair hangs loose down her back, I'm not sure how it stays so neat, but women's grooming is a mystery to me.

'My darling, sister.' Morgana kisses her friend on both cheeks before pressing their foreheads together for a long moment. 'Can I introduce my beau, Ricky.'

I stand, though my legs seem unreliable under me. 'Wonderful to meet you,' I say, sticking out my hand to shake Arcadia's. Her hand is cool, and smooth, almost as though it belongs to a statue and not a person. My tummy is in knots, and I feel sweat drip down my back. I had a similar reaction the first time I touched Morgana, though I was full of sexual desire at that time, I'm just as drawn to Arcadia, but my genitals seem uninterested.

'You're much more handsome than your picture,' Arcadia says, she drops my hand and turns to her friend. I expected the two women to talk to one another, and not me, but I'm still a little stung that Morgana's attention had so easily been drawn away. Stupid I know, since she has all but promised me a night of athletic sex later, but feelings aren't always rational.

'Come with me, we'll sit at the table,' Arcadia says, before sweeping off deeper into the restaurant. I suppose it's a perk of knowing a staff member that she can swan around like she owns the joint, I grab the wine and follow, but look around for a waiter to wave over at the first opportunity.

'Hey, gorgeous.' A sultry male voice speaks from behind me as I'm holding out the chair for Morgana. I turn to see a deeply tanned Latin looking man, his slicked back black hair is in a ponytail at the nape of his neck, and he's wearing all black.

'Hey yourself,' Arcadia replies, her voice like a purr and her body takes on a languidness it hadn't had before. She takes his hand in both of hers, caressing it; I feel indecent watching though they were only holding hands. He only has eyes for her, unaware of the looks he's getting from the other staff.

'Are you being looked after?' he asks, seeming to remember his job.

'We've only just sat down, we'll need another minute, *mi amor*,' Arcadia replies. He nods and backs away, letting his hands linger in hers for as long as possible.

'He's lovely, what's his name?' Morgana asks.

'Julio.'

'Gorgeous.'

I say nothing, still feeling soiled from watching their display, and miffed we weren't introduced, though at least Arcadia had forgotten both of us. She starts to tell Morgana about Julio, and I decide to study the menu rather than listen to more details I don't want to know.

The food is strange, the names make it sound like the dishes are made with meat, but there is a tiny asterisk at the bottom of the page to say the meat is all imitation, made from soy and gluten products. I always think if you're going to be vegan you should stop eating meat-type foods; surely food that tries to copy animal products should be avoided but given the proliferation of meat substitutes, I'm in the minority.

When Julio returns, he's much more professional. 'I'm Julio, I'll be your waiter this evening, my darling Arcadia has explained to me that you are good friends and that I should take good care of you,' he pauses to place his hand over his heart, 'I plan to do my very best.'

'Delighted to meet you, I'm Morgana, this is Ricky.' Morgana says, gesturing to me without looking away from this chiselled, smooth-skinned man. A prickle of jealousy rises in my stomach, her face was alive with pleasure in a way I hadn't seen for a while. If only I weren't such a slug of a man, I might have made a fuss, or tried to wrestle her attention back, but I know it's pointless.

The meal is pleasant enough, the two women mostly speak to each other, and don't include me in the chat. I have some sort of rice stir-fry thing, Morgana and Arcadia both have salads, which seem unappealing on a such a chilly night.

After clearing away out plates, Julio comes back to take the empty chair at our table. The restaurant has emptied while we had our meal, and he isn't needed to run around doing this and that.

'Morgana says she took you up to the forest, Ricky, on the equinox too. That's an important day,' Arcadia says.

'Uh, yes.'

'It's okay, you can speak freely in front of Julio, he knows all about our religious ceremonies.'

'Do you get involved too?' I ask him.

'No, I am not yet invited. I hope that over time, this may change. Perhaps I will also be taken to the forest.' Julio looks at the table, perhaps embarrassed he hadn't been asked.

'There will be an important ceremony on the winter solstice, in a few weeks,' Morgana says. 'Arcadia and I, along with all of our coven, will be there, but we need to do some other smaller things before that.' She takes my hand and I turn to look into her deep, cool, eyes.

'In our religion, we are much freer with sex than the rest of society. We think this prudish attitude only represses people's natural urges. I would like to invite Arcadia and Julio to join us, to make love with us.'

I'm stunned. Wherever I thought this meeting was going, it isn't here. 'Have you discussed it already?' I turn to Julio and Arcadia.

'We've had this conversation with a few of our coven, and we've been able to join with some already,' Arcadia says, squeezing Julio's hand as he smiles back. He's clearly loving this sex-positive arrangement.

'Is this what you've done with other boyfriends? Are you a swinger?' I say to Morgana. My cheeks are heating, I want to run away but it wouldn't help.

'It's something we can work towards. For the first time, I thought we would stick with our usual partners, but perhaps play in front of each other. It can be hard the first time, and I haven't given you any time to think about it.'

'Right,' I say. I nod my head, more to buy time than in agreement. 'I need to pop to the bathroom.' I dash out of my seat and rush to the bathrooms at the back of the restaurant. Is this why she hasn't wanted to introduce me to any of her friends, because they're all fucking each other? Am I jealous or just intimidated by how hot Julio is? If we did swap partners, would Arcadia agree to be with me? I've never been a handsome man, and if Morgana is out of my league, then so is her friend.

I look at my reflection, round flabby cheeks and thinning hair, but I'm not bad company, and my body is definitely in much better shape than when we first started dating. Morgana has probably shown her friend photos, why would they have dinner if she hadn't already said yes? Am I the prude for being put off?

On the other hand, what do I have to lose? I might be a common-looking fellow, but I know my way around Morgana's body, I know how to pleasure her, so I won't embarrass myself. Perhaps it's exactly the shake up I need to get out of my funk, with all my crappy health stuff, my ego could use a boost.

'Sorry about that,' I say, retaking my seat at the table. 'I was a bit taken aback by the suggestion but I'm willing to try it.'

'I'm so glad,' Morgana says, beaming. 'What about tonight? We can all go to my place, but you won't be able to stay the night I'm afraid. That goes for you too

Julio, Arcadia and I have business tomorrow we need to attend to.'

'Tonight?' I don't know why I didn't expect it, Morgana is impulsive, and demanding when it comes to sex, and having to arrange the dinner to introduce me probably cramped her style enough as it was.

'If you'd like to, of course.' Morgana's hand moves into my lap, brushing against my groin. I'm helpless to resist her, my desire for her is stronger than any other feeling and if there are other people in the room, then I won't even notice them.

'Alright. Yes, I'll do it.'

'Wonderful.' Morgana smiles at her friend, a flicker of something crosses her face that I can't read, but I'm soon distracted by her hand in my lap.

*

The four of us take a taxi to Morgana's place, about ten minutes away. I feel euphoric, perhaps the wine was stronger than I anticipated, or perhaps the idea of being with Morgana is overriding all my modesty, whatever it is, I'm drawn inexorably into a situation I would never have dreamed of even six months ago.

Morgana sits next to me in the back of the cab, Arcadia on my other side and Julio in the front. Morgana spends the ten-minute journey rubbing my leg aggressively and kissing me. I'm dimly aware the driver is probably not keen to witness our public display, and possibly nor would the other couple, given they weren't able to do the same. At one point I'm sure I felt a hand on my other leg, perhaps Arcadia getting a little frisky, but before I can look, we've stopped.

Julio pays the driver, and Morgana grabs my hand, dragging me behind her into her building. Both women are flushed, and not from the cold.

In the apartment, we waste no time piling onto Morgana's enormous four poster bed. She pushes me down and straddles me, covering me in kisses and pinning my hands down. Arcadia has Julio in the same position next to me. The two women share a meaningful glance, and something tells me they had done this many times before. Arcadia closes the distance between them and they kiss.

I expected to be jealous of my gorgeous girlfriend kissing someone that isn't me, but my cock has other ideas. Where it has been pushing against my trousers in a semi-aroused state since the restaurant, it starts to throb and strain. My hands are roaming over Morgana's torso above me, she takes one hand and moves it to Arcadia.

The sensation is hard to describe, it's as though they share a body, their skin, their flesh feels almost the same; cool, porcelain skin, pert breasts, soft belly and hard, powerful thighs. Running my hands over the two women it would have been hard to know who was who if I closed my eyes. I pull my hand away, back to Morgana, so my brain doesn't have to process the strange similarities. Julio's hands start to wander over Morgana, slipping down to caress my thigh on occasion. It isn't unpleasant, though I've never been touched by a man like that before; perhaps his being an Adonis helps.

My mind starts to feel fuzzy, my eyes drift closed for a moment before I snap them back open. I don't want to miss anything but I'm so sleepy.

After that, I can only remember bits and pieces; Morgana's smooth naked body on top of me, Arcadia kissing me as Julio fucks her from below, kissing Julio. I'm fairly sure we swapped partners for a while, Arcadia's dark, shiny hair falling into my eyes as she rode me.

I start to get my wits back as we're lying afterwards, limbs entangled, slick with sweat and thoroughly spent. The fog clears, perhaps I'm sobering up, and I wonder how I found myself in this situation. If I had known what it would be like, the joy, the abandon, leaving all my hang-ups and limiting beliefs at the door, I would have said yes immediately, but without the wine, I doubt if I'll be able to do it again.

'I hope you don't mind, I gave you a little … potion, to help get you in the mood,' Morgana whispers in my ear.

'Really? When?'

'Julio put it into the dessert wine. We all had it. It's a special recipe the coven uses for sex rituals, although that wasn't exactly a ritual,' Arcadia says.

'That was for fun. Since you'd never done anything like that, I thought it would be easier if I … helped you along a bit.'

Morgana, My Queen

I press my lips together, trying to get my brain to think straight. I'd done things I'd never even hoped to do. The night had been blissful, but I feel violated. If she'd asked me, I would have said yes to her potion, but she didn't ask. She just did it. It's too late now, but if I have to keep a look out for drink spiking with my girlfriend now, as well as the weird illnesses and fatigue, it might be the end of my rope. It's one thing to date someone much hotter than me, but it doesn't mean she can do whatever she likes to me whenever it takes her fancy.

My eyes drift closed, and I can't hold on to my anger, perhaps the potion is still hanging around a bit.

'I'll call you a taxi to take you home,' Morgana says, propping herself up on one elbow to look at me.

'Huh?'

'I told you before, you can't stay tonight.' She strokes my hair. 'I'm so glad we were able to do this together.'

'Right. Of course,' I say, my brain still trying to catch up. Arcadia and Julio are starting to dress, the night is over. The clock shows a little after one in the morning. I'm definitely going to be hungover tomorrow. What am I doing with this woman? How does she keep reeling me back in?

*

I wake late feeling seedy; my tongue furry and dry, my eyes scratchy and my head pounding. Whatever Morgana slipped me didn't agree with me, I'd only had a couple of glasses of wine.

Why had she done it? We had a great sex life, I thought we were developing our relationship, the ritual in the forest seemed to be an indicator of seriousness on her side. Had I misread the signs? Or was this the next logical step for her? Introducing other people and drug-fuelled orgies to my relationship is not what I consider serious, and certainly isn't what I'd signed up for when I started dating Morgana.

I have two glasses of water and find a couple of Panadol before crawling back into bed. Under the throbbing headache, I'm fuming at the deception. If it was important to her, I would have taken the potion willingly, but instead, she dosed me without my consent. As soon as I'm feeling better, I'm going to call her and confront her.

I doze for most of the rest of the day, at one point getting up to try to eat something but find my belly is too sensitive and give up on food.

Work on Monday is a struggle, my brain feels full of cotton wool, but my anger at Morgana hasn't abated. I didn't feel strong enough to speak to her that night, but after dinner on Tuesday, I'm ready.

'Morgana?' I say when she answers the phone.

'Ricky? What are you calling me for?' she says, her voice clipped and irritated.

'We need to talk about Saturday night.'

'Did you have fun? I'm so glad you were able to meet my friends—'

'You dosed me. I want an apology. I want you to promise not to spike my drink again.'

'I . . . I didn't think you would react like this.' Her voice is soft, and completely unlike her. I wait for more, listening to her breathe down the phone.

After a long pause, she sobs. 'I'm sorry, Ricky. I—' More sobbing.

At first, I want to remain hard, distant. I'm the one who's been tricked and violated, I won't get sucked into her emotional response, it's her responsibility to apologise.

'I thought you would be okay with it, it's just…' Morgana sniffs as though trying to calm herself.

'It's just what? You thought you could do whatever and I'd be okay with it?' This conversation isn't restoring my faith in her. She has no concept of how hurtful her behaviour is.

'I've had some bad news today. I don't think I'm handling this very well.'

I hold my mouth firmly closed; it could be a ploy to distract me.

'My snake, Wilson, he's sick.' She sobs aloud again. 'I think he's dying.'

'I'm sorry to hear that. I know how much he means to you.' I clench my teeth. Her snake is sick? That's her big tragedy? The tears only make me angrier, I want to talk about her behaviour; not only her immoral, but criminal, decision to slip a psychoactive substance into my drink and she wants me to feel bad about her pet snake.

'Ricky, I wish you could be here, I would feel so much better in your arms.' Her voice is shaky but has taken on a little of that characteristic purr she uses when trying to seduce me.

'I'm trying to talk to you about something serious. You did the wrong thing. You hurt me and you want me to come comfort you?'

'Why are you being so mean? Don't you love me anymore?'

'I'm going to hang up. This conversation needs to happen before I come back to comfort you or do anything else with you, so when you're feeling more like talking like grownups, you can call me. Otherwise, maybe Julio and Arcadia can come and hold you tonight instead.' I stab the button on my mobile to hang up and drop the phone onto the dining table. My hands are shaking. I hadn't thought I could feel more enraged with her, but I do.

I pace up and down my apartment, trying to make sense of why she's being such a bitch. It isn't helping, so I grab my jacket and shoes and go for a walk. My hands are clenched into fists for a long time, I walk fast, pumping out feelings I can't channel anywhere else.

The next time I look up, I realise I'm a long way from home. I'm sweating from walking so fast, and the chilly evening air is freezing on my nose and ears. The anger has drained away and I'm tired and sad.

My girlfriend's behaviour is appalling. If she's just heard about her snake being sick, then dosing me on

Saturday wasn't because of the grief, but her response tonight definitely is. I turn around and start walking home, slowly this time, as my feet are starting to ache.

I'll give Morgana a few days to think about things and try to talk to her again at the weekend. Maybe some time without my company will give her perspective.

5.

At nine on Saturday morning I wake to insistent knocking on my door.

'Isn't it a bit early for visitors' I ask as I pull the front door open.

'Maybe.' Morgana stands on my doorstep. She looks terrible, her skin usually glowing with otherworldly pallor, is grey and stretched taut over her features. Her eyes are red-rimmed as though she's been crying.

'I . . . wasn't expecting you.'

'I know. Can I come in?' Her arms are wrapped around her front, as though hugging herself.

'Sure.' I step back and she walks into my home. She's been here many times before, but today is different. She's smaller somehow. Last time she swept through like royalty, assuming I would follow in her wake, and do whatever she wanted, but today she looks back twice in the short distance between the front door and the couch to check if I'm there.

Morgana folds herself onto the brown leather couch, her legs tucked up under her in a childlike way.

'Are you okay? You look awful.'

'Wilson died. Last night.'

'I see.' I'm standing, my bottom perched on the dining table, unwilling to sit with her, unwilling to comfort her.

'I know you don't understand, but I loved him.'

I say nothing. I'm still furious she hasn't apologised, and while I acknowledge her pain, I'm not going to jump to her side after the stunt she pulled.

'I'm sorry about . . . last Saturday.'

'Really?' My voice drips with sarcasm, I can't help it, even though I want to be the bigger person.

'Yes. I—' She rubs her hand over her face, dashing away a tear. 'Wilson has been dying for a while. I've known it was coming, but I didn't say anything to you because, well, it's not your problem, is it? Anyway, on Saturday Arcadia thought it would be funny to slip something into your drink. I must have been out of my mind because I agreed with her; it can be hard to say no to her, I'm sure you wouldn't find that hard to imagine.'

I wait.

'When you called me afterwards and were understandably upset, I was . . . I didn't know what to do. I've never done anything so stupid before. I didn't want to admit I'd been wrong because the more I thought about it, the more I hated myself for going along with her.'

'And now?'

'It took me a couple of days to really understand t I was an idiot. I was losing Wilson, there was nothing I could do about that, he was an old snake, he's been with me through a lot. And as I held him last night, knowing you were still angry with me, I realised I couldn't lose both of you. I had to put on my big girl pants and beg your forgiveness. So here I am.'

'Right,' I say. She looks so cold, so small and vulnerable sitting there. She admitted she was wrong, she's here to make things right but I feel like a fool giving in. 'And what are you going to do to show me I can trust you?'

'I'll do anything you want. I came here as soon as Wilson was gone, I was up all night holding him, trying to make his passing easier, and then I came here. You were the first person I wanted to see, the person I wanted to comfort me.'

There it is again, she wants something from me, she isn't interested in being in a two-way relationship, she only thinks of how I help her, and what I can do for her. 'I don't know if that's enough.'

'I've never been here before, Ricky, I have never fucked up this badly. I don't know how to make it right.'

I close my eyes and pinch the bridge of my nose between my thumbs. 'Why don't I make coffee and we can chat? No promises though.'

'I would like that. Thank you.' Her lips turn up in an attempt at a smile, though her bloodshot eyes remain sad.

I turn away and go into the kitchen to make the hot drinks. I haven't had much sleep, I was up late last night watching stupid videos and cursing Morgana's name. Now she is here looking pathetic, saying she's sorry, that she was an idiot, and that she would do anything to have me back.

Six months ago, even three months ago, I would have forgiven anything she did. I would have eaten shit off her shoes and said thank you but now—something of her shine had worn off. The sun that had seemed to shine out of her arse has dulled and I see her as a beautiful, yet deeply flawed person. It's as though a switch was flicked when we did the forest ritual, my eyes opened after that and I started to see things differently.

I fill the kettle to boil and clean out the coffee plunger, unlike Morgana I don't have a fancy machine to make coffee in, but it does the trick, even if it isn't the single origin espresso machine version she's used to.

'You know that trip to the forest?' I say.

'Yeah.' She doesn't look up.

'I know you said it was like, a bonding thing, and that it would bring prosperity, but was that the whole story?'

Morgana's large green eyes pull away from staring at the floor to gaze at me. 'The whole story?'

'I mean, was there another part you didn't tell me about?'

'I don't know what you're getting at.' Her frown deepens.

'Since that day I've felt . . . well different, around you.'

'I guess that makes sense,' she says, her eyes softening, the anger in them replaced with more sadness. 'A ritual like that is a bond that goes to the heart of a person. All the things I've tried to change about myself, all the parts of me that I hide because I want to be a better person, I can't hide them from you now. You see me more the way I see myself.'

'Why would that make me feel distant?'

'I don't think I've ever really talked about my childhood.' She holds up her hand as though to stop me interrupting her, not that I'm going to. 'When I was little, my father and mother were always having parties, lavish affairs where all their important friends would come for dinner. There would be food, wine and musicians, very Bacchanalian. It was a version of themselves that all their friends believed in completely. But they were cold people, both of them. I was only ever a prop to them, a way for my mother to fit in with the other women in her set, or so my father could talk about me to his work friends. They barely knew who I was, what I liked; they never hugged me or said a kind word unless there was someone there to witness it.'

Morgana takes a deep breath and stares towards the dull grey clouds outside the window.

'I always thought there was something wrong with me. I'd done something to make them dislike me, that I deserved to be treated in that way for a reason I didn't understand. I grew up cold and distant like them, I didn't know how to be affectionate with friends, the few of them I had. When I was older, I found Wicca, and my coven. It was the sort of family I never had growing up, and it showed me a way to be that wasn't so calculating.

It didn't come naturally, I spent a long time making mistakes, and I'm still making them, but there are days when I don't hate myself quite so much.'

'It wasn't your fault your parents were like that.' I say, pouring the coffee into mugs I quietly removed from the cupboards as she spoke.

'I know that, in my head, unfortunately my head doesn't rule how I feel. Now that we're bonded, you might be picking up on that feeling of inadequacy. Perhaps all the love you have for me isn't enough to override the loathing I have for myself.'

She looks down at her hands and is quiet. I don't know what to think. Wicca is a fiction, a religious metaphor. The magic is symbolic not real so whatever happened up in the forest must have been some sort of psychological trick. We've been dating for a little while and maybe the initial honeymoon period has worn off, maybe I'm less—what was the word Brad used—cunt-struck? than I was when we started out and I can see the things about her that aren't perfect. Either way, this is a turning point. She's hurting, I have to decide if I will accept the apology and give her another chance or lose something that was making me so happy up until a couple of weeks ago.

'I'm glad you told me about your family. I'm sorry you went through that. I hope you know how much you hurt me with what you did last week, and that you know I won't forgive you a second time—'

'Does that mean you forgive me now?' she interrupts me. I walk over to the couch, putting the coffees down on the small table and sitting down.

'I think so. I'm not ready to lose you after our first proper fight.'

'I'm so relieved, oh Ricky, I thought I was going to lose you too.' Morgana unfolds herself, closes the distance between us and embraces me. She's freezing and holds onto me so tightly I think I might have to unhook her arms to breathe properly, but she relaxes after a minute or so. I settle back into the couch and she curls into the space next to me; she fits so perfectly into that space. We sip our coffee without saying much and I'm happy we worked it out. But I'll be wary from now on, fool me once and all that.

*

For almost a month we're happy. Morgana seems to take what I said to heart and is really looking after my needs. The tiredness is still present after we're together but it lessens a little. The coven is doing a big ceremony for the winter solstice, and Morgana invites me.

'Tell me again what's going to happen on Friday night?' I ask, as we lay on her bed after a rare midweek date.

'Are you still anxious about the ritual?'

'Yes. I'm still hurt by that time you drugged me. Remember?'

Morgana's cheeks flush red with embarrassment. 'I told you I wasn't going to do that to you again. We're going to say some words and do some symbolic stuff with ribbons and what not. Very similar to the equinox thing.'

'But that ended in sex, remember? I'm not really okay with sex in front of people.'

'I promise there won't be anyone watching if we have sex after the ritual. Cross my heart. And, I promise no other people will be invited into the sex. Just you and me.'

Her eyes are clear and I want to believe her. I guess I'll find out on the night. If there's any shenanigans, I owe it to myself to leave her. She might be out of my league but I'm done being an accessory for her to use in whatever way she wants. Being single isn't so bad that I'll let someone treat me like that, even if she is beautiful and charming.

On the day of the ritual, Morgana asks me to take the afternoon off so we can prepare. I wouldn't have done it, except we have to drive up to a section of redwood forest in Warburton to the east of Melbourne, and we need to be there before dark sets in at about five-thirty.

'Ready to go?' I ask Morgana when I greet her out the front of my office building. Given she works down the road it makes sense for us to have a late lunch break and travel together in her car.

'All ready.' She grins and adjusts her handbag on her shoulder. She looks drawn, and older than usual, with dark circles under her eyes.

'Are you feeling okay?'

'I didn't sleep so well last night. Nervous about the ritual I suppose,' she says, her smile is weak and doesn't quite reach her eyes, hopefully, it's nothing more than a bad night's sleep. She's been looking unwell for a while, deteriorating a little each time I've seen her since the orgy. I tell myself it's nothing, but if it doesn't improve soon, I'm going to ask her to see a doctor. Maybe she has an iron problem.

The road is beautiful once we get out of the suburbs, long winding forest roads and few other vehicles. Even though we left early it's starting to get dark as we approach the property.

'It's this driveway to the left, where the big flag is, you see it?'

Up ahead on the left a long thin flag is planted in the ground, purple and green tie-dyed patterns, flapping in the wind to mark the turn. As I get closer and slow down, I see the flag is tattered at the edges, and some of the patterns are stained and faded.

'Whose place is this again?' I ask, as I ease the car up the narrow dirt driveway.

'It belongs to Arcadia's cousin, Gwen, the founder of the group. It's a sacred site for us. Gwen lives here full-time, with a couple of other women, and we use the main house and surrounding forest for our important ceremonies.'

'Right.' I wonder why the equinox ritual was done in a national park when they have this property, but maybe that was only for me and Morgana. This will be the whole coven; twelve women.

'This is a big night for me, every seven years we have a special anniversary, and this year is one of mine. Not everyone gets to bring a guest with them, but I do, and Arcadia does, it's our year.'

I glance at her in the passenger seat beside me, she's solemn, her eyes are hooded. 'I'm glad I'm able to share this with you.'

I'm not sure what it is I'm sharing but it feels momentous, perhaps indicative of good things to come between us.

At the end of a very long, pot-holed dirt driveway we enter a clearing. Darkness has set in, and the headlights shine hard beams across the landscape. Short wild-looking shrubs are scattered around the garden, perhaps an artfully designed native plant garden, but equally likely to be unkempt. The house is low and wide, the peaked tin roof spreading out to the left and right of the main path, and a veranda along the front. Lights glow inside, and smoke comes from two chimneys. It's hard to know if it looks like the start of a romantic comedy or a horror film.

I squeeze Morgana's knee briefly as I pull up next to half a dozen other cars, she feels cold even under her skirt. She pats my hand and lets herself out of the car before I turn off the engine.

I follow her inside; the wooden planks of the veranda are grey with age but seem well-maintained. The farmhouse is built of untreated wood and has a warm, rustic feeling; a broken wagon wheel propped next to the main door gives it a distinctly rustic vibe that borders on kitsch but never quite gets there.

Morgana steps into the house first, the glow of the open fireplace to the left and the low lights are very romantic, giving her a radiance I haven't seen in her for a while. She smiles at the others in the room and hurries over to say hello. I follow a few steps behind, closing the door and putting our bags down where they won't be in the way.

Arcadia and Julio I recognise, a slightly older blonde woman I assume is Gwen given her resemblance to Arcadia, and an unknown mousy-looking man in his late twenties who sits alone cradling his hands around a mug. The voices of several others come from other parts of the house, laughing and talking.

'Ricky, come meet Gwen,' Morgana calls to me. I'm right about the blonde woman, she's the owner of the impressive house. As I approach, she becomes more magnificent, her eyes are ice-blue, and hard like a bird of prey, though her hair is soft and voluminously arranged around her head. She wears many layers of clothing, bohemian and flowing, and wears far too many necklaces, bracelets, and rings. She stands, and holds out her hand to me, she jangles when she moves.

'Is this the man I've heard so much about?' Her voice is dark, deep, and husky, like a fire. My cheeks heat, there's something immediately attractive about this woman, I try to push down my feelings as I take her hand to shake it. She covers my hand with hers and turns it over a couple of times. Shivers run up my arm, a warmth starts to pulse in my groin.

'Thank you for having me,' I manage to say after a very long pause.

'It's okay, Gwen has a . . . talent for being exactly what men desire,' Arcadia says. My flush deepens and all three women laugh. 'I'm sorry, it was too good to resist, everyone who meets Gwen for the first time lusts after her. Some will always want her, but for, others it's a fleeting feeling.'

I can't think straight, my mind is consumed with where her skin touches mine, my eyes linger on her lips. What would they feel like to kiss?

'Even I feel it sometimes,' Morgana says, her mouth tilted in an uneven grin. I'm relieved she isn't jealous, although given her antics with Arcadia perhaps jealousy isn't what I should be worried about.

'The others are in the kitchen preparing our feast, I'm so glad you could join us,' Gwen adds, finally dropping my hand. As she does, the spell is broken, and I have no idea why I wanted her moments ago.

Gwen takes her seat again, leaning back with her arms spread like the queen of her own special domain. Her icy blue eyes remain on me, and I feel like she might be silently dissecting me. I shift to face Morgana.

'She does it on purpose, you know,' Morgana says.

'What?'

'Makes people want her, and then stares at them as though she might eat them. She thinks it's funny but don't worry, she won't actually eat you. Or force herself on you, I told you that it's just you and me this weekend.'

My shoulders drop, as though I'd been tensing them without knowing it. 'That's good.'

The three women chat amongst themselves for a while, Julio watches Arcadia's conversation, which leaves me to look around the room. It's more of the same rustic farm aesthetic: large, exposed beams in the ceiling, and huge metal farm equipment hangs from the beams and walls as decoration. The wooden floor is covered with an enormous boucle flax mat, on top of which are laid several cow hides. The couches are large, and soft, the sort of couches that are difficult to get out of as though they want to swallow you.

The mousy guy sits even more quiet than I am at the other end of the couch.

'Hey,' I say.

'Hey,' he replies, his voice very soft compared to the women next to us.

'Is this your first time?'

He nods.

'I'm Ricky.'

'Jonathan.' His mug appears to be empty, but he doesn't put it down, or put his hand out to shake mine. A little rude, but for a shy person the situation is overwhelming.

'Did you come with someone?'

'Yeah, my partner, Helene, is in the kitchen.'

'Oh, cool.' I nod. So, we were the three partners. 'Have you known her long?'

'Not really, we've been dating a couple of months.'

'That's nice.' I frown and look away. Was it suspicious all the men were relatively recent relationships? Julio and Arcadia were new, according to Morgana, and we'd been together a little more than seven months. Then again, I'm not much good at having long-term relationships either so I shouldn't judge.

*

Dinner is served an hour or so later, four women come out from the kitchen carrying plates and plates of various foods to join us in the dining room, and another five from other parts of the house. Perhaps they were resting or preparing for the ritual.

I don't catch some of the names. All of the women are beautiful, though not all have the eerie, otherworldly beauty of Morgana and Arcadia. A few are gorgeous in a soft way, others in an angular way. They share a resemblance that could have made them family in some distant way, though it isn't mentioned.

The meal is extravagant; roast beef and chicken, potatoes and pumpkin piled high, salads, steamed vegetables and bread along with a variety of sauces spread along the centre of the table. I sit next to Morgana at the long redwood dining table, it's rough-hewn but waxed and rubbed smooth by long use. Waiting until everyone is seated, Gwen takes her place at the head of the table.

'Thank you for joining us, on this, the night to celebrate the return of the light. We welcome our special guests, Julio, Jonathan and Ricky, who are integral to the success of our ceremony tonight. I bless us all, in the name of the great mother and father spirits, may we live long, eat well and be happy. Dig in.' Gwen smiles, though it doesn't reach her icy eyes.

I wait until Morgana has served herself before reaching for the food. It looks wonderful, and smells even better. I try to restrain myself; I don't want to appear greedy in front of the coven, but it's hard not to try some of everything.

Morgana eats more than usual, her appetite is small, and she grins, chatting with a woman on her other side, as I take another slice of the roast beef. She squeezes my hand in reassurance.

It's hard to follow the conversations around the table, half-finished stories, indicating their long friendship. Looking at the women, it's hard to judge any of their ages, but I could swear some were in their early twenties, though they seemed to have known each other much longer than that. I put it from my mind, perhaps their mothers were in the coven before them, and they'd grown up in it.

The time creeps on towards nine o'clock before we start to pack up the meal and the conversation turns to the ritual.

Morgana, My Queen

'We'll be heading out into the garden at the back of the house for the ritual. The first part involves all of us, and then it will be those of us with an anniversary to do the second part,' Morgana says.

My stomach, which is so full I think I might need to lie down, does a small flutter. Morgana promised we wouldn't be watched but now I'm not so sure. Sex magic is important to the group, and I start preparing myself to be drawn into another orgy. As long as Morgana doesn't try to drug me again, it might be okay.

The garden behind the building is much like the front—slightly unkempt. Two huge fire pits blaze high in the middle of a large circle of gravel. After the food has been cleared away, Gwen invites everyone to join her in the garden.

The women form a circle; it's freezing out here but the heat of the fire makes it bearable. Somehow the smoke rises straight up and doesn't get in my face like it does every other time I've been around an open fire.

'Join hands,' Gwen says, and we all clasp the hands of the people next to us. I stand next to Morgana, and Arcadia, Julio is on her other side.

'Tonight, we renew our vows to the spirits. We come together to thank them for their abundance, for their guidance and protection for another year. We welcome the return of the light, the sun, and the beginning of a new cycle.' Gwen's husky voice now loud and carrying into the cold, cloudless night.

The women chant some words I don't understand; I remain silent. As they speak, I start to feel weird, my heart races, my ears pound, and my vision pulses in time with the words. I close my eyes, and when I open them again my sight is normal again.

I try to calm my breathing, the chanting increases in speed and volume; they're working themselves up to a fever pitch, raising their hands as they gather momentum. I glance at the other men's faces, they look glazed and possibly high. A small seed of panic starts to surface, what if there was something in the meal? We'd all eaten the same thing, so if I was dosed, then everyone was dosed, but the women's faces are slick with sweat and glow with a kind of manic internal light.

The fires dance and crackle, it's hard to look away once I start to look at them. Part of me wants to get closer to the flames, to feel them on my skin, to dance between them, something I'd never had the urge to do before.

At some point the chanting winds down.

'I thank the spirits on behalf of everyone here today. The circle is now open, but never broken,' Gwen says, dropping the hands of the two women beside her. As she does everyone else lets go and something changes in the atmosphere, the only thing I can think that is similar is popping my ears on a plane but at the same time it's completely different.

My legs are weak and wobbly, and I sit down suddenly on the damp gravel.

'Are you alright, darling?' Morgana asks, her face pink and flushed beside me.

'Felt a bit funny.' It's as though my arms and legs are not really in my control.

'You stay there for a moment; I have one or two things to collect for the next part.' She kisses my forehead and my skin tingles where her lips touch. My eyelids are heavy, but I blink back the fatigue to see the other two men also sitting on the ground alone.

I should say something, I think, my brain sluggish and full of cotton wool. I blink, and when I open my eyes, Morgana is returning. I try to raise my hand to greet her but nothing happens. I should be concerned, but I'm not.

'I'm back my darling,' she says, kneeling beside me. 'The next part is very easy, I promise.' She stands up and sets out a woollen blanket on the ground beside me, from the corner of my eye, I see Arcadia doing the same, and another woman with Jonathan. Morgana takes my shoulders and steers me to lie on the blanket. I look at the stars above me and marvel at how many there are.

Morgana is straddling me, she takes my clothes off, pulling me around like a rag doll. I don't want her to, but there isn't anything I can do to stop her. My limbs are not responding, my brain is like warm mush. At least I don't feel cold.

The next thing I know, Morgana is naked too, she presses her body onto mine, her skin hot and slick, she's usually so cold to the touch; it's strange but it feels so good. She kisses me, and I kiss her back, at least I try to, I'm not sure my mouth is working either.

My skin tingles all over where she touches me, and then she lowers herself onto me, I must have been hard because it was the tightest she's ever been, wrapped around me. Then she's fucking me; it's amazing, I'm floating above myself, my body lying prone on the cold gravel being fucked by the most beautiful witch in the world. Jonathan and Julio are in the same position, under their partners, though I can't seem to keep my mind focussed on them.

From my position above the garden, I can see the remainder of the coven standing back, still in a circle behind the fires, their mouths moving, perhaps in silent prayer. It's so nice on the warm blanket above the world.

Morgana sits back, her head turned to the sky. Her skin starts to glow and pulse. At first, I think I'm imagining it, it's so subtle, but as time goes on her body shines brighter with the greenish light. It beats in time with her thrusts above me. I look at myself, and it's as though I'm fading as she becomes brighter. It must be a trick of the light, or part of this strange waking dream. Jonathan and Julio are floating in the air above the circle too, their eyes drooping in ecstasy.

My groin is on fire, all my nerve endings feel as though they're all firing. Agony and ecstasy at once. Nothing exists apart from Morgana's pussy around me. And then there's a moment of blinding light from Morgana and the other two.

Morgana, My Queen

When my vision clears, I can't see myself at all.
Morgana is kneeling above the blanket, panting and
leaning over as though she's going to vomit. Her body
writhes, and heaves a few times before she starts to expel
a long green snake from her mouth.

I must be dreaming, or hallucinating, I tell myself.
Morgana struggles to expel the snake, grasping it gently
in her hands to help it out. Then, as the tail is about to
leave her mouth everything goes black.

*

I must have passed out, because when I wake up in
the living room the grey early morning light is creeping
in. My arms and legs seem to be asleep, and I can't move
properly. Turning my head, I see the living room inside
Gwen's house, though it is strangely colourless and a
little bit blurry. I must have had more to drink than I
thought.

Morgana walks towards me, I know her shape and
gait anywhere.

'Hello, Ricky, how are you feeling?' Her long slender
hand moves towards me, then closes around my neck.
She lifts my body, somehow it isn't heavy for her, and I
wonder if I'm dreaming.

'You look okay, nice clear skin, but I'm sure you're
very confused.'

I open my mouth to reply, but no words came out.

'Don't try to talk, darling. You might have seen that
snake come out of my mouth before you blacked out.

Consciousness usually lasts that long before the transfer.
You're the snake now.'

I try to get away from her, I twist and writhe. I try to
shout but nothing happens; a low sort of hissing sound
was all that comes out.

'I know you're angry but there is no need for that
behaviour.' Morgana puts me down. I continue to twist
my body, it is the only thing that seems to work, and I
catch sight of the long scaly body. Deep green, almost
the colour of Morgana's wallpaper. Nothing makes
sense. My brain isn't working properly. She couldn't
have said I was a snake. I close my eyes and try to wake
up.

A while later I come to my senses as I'm jolted
around. The world is blurrier, and I feel cold plastic
against me.

'We're going for a ride, Ricky. I'm taking you home
now. Good thing we came in my car.' Morgana is
carrying me in some sort of travel cage and puts me in
the dark car boot.

The ride home is bumpy and frightening, the cage
slides around the back of the car violently, I wonder if
she's doing it on purpose, or just careless. I was always
the driver when we went on adventures, so I haven't
experienced her driving before. When we arrive at her
apartment, I'm tired and stressed and feel very unwell
indeed.

'We're home, honey,' Morgana says, taking the box
out of the back of the car. 'You've got your own big

tank, and a nice heat lamp. I'll feed you mice, you won't need to eat much now, you're much smaller than you used to be.'

She puts the plastic box inside the larger glass tank she has in her loungeroom. I see the snake skeletons on her wall, there is another there now. I guess she must have cleaned her old snake and put him up there.

'Here we are. You're part of a long line now, and once you've been with me for seven years, it will be time for you to go on the wall. I love you, Ricky.' She tips the box and I slide out onto the sandy bottom of the tank.

I curl up on myself and try to wake up, over and over, but every time I open my eyes, I'm still inside the tank in Morgana's loungeroom.

The Tarot Reading

1.

My friend, Jerome, asked me to go with him to the Night Markets. It wasn't really my jam, you know the sort, they have live music—the shitty world music kind played by white dudes with dreadlocks and hemp clothing—and food trucks selling overpriced *banh mi* and *paella*. There were far too many people, and not much in the way of stalls selling market things.

Jerome and I wandered around for a while, me sweating profusely through my thin summer dress in the sticky Melbourne heat, looking for something to catch our eye when I saw a couple of stalls offering tarot card readings, psychics, and clairvoyants to tell you your future. I couldn't resist.

'Let's get a tarot reading,' I said, tugging on Jerome's arm, pulling him in their direction.

'Seriously, girl? You know they're making it up, right?' he said, one dark eyebrow arched gracefully.

'I know. But sometimes I like to have a hippy tell me my life is destined for greatness in a soothing voice. Come on.'

He sighed. 'I'm not getting one, but I'll come watch so I can give you shit later when none of the predictions come true.'

I grinned, I didn't need him to get a reading, just to come with me for moral support. Not that I really needed it, but there was something unsettling about the idea of sitting alone at a card table across from a charlatan who would tell me a bunch of nonsense in exchange for fifty bucks. With Jerome there, at least I would have someone to talk to later about how bonkers it all was.

We picked and pushed and finagled our way through the throbbing mass of people towards the three tables lined up under brightly-coloured tie-dyed banners. The first person had a square card table, about eighty centimetres on each side, covered in a deep green crushed velvet tablecloth. Two flimsy-looking, black, plastic folding chairs sat in front of the table. The sign read:

Best psychic tarot card reading in the market. Positive results only $50.

The woman behind the card table was a short-statured, bulky woman wearing layer upon layer of lacy, purple clothing. Beads of sweat collecting on her upper lip and chin demonstrated it was far too hot to have so much on, but she was a performer; the costume had to be right. We moved past her, as she was in the middle of a reading already, and I didn't want to wait.

The second table was round, covered in a black satin tablecloth, with a huge crystal ball sitting on an ornate gold and black stand. The chairs looked a little sturdier than the first reader's, but the man behind the table was frightening. He had long silver and black hair in a plait running over his shoulder; his face was gaunt, cheekbones and brow protruding like a skull. He wore all black, perhaps linen, and perched on his narrow nose were small wire-rimmed glasses. If I imagined an evil tarot reader this man would definitely fit that image. The sign on his table was simple:

Clairvoyant Tarot Reading, $50. No refunds.

I nudged Jerome. 'No refunds if his reading portends evil then.'

His eyes widened in comic surprise. 'Go to him, it'll be the most entertaining, plus I can bet you on whether he'll predict your death. Do it, go on.'

I looked to the third table, square again, purple crushed velvet this time, no ornaments. The woman seated behind it was older, perhaps in her sixties, round and fleshy in the face, and her body looked squishy too. She reminded me of my grandmother, a soft woman who gave great hugs before she got sick. I started to walk towards the third tarot card reader when a young man swept in from my right and took the seat in front of her.

'Damn it,' I said aloud.

'Now you have to go to the black crow in the middle. This is going to be so much fun.' Jerome's face was alight with malicious glee, the bastard.

'Fine.' I took a deep breath and strode toward the middle table and the man in black seated at it.

'Uh, hello,' I said.

'You've come for a reading,' he said. Great psychic abilities there.

'Yes.'

'Sit down. Your friend will have to wait somewhere else; I don't allow an audience.'

'He's getting a reading too—' I started to say.

'He has no intention of doing so and is only here to laugh at me, and you.' The man stared hard into my eyes, I wanted to squirm and look away but somehow, I couldn't.

'I'll do a lap and come back,' Jerome said, the Cheshire cat grin never leaving his face.

'You can call me Raven, though it isn't my name,' the man said as I sat down.

'Okay.'

'The fee is fifty dollars, cash only.'

'Okay,' I said again, fishing my wallet out, and handing him a yellow bank note.

'You want a general reading, something fun and light to talk about with your friend, but I cannot guarantee what the cards, spirits, or ball will reveal.' Raven pulled a large deck of tarot cards from his lap and started to shuffle them with long, thin, nimble fingers. At least his nails were trimmed short, I would have turned around and run if he'd had talons.

'I have shuffled the cards, now you will shuffle.' He handed me the cards using his right hand but he didn't lean over the crystal ball that was still in the centre of the table. I took the cards, they were much larger and harder to hold than ordinary playing cards, and started to inexpertly shuffle them around. I looked up and Raven had closed his eyes, set deep into his face and half-hidden behind his glasses, he looked corpse-like. I shuddered and his eyes flicked open.

'That's enough. Put them face down on the table.' He pointed to a spot left of the crystal ball.

I did as he said; he closed his eyes and his hand hovered over the pile of cards, his lips moving silently.

'A few basic questions to start. What is your name?'

'Anya,' I said.

'What is your star sign?'

'Aries, and I'm a year of the tiger if you want that too.'

'What a fascinating combination. Now, what do you want to ask the cards?' he said, opening his eyes to stare at me in a disconcerting, unblinking way.

'I, uh—' Now that I was here, I didn't know what to ask. I chewed my lip for a moment. 'I'd like to ask where I should look for romance.'

Raven flared his nostrils briefly, his lips compressed in disdain. 'I get that a lot. No one seems to be happy with the lot they have, sometimes you are single for a reason. However, it is your reading so, let us begin.' He inhaled, closed his eyes briefly, and scooped the cards back into his hands.

The Tarot Reading

'While I put out the cards, I want you to hold your question in your mind. Try to keep your focus, the cards can be easily confused if you are not consistent.'

I nodded, and he started to deal cards onto the table, face down. The seven cards formed a V-shape around the crystal ball in the centre.

'The first card represents your past influences.' He flipped it over. 'The Hanged Man reversed. This represents a focus on the self, egotism. This could provide insight into why you are single.

'The second card shows your present issues. Ah, the ace of rods, also reversed. This card shows me that you are too focused on decadence and not enough on spirituality. Too much time and money spent on wine and parties and not enough on choosing your friends wisely.'

How dare he, he doesn't know me.

Raven's eyes flicked over my shoulder, I turned and saw Jerome wandering back towards the stall.

'Card three is for future developments—my, the tower. This is for unforeseen catastrophes. Are you sure you're focusing on your question as I turn the cards?' He frowned.

'Yes, I'm concentrating.' To be honest, I wasn't, my mind had been taken up with angry thoughts about this reader casting aspersions at my best friend.

'Four, this card is advice you should consider to achieve your goal. Eight of swords, another poor omen. This could mean you are unable to extricate yourself from a bad influence or situation, but it seems to be different from the earlier warning about choosing your friends wisely.' Raven frowned again; his dark eyes narrowed in their deep sockets. 'Do not take this lightly. There are bad energies around you. You must take heed or something terrible will happen, I fear more than being lonely or broken heart. Concentrate now, the next card relates to those around you.'

I clenched my teeth and said nothing though he was clearly being dramatic. In the sweltering heat of the marketplace in January, a chill wind caught the back of my neck as he turned the next card over.

'The devil.' He sucked air through his teeth, as though steeling himself to go on. 'What are you involved in woman? This is the worst reading I've ever given. The devil is an inhumane and destructive force that has attached itself to you. No doubt you're not even aware of it.'

If I hadn't already given him my money, I would have left right then. I don't need some scrawny old Goth telling me my choices are going to lead to ruin, I have my mother for that.

'The sixth card represents hidden obstacles or influences.' He flipped over the card; I should have left. 'Judgement, reversed. This card can mean threat to physical health or loss of worldly goods.' He closed his eyes for a moment, before reaching for the last card.

'Five of swords. Dishonour, corruption and loss. I don't understand it in that position, this should indicate what you must do for a good resolution but there is no good to be taken from this card in this place.'

The cold wind blew again, the hairs on my arms stood up, and the devil card flicked off the table landing in my lap. I reached for it to hand it back to Raven, and as my skin touched it, a chill spread through me. The heat and noise of the market faded and all I could feel was a cold, lonely silence. It felt as though I couldn't move, I registered briefly that Raven had reached over to pull the card from my fingers.

'Well. I've never seen anything like it. I think you should leave; you bring evil spirits with you, and I would rather be rid of you. I wish you'd never come to me.' He dumped the cards on the tabletop, stood, and grabbed the edges of his black tablecloth. In a swift movement, he had wrapped the tablecloth around the objects on the table and stuffed it into a black leather doctor's bag that had been sitting under the table. I sat on the folding chair, dumbstruck by his sudden and urgent need to get away from me.

'Shoo. I'm going home to cleanse your influence from my aura.' Raven's hands were shaking as he pulled on the lever to collapse the table. I stood; my brain was not keeping up with whatever was happening, and then stood and started to back away.

'What's he doing?' Jerome had come from the crowd to stand beside me at some point during the fracas.

'I'm an evil omen, apparently.'

Jerome laughed, but when I didn't join in his smile faded. 'For real?'

'Yeah, cursed by some sort of bad influence that's going to destroy me. It . . . escalated quickly.'

'I can see that.'

Raven had pulled his signs down and was rushing off towards the car park carrying as much as he could. He'd have to make a return trip, but I planned to be long gone by then.

'I need a drink.' I turned to Jerome, hoping to lighten the mood.

'You read my mind.'

'You're so funny,' I said, lightly slapping his arm.

*

We had a drink around the corner at a skeevy-looking bar with overpriced beers. I guess that's what I get for trying to have a drink in a tourist area. I told Jerome what Raven had told me, and he didn't seem surprised.

'What did you think was going to happen? He was the most tragic Goth-looking guy there. Of course he tried to scare you. I bet he made up half of the card meanings so they'd be more alarming.'

I raised my eyebrows.

'I would put money on him being back there right now, doing the same thing to some other unsuspecting person,' Jerome picked at a manicured fingernail.

'You think the freaking out and leaving was part of the act?'

'Honey, you thought that was real? Bless your heart.'

I hate when Jerome gets all fake-Southern; it's so patronising.

'I'm sure he storms off several times a day. They all have their acts, and that's his. I guarantee it,' Jerome said.

'Maybe.' I wasn't convinced; he'd seemed so upset.

'Sweet Anya, you believe in people too much. He's a con man for sure. They all are.'

'You're probably right.' I took a sip of my beer. Raven had said the people around me were bad energies, and that one of them was the devil. I made a mental note to look it up when I got home. Surely, they don't mean the actual devil, the tarot didn't use Biblical imagery as far as I knew. He must mean someone with a devilish influence. Inhuman and destructive were the words he'd used.

'Hello?' Jerome waved his hand in front of my face.

'Hmm?'

'You weren't listening to me. I said, I saw a cute boy in the market, and I got his number while you were being rattled by that charlatan. How long do I wait to see if he's free to meet up?'

I looked back at my friend, he was staring at his phone as though the answer was there, no doubt imagining having a quickie in a Portaloo instead of sitting here listening to me worry about an apparently psychic card reading.

'You want to call him and see if he's free now?'

'Ooh, no calling is so last century. But you don't mind if I cut this short, do you? He was giving me intense bedroom eyes, and I don't want to lose the opportunity—what if he changes his mind while I'm here gasbagging and I miss out?'

'You're right, you should go find him.' I didn't mean it, of course, I wanted him to stay here and comfort me, but Jerome was who he was. He always put his conquests before his friends.

'That's why I love you, doll. I'll see you around.'

'Okay, don't get murdered.'

'As if.' He beamed and stood up, rushing out the front door of the bar without a backward glance. I worried about his tendency to hook up with strangers; I'd listened to enough true crime podcasts to know that it was a dangerous world out there but then again, women were the number one choice for murder victims, so perhaps he would be alright.

The tram ride home was jammed for a Wednesday night. I ended up stuck under the armpit of a man whose deodorant was not coping with the heat. It wasn't his fault, it had been stinking hot for days, over thirty in daytime and only dropping to mid-twenties overnight. It had been a while since Melbourne had had such a long hot streak like that. My place would be sweltering when I got home, we didn't have air conditioning.

As I finally stepped off the tram at the end of my street, the same cold breeze I'd felt with Raven ran down the back of my neck. It must have been from getting out of the packed tram, or maybe because I was so sweaty, but I shivered.

I'd almost forgotten about the strange chill when I got home, the hot stagnant air in Brunswick was stifling. The front door was wide open, and only the screen door closed to keep out the flies and mozzies.

'Anya? Are you back already?' My housemate, Bekky was lying on the enormous beige sofa in front of a fan.

'Yeah.'

'I didn't think you'd be back till later. Was it no good?'

I flopped onto the other couch, a matching fabric two-seater. 'It wasn't as good as I had hoped. Plus, Jerome ditched me to hook up with some random he met there.'

'How does he manage to pick up so easily?'

'He's gorgeous and slutty.'

'True.'

Jerome had the cheekbones of a runway model, and an insatiable appetite, there were very few offers he turned down so I shouldn't be surprised he was always able to find someone to spend his time with.

'Did you get anything?' Bekky asked, her head back against the cushions.

'Not really.' Did I want to tell her what had happened? I couldn't stand for two people to give me grief for believing in the reading in one night.

'Shame. I was thinking of going next week. Maybe I'll give it a miss then.'

'Yeah. Might be wise.'

Now I was home, a great wave of weariness flooded over me. I let my heavy eyelids drift closed, the soft burbling of whatever was on the T.V. barely registered.

*

For two weeks after that terrible tarot reading, I waited for something bad to happen, but apart from losing two socks, from different pairs, nothing out of the ordinary happened. Work was boring, but predictable; the boss was busy with doing six-monthly reports and I was busy avoiding being delegated any of the work for them.

When I got home from work on a Thursday there was a package on the dining table addressed to me. It was a small box, a little smaller than a shoe box, wrapped in brown paper, and addressed in sharpie with bulky block capitals.

'Bekky, do you know what this is?' I called into the depths of the house. She was usually home before me and must have brought the parcel inside.

'Huh?' she said, popping her head out of the kitchen.

'The parcel.'

'It was there when I got home. I thought you'd put it there.'

I frowned. I would have remembered a parcel; I wasn't waiting on any online shopping orders, drunken or otherwise. The cold shiver I hadn't felt since the night of the market ran down my neck when I touched the brown paper to pull the parcel towards me. I shook it off, it was a draughty old house after all.

There was no return address, so I ripped the paper off and opened the plain white cardboard box underneath. Nestled in a bed of shredded paper, I found a small fabric doll.

'What the hell?' I said aloud.

'What have you got?' Bekky came back out from the kitchen immediately. 'Who sent you a doll? Did you order a doll?'

'Why would I want a doll? It's weird.'

'She looks cute,' Bekky said, holding out her hand. I passed it over and she started looking at it. The doll was similar to a Raggedy Anne doll, but less cute, like it had been handmade. It didn't seem like something I would have bought or a gift from anyone. It didn't even seem like a joke I wasn't in on. It was just weird.

'There's no return address, I guess it's mine now even if it is a mistake.' I laughed, the coldness on my neck wasn't going away like it had the other times. It lingered and fizzed on my skin, I brushed my hand over the area, and it dissipated.

'You had dinner?' she asked.

'Not yet, what are you thinking?' Sometimes we cooked together.

'I was hoping you would want pizza, so I didn't have to order and eat it alone.' She smiled.

I eyed the doll. 'Twist my arm. I'll have supreme, I'll pay you back later if you order?'

'Deal.' Bekky pulled her phone from her back pocket and started tapping away on it. Ordering from the food apps was a common occurrence for her, though I tried to be conscious of both my wallet and my waistline.

The creepy doll sat on the dining table looking at me. While we waited for dinner to be delivered, I grabbed it and took it to my bedroom. Not that I wanted her in there either, but I thought it would be safer to have her in a box in my wardrobe, that way I could try to forget about it.

Where did she come from? I wondered as I closed the wardrobe door. My reflection stared back at me from mirror on the back of the door, I had dark circles under my eyes, and my skin had the greenish undertone of fatigue and possibly sickness. I felt okay, at least I thought I did, but my face told a different story.

The pizza was good, not great, Bekky had ordered from a place close by, reliable but never gourmet. When I flopped into bed, a little after ten, I looked at the wardrobe. No outward signal betrayed the weird, creepy doll inside, but I knew she was in there.

You're being silly. Go to sleep and don't think about it, I told myself.

2.

The next morning, I woke to my alarm blaring in my ear. I have to have it turned up all the way and set to the most obnoxious tone I can find or else my tendency to sleep in takes over. My blinds were not good at blocking the sunlight and bathed the room in pale orangey-pink light. I turned over, stretching my limbs out from under the sheet when my eye fell on the doll. That Raggedy Anne doll I had put inside a shoe box on the top shelf inside my wardrobe was sitting on the chair next to my desk. The pale white fabric face was turned towards me, the feeling of being watched was inescapable.

I leapt out of bed and dashed into the hall. I pounded on Bekky's door.

'That's not fucking funny,' I yelled through the wood.

'What the hell?' Her voice was muffled. I continued to bang on her door until I heard footsteps.

'What are you on about?' Bekky's short blonde hair made a dishevelled halo around her head.

'The doll.'

'What doll?' She rubbed the heel of one hand into her eye.

"You knew I was scared of the stupid thing, so you took it out of the wardrobe while I was asleep.'

'You've lost your mind.'

'Look.' I grabbed her hand and dragged her back to my room, pointing at the demon doll sitting there grinning.

'Yeah, that's the doll you got in the mail yesterday.'

'Right. The one I put in the wardrobe, inside a box, behind a closed door, and now it's there.'

The colour drained from Bekky's face.

'I knew it.' I said, triumphant.

'No, hun, I didn't do that . . . do you sleepwalk?'

'What do you mean you didn't do it?' My mind spun with the ramifications. If Bekky hadn't done it, and I hadn't done it, how had the doll got there?

'I didn't move the doll. How would I even know where you'd put it? Last I saw, you had it on the dining table, and then you took it away while I was on the phone. And now you've woken me up on my day off to yell at me.'

My mouth worked up and down, my brain seemed to have taken a holiday, nothing made any sense. 'Dolls can't move on their own,' I heard myself say.

'No, they can't.' Bekky put her hand on my shoulder. 'I think you must have done it in your sleep and not remembered. Nothing to get worked up about.'

'I'm sure you're right. Sorry I accused you.'

'Hey, I like a prank as much as the next guy, but this isn't funny. I wouldn't have done it even if I'd thought of it.'

Silence pulsed in the air between us.

'Maybe put it in the storage cage? Put it back in the box and then out in the garage. Then you can't go and get it while you're asleep and give yourself the willies.'

I nodded. 'I think I'll do that.'

I had to hurry, I was due at work in an hour and the morning's drama had put my schedule out of whack. I locked the creepy doll in the storage cage and walked to the tram. I arrived at work with five minutes to spare.

I didn't think about the doll for most of the day, we were slammed with customer queries running up to month end. When I arrived home that night, Bekky was out, maybe hanging with her new boyfriend, and the doll was nowhere to be seen.

I flopped down on the couch, closed my eyes and rested my head back. I realised I had fallen asleep when I was woken by my phone ringing.

'Jerry,' I said.

'I've told you I hate that name,' Jerome replied.

'I know, but you're so funny when you get mad.'

He sighed loudly.

'How's things?' I asked.

'Same soup, just reheated.'

I laughed; he always had the most bizarre ways to say he was fine.

'It's been ages since we hung out, I was checking you weren't dead.'

'It's only been a couple of weeks. And we've been texting most days, I hardly think I would be dead.' My voice was light, but with the tarot reading and the creepy doll, his comment sounded sinister. 'You didn't send me something, did you?'

'Send you something?'

'Yeah, in the mail.'

'No darling, why would I spend my time mailing you crap?'

'That's true. I got a package yesterday with this creepy doll inside. I thought you might have done it as a joke.'

'I'm offended you would think such a thing. That's not funny.'

I nodded, if not Jerome, then who? It would have been a weird choice for him, but I would have understood. Now he'd denied it, and I had no reason to think he was being untruthful, I was even more perturbed by this doll that had appeared from nowhere.

It was addressed to me, so it wasn't a delivery error, whoever had ordered it had my name and address. I scanned through my friends in my mind, there weren't many so it didn't take too long, and none seemed the sort of person who would send a gift without telling me, especially not a creepy one.

Even if I worked out who had sent it, I still had the problem of her moving during the night. It was possible I had done it, but I hadn't ever moved things while I slept before. Twenty-seven seemed a strange age to start sleepwalking.

'Anya, are you listening to me?'

'Hmm?'

The Tarot Reading

'I'm telling you about my dilemma with this guy I've met and you aren't listening at all. And you call yourself a friend.'

'Sorry, I drifted off there for a moment.'

'The world doesn't revolve around you, you know.'

'I'm sorry, tell me again.'

Most of the time, when Jerome said things like that, I found it amusing, he was such an over-the-top person, but today it rankled. Something was going on in my life, something that could be dangerous, what if I had a stalker? And he was dismissing it to ask about whether a person who didn't bleach their eyebrows to match their hair was worthy of a second date.

The image of the Devil tarot card flashed into my mind, a destructive force that had attached to me, what if it had meant Jerome?

'So now I don't know whether to text him back and arrange another hook-up tonight, or to block him,' Jerome said.

'Are those the only two options?'

'I need to find someone for tonight babe, I have needs.'

I looked at the clock, after nine, I certainly wasn't going out again at this time of night, but Jerome often partied on a weeknight, sometimes even coming to work straight from whatever party he'd been at through the night. How he managed to keep his job was beyond me.

'I don't know, hun. If it was me, I'd go with the guy you've already met, you know what he's like, and you know he's keen, why not give it a try a second time.'

He chuckled. 'I guess that's what I get for asking your opinion. You're a darling heart, but you don't know me very well if that's your answer.'

I sighed. He had wanted validation to ditch the man he'd already met on the path to a new conquest. It all sounded so tiresome, meeting people every night, spending all his money on alcohol and drugs, sleeping with strangers. 'I guess I don't.'

How have I not noticed how vapid he is before now? The conversation was starting to irk me, and I heard Bekky coming out of her room. 'I have to go, I hope you find a new playmate that is better groomed than the last guy. Kisses.' I hung up, no doubt he would be raging about it next time we spoke but for some reason I didn't care.

'Who was that?' Bekky asked.

'Jerome. Who else?'

'You sounded really pissed off.'

'I asked him if he'd sent the doll, he hadn't, but he didn't even care that someone sent me a creepy gift. He called me so I could give him an excuse to ditch some poor guy he's fucked once so he can move on to someone else.'

'You don't think he should?'

'The reason he didn't want a second date is his eyebrows don't match his hair. If there was ever a shallow reason to dump someone that's up there.' I shrugged. 'It seemed petty, and I wanted him to show more interest in my thing.'

Bekky leaned on the door jam. 'It's really bothering you.'

'I've never moved something in my sleep. I don't usually drunk order things online, and if I did, they wouldn't be fabric dolls.'

'It's not someone who thinks it's funny?'

'I can't think of anyone who would think it was funny. My friends are pretty boring, with the exception of Jerome, who does all of our partying on our behalf.'

I went through the motions getting ready for bed with my mind still on the damned doll. I needed to figure out where it had come from, but where to start?

I should apologise to Jerome for being short with him too, I don't know what came over me. Throughout our friendship his borderline narcissistic obsession with hooking up and partying usually gave me a vicarious thrill. Since the tarot reading, I'd been less inclined to text him, a distance was opening between us, and today I had been harsh. He hadn't changed, I had, and he didn't deserve to be cut off like that.

I'll text him tomorrow.

Assuming the doll doesn't appear on my chair again tomorrow morning, I was hopeful for a more productive day.

*

I woke before my alarm and lay awake with my eyes closed until it went off at seven. I turned over and looked at the chair, my heart pounding in my chest, but it was vacant.

It must have been me moving the doll in my sleep, I thought. I checked my phone, the adrenaline in my system starting to drain away now I knew I was alone in my bedroom. I'd had four missed calls from Jerome overnight. I had my phone set not to ring unless it was family.

Jerome had been through a particularly annoying phase a few years ago where he would call me at two, three, or even four in the morning to talk to me while he was out partying. He was always off his head on some substance or other and didn't make a lot of sense. Half the time when I asked him about it, he wouldn't remember.

I listened to the voicemail he had left after the third call.

'Anya, you bitch, I can't believe you aren't answering the phone. This guy is amazing, he's got a dick like a horse, and stamina for days. Come out and join us, he has a really cute friend who likes women. God you're so boring.'

I sighed, four calls could have meant he'd had an accident and was in the hospital, but of course he wanted me to come and party with him. I deleted the voicemail.

After scrolling through social media for a while, I realised I was going to be late if I didn't get a move on. I extracted myself from the bed, pulled on some clothes that smelled clean enough, though they probably could have used a wash, and stumbled into the kitchen.

And there it was. The fucking doll, sitting on the dining table, facing me as I stepped out of the hallway. I blinked slowly in case I was imagining it, but when I reopened my eyes, she was still sitting there, her grinning face mocking me.

'How did you get there?' I asked aloud. I took three steps to the table, snatched her up and threw her into the rubbish bin. I'll have to take it out later today so she can't come back in.

My nerves were twanging with stress, all the calm I had managed to find when she wasn't on the chair was long gone. My hands shook as I poured my coffee, and I wondered if I should be having caffeine after all the stress and adrenaline.

Somehow time had gotten away from me, again, and I dashed out of the house, coffee in my travel cup and no breakfast, hoping I would be at work by nine.

I missed the tram; it was rolling away as I approached the stop.

'Fuck,' I said aloud, startling an elderly woman passing the tram stop. 'Sorry.'

She frowned but said nothing. If she knew the morning I was having I'm sure she'd forgive one expletive, but some people are judgemental about swearing.

The next tram trundled along about ten minutes later and was jam-packed already. I was definitely going to be late. I squeezed on board and stood next to a thin young man with an enormous backpack that he'd put on the floor between his feet to save space, not that it helped much.

Stuck in a really slow tram, might be late. Sorry.

I texted my boss with one hand while I hung onto the overhead rail. I wondered if I should check in on Jerome. My thumb hovered over his name, but I decided not to call. If he was on the way to work, he wouldn't appreciate the interruption and if he wasn't, it wasn't my responsibility.

If he was the devil from the tarot reading, he was a bad influence on me, but on the other hand I was selfish and decadent so I should be more community minded. The whole reading was contradictory and confusing.

Ever since that day my mind hadn't been settled. My thoughts were confused, I forgot things, and became more easily stressed. It was as though the reading was a curse that had been put on me, instead of revealing what was happening around me.

The tram lurched to a halt in Elizabeth Street, near the corner of Bourke, and I threaded my way to the exit. At the crossing, the green man turned on, and the blipping of the crossing alert sounded. I stepped into the street and didn't see the motorcycle until it was too late. It slipped on the tram tracks and was skidding out of control into the pedestrian walkway. The world slowed down, I knew it was going to hit me, but there was nothing I could do about it. I half-turned away and felt the chassis collide with my side.

A sudden, burning pain split through my body, and I heard a bloodcurdling scream. My feet went out from under me, I rolled over the body of the bike, crashing into the rider as I went.

I ended up on the pavement, crumpled in an unnatural mass of limbs. Everything hurt, but my left leg, and hip felt like I was on fire. I tried to breathe, to call for help, but nothing came out of my mouth.

I looked around, I couldn't focus. I started to panic.

'Don't try to get up. Stay still.' A calm male voice said from somewhere behind me. 'Someone's calling the ambulance, but it's better if you can stay still.' His head came into my field of view, a forty-something-year-old man with kind eyes, deep tan skin, a neat black beard and a Sikh-style turban on his head.

'I'm Parminder, try to stay calm, okay?'

My eyes rolled around in their sockets trying to get a grip on where I was. A moment ago, I had been trying to get to work.

'I'm going to be late for work,' I said.

'Alright, don't worry about that now.' Parminder had put his hand on my shoulder, it was warm and he was reassuring although I didn't know who he was. The pain in my side came in waves, I tried to breathe slowly, in through the nose and heavy out through the mouth. I don't know why I thought that would help.

'Yes, that's good, keep breathing. I'm going to stay here until the ambulance arrives.' He said some other vaguely soothing things, but I found it hard to concentrate.

'Where's my bag?' I couldn't feel it on my shoulder or see it anywhere.

'The blue and grey one? It's a little way behind you.' He waved to someone I couldn't see, and the bag appeared above my head. 'I'll make sure it stays with you, no need to worry.'

He kept saying that: no need to worry, but I was in more pain than I had ever been in, lying on the footpath in the city after losing an argument with a motorbike. If there was ever a time to worry, it was now.

'Where's the other guy?'

'There is someone with him too. I saw the whole thing, very scary. He lost control on the tracks and then came crashing into you. It's not like in the movies, it was all too quick and too slow all at once.'

I moved my eyes over the scene in front of me, I could see the bike over to the left of my field of vision. The rider was partially under the bike.

How did that happen? Whether it was shock or pain my brain wasn't making sense of what was going on around me. I wanted to close my eyes, but the pain wouldn't let me relax. Breathing was hard, thinking was harder.

At some point the ambulance arrived, I heard the sirens coming for a long time before they stopped. The paramedics gave me a green whistle filled with painkillers.

'Breathe deeply on that.' A young man in a dark blue uniform said to me.

I took a massive breath, and I choked on the powder inside the whistle. I took it out and coughed. The paramedic gently guided the whistle back to my mouth.

'Keep breathing on that, okay?'

I nodded, the second inhale was better, and everything got fuzzy after that.

*

The next time I felt anywhere close to compos mentis was several hours later in the emergency department. Time had gone quite strange when I'd taken the drugs the paramedics gave me.

One of the doctors came around, his face taught with concern. 'You managed to get quite banged up there, Anya, but I have to say on the whole it could have been much worse.'

I blinked. 'Really? I feel like he did a pretty good job.'

'You've got extensive bruising down the left side, and a greenstick fracture of the left tibia. You'll need to wear a plaster cast for a while, then a moonboot for about six weeks, and won't be able to put weight on that leg for that time, but it was a nice clean, contained break.'

'Great,' I said, not meaning it.

'Now, you said you didn't hit your head on the way down, so that's a good sign, seems like we don't need to worry about concussion. We'll keep you here a night or two to make sure, but then you should be okay to go home.'

'No surgery?'

'Nothing in your scans suggests we need it. Of course, if things change, we might need to reassess but, honestly, you've come out of this with fewer injuries than we might have expected.'

I nodded. It all seemed a bit surreal.

'Do you have any other questions?'

'I don't think so.' I paused. 'Do you know where my things are?'

'The nurses have your bag; we'll make sure you have it on the ward.'

'Okay.' My eyes were getting heavy. All this talking was exhausting.

It occurred to me as I was lying on the gurney that I hadn't shown up to work, and I hadn't called them. I guess I'll have to let them know I won't be in for a few days. Maybe I'll even try to work from home for a few weeks.

Some time later, I was wheeled up to the ward, then given some dinner: bland fish and boiled veggies. The nurse left a blue plastic garbage bag with all my stuff in it on a chair next to my bed.

Rolling over to find my phone, my bruised left side screamed in protest. I shouldn't have done that. I lifted up the hospital gown to look, my hip, thigh, and some of my ribs were red and tender where the bruises were starting to come out. The plaster cast came up to my knee and was elevated on a couple of pillows. I rolled onto my back and tried again to reach for my phone without putting pressure on the bruises.

After a long five minutes of feeling around blindly, I found it. I had two missed calls from work, and a few other notifications.

I listened to my voicemails.

'Hi Anya, this is Joe,' my boss's voice was concerned but not yet worried, 'just wondering when you'll be in today?'

That was at nearly ten o'clock. Nice of him to wait an hour before calling, I thought.

'Hi Anya, Joe again. We were expecting you in the office. Can you give me a ring when you get this. I hope you're not dead in a ditch or something.' He laughed but it was hollow. Definitely starting to worry by three o'clock. It was after seven now, no use calling him back now, better to text.

> **Hi Joe, sorry about today. I was involved in a traffic accident on the way to work. I'm okay mostly. Broken leg. I'll be in hospital for a couple of days they reckon, should be back at work in a week or so. I'll call you tomorrow.**

He'd get a surprise in the morning, unless he checked his work phone outside work hours. I laid back on the bank of pillows and closed my eyes. I wasn't sleepy but must have fallen asleep.

'Anya?' a soft male voice asked.

'What?'

'It's time for some painkillers.' The nurse came into the room carrying a small paper cup.

'Thanks.'

'Let me know if you need anything, you can use the bell here.' He pointed to the small white controller attached to the side of the bed. It had the nurse call button as well as the controls for the TV. The nurse went back out into the hall.

I sat up a little more, trying to get comfortable, not that any position was comfortable. Now I was awake I was glad to have the extra painkillers, there was a dull ache in my leg that I hadn't been aware of.

'I almost forgot, someone left this for you,' he said, coming back in carrying a small shape. The room was quite dim, as he approached my bed, I saw what he was holding.

'Oh no, I don't want that.'

He was holding that fucking doll. This time it had a small, fabric crutch sewn under one arm and a white fabric cast over the left leg.

'You don't want it?' His eyebrows rose in confusion.

'I don't know who sent it. I got one to my home a few days ago and now here. I haven't told anyone I've been in an accident so I don't know how they knew but—' my throat had dried up and my words faltered. 'Can you throw it out? It's really creepy and I don't want it in here.'

The Tarot Reading

'Oh . . . I'm sorry, I didn't know.' He pulled the doll away from me, holding it awkwardly against his chest. 'I'll take it away.' He nodded and stepped outside again, his blank face demonstrating his incomprehension. *At least he did as I asked*, I thought.

If I didn't know any better, I'd have thought the doll was following me, but that can't be true. Dolls can't move on their own. I'm being silly. Maybe they called Mum and I didn't remember or something. She might have sent something along from the gift shop. That would be a reasonable explanation.

With that settled, some of the tightness in my chest released. I sent a text Jerome and Bekky to let them know what had happened, before the waves of fatigue pushed my head back down and I fell into empty sleep.

*

The next morning various medical professionals came to see me, the doctor was first, giving me a rundown of the injuries again. I appreciated it, since despite him having definitely told me yesterday my brain wasn't functioning at the time, and I had forgotten.

'You'll need to do exercises at home to make sure your leg doesn't get too weak when you're not using it. The physiotherapist will come later. At the very least you need to get up and do a lap around the house or the ward every couple of hours. Your bruises will be painful for a while, especially if you bump them, but they should heal up quickly.' He was a very charming, good-looking blond man with an English accent. I tried to keep my mind on his instructions, but it was much harder than normal.

'I'll be back tomorrow and then we should be able to send you home. Okay?'

I nodded, and he took his leave. A while later the physio came to show me some stuff to do at home and wrote out a program for me on a piece of paper. Each exercise was accompanied by a little stick figure drawing in case I forgot what I was supposed to do.

When the nurse came in with my medication at lunch time I was exhausted again.

'You can have a little nap this afternoon, it's very tiring being injured.' She was an older lady with a pudgy, kind face.

'Thanks. I'm surprised how wrecked I feel.'

'It's perfectly natural. Listen to how you're feeling.'

I nodded, took my tablets with the last of the apple juice I had with lunch, and saw the damned doll was sitting on the bench on the opposite wall.

'Did you put that there?' I said, trying to keep the wobble out of my voice.

'Yes, it was in the nurse's station with your name on it.'

'I—' I swallowed and started again. 'I asked the nurse last night to remove it. I don't want it in my room.' My voice was rising in pitch, I sounded hysterical.

'It's alright dear, I'll move it. It seemed such a sweet little gift. But I can see it's upsetting so we'll get rid of it.' Her eyes were wide, her small, plump mouth pursed in concern.

How did that fucking doll keep turning up? If I wasn't so exhausted, I'd follow her into the nurse's station, cut the damn thing into pieces, and stuff them in the incinerator, assuming they have an incinerator.

I sat back, trying to calm my racing pulse, and jumped when I heard my phone buzzing.

'Hello?'

'Anya! My God, what happened?' Joe, my boss sounded wild, almost shouting down the phone. Clearly, he hadn't seen my message until today.

'I'm okay.' I told him the story, as I was talking, I recalled the accident in vivid detail, but was somehow detached.

'My God, my God. You poor thing. Of course, we'll do everything we can on our end. You can have as much time off as you need and if you need to work from home, you can do that. How is your family taking the news?'

Shit, my family. I hadn't told Mum. 'Uh . . .'

'Never mind, sorry that was too personal. Um . . . I'm not really sure what to say. Do you need anything?'

'That's very kind of you to offer, but I'm okay.' All things considered, and not counting the creepy doll that is stalking me. Bekky and Jerome both claimed not to be involved with it, and no one else knew about the accident.

On the other end of the phone, Joe was babbling about the work I had been in the middle of before my unexpected absence, I was too tired to participate in the conversation, I let the words roll over me. He didn't need me to reply, there were no pauses in his monologue for my input in any case.

'Goodness, is that the time? I'm late for a meeting with the exec. Reach out if you need anything, otherwise I'll leave it with you to tell us when you're well enough to come back. Even a few days, a week, whatever you need. Okay, well, take care. Bye.' Joe tended to talk when he was nervous, and he must have been very worried about my being away from work. He'd done some digging around in what I was up to, based on the rundown of outstanding stuff he'd given me, and I felt less guilty about leaving them in the middle of everything. Not that I could do anything about it, even if I'd wanted to.

I needed to tell Mum, but I was dreading the conversation. She'd want to come and see me, which would have been fine if she wasn't so over the top. I love her, but she had a knack for making any time I was unwell into a performance of how good a mother she was. Her new partner was just as bad, being supportive to the point of intruding on family business.

'Hi Mum,' I said when she answered the call.

'Hi darling, lovely to hear from you, but aren't you supposed to be working?' She sounded breathless.

'Yes, normally I would be at work, but—'

'I'm in the middle of a workout with George, can I talk to you another time?'

I hoped workout didn't mean sex, I was all for Mum having an active sex life, but I did not want to know any details. 'I'm not calling for a chat. I need to give you some news.'

A beat of silence. 'What sort of news?' I could almost see the narrowing of the eyes, and the suspicious expression on her face.

'I've had an accident. Well, been involved in an accident—'

She tried to interrupt but I pressed on. 'I'm in hospital, broken leg, but I don't want you to worry, I'm fine, there's no need for you and George to come.'

'Hospital? Broken leg? What do you mean not come, of course we have to come.'

'Please don't. I just want to rest. I'd much rather you come when I'm back home, maybe you can make me a casserole or something.'

If I manage to get away without naming the hospital, I should be safe, I thought. I could hear Mum relating the story to her partner, who was clearly in the room.

'I'm putting you on speaker, George is here too.'

'Hi George.'

'Tell me what happened. I know you don't want me to visit, which I think is very unfair of you, but at least tell me the story so I don't worry.'

'Okay.' I told the two of them the story, which took much longer than it should have with all the interruptions, exclamations, side stories and anecdotes about people she knew.

'Are you sure you're being looked after?' Mum said when I'd finally got to the end of the story.

'Yes, they're doing good, I'm fine I promise.' *Please don't insist on coming.*

'Alright, well, you know we're here for you, I'll start on some food parcels for you. My poor baby, such a terrible thing to have happened. I knew something bad was coming, I've had a sense of foreboding for weeks.'

She had foreboding feelings all the time; it was mere chance this time she was right.

'I love you, I've gotta go.' My eyelids were leaden, I'd given up and closed them a few minutes earlier, and had to force them open to end the call. Mum could never find the button and I didn't want to talk her through hanging up after everything else.

I dozed through the afternoon. Dinner in the hospital was served at quarter to six, very early for my usual standards, but when there wasn't much to do except sleep and eat, I was grateful for a break from daytime TV. As I was about to start eating, I heard a familiar voice.

'Yoohoo bitch, I'm here.' Jerome burst into the room through the open door to the rest of the ward. At some point in the afternoon my roommate had been cleared out and the now empty bed made the room feel bigger and more sterile.

'Hi.'

'I can't believe you got hit by a runaway motorbike. Only you could get injured in such an extra way.' Jerome leaned over the bed to hug me and kiss each of my cheeks.

'I made it dramatic just for you.' I wasn't in the mood for banter today, Jerome was often acerbic in his humour, and I didn't have the stamina to be the butt of jokes today. I hoped he would get the message without me having to tell him.

'I know it wasn't your fault, of course darling, I was trying to bring a bit of levity. I hate hospitals you know.'

'I know.' *If there was any other choice, I wouldn't be here either,* I thought.

'You're going to miss out on so much stuck in here, I'll have to do all your partying on your behalf.'

You do that anyway. 'Sounds good.'

'Work is doing my head in.' He showed no interest in asking me how I was doing, I suppose I should have expected as much, the relationship seemed very one-sided. I took the place of a boyfriend, or silent partner, a person that Jerome could talk at and hash out his plans and aspirations, since he was uninterested in sleeping with anyone more than once. It had become more and more clear that he did not do the same for me in return. He dominated every conversation, we only ever met when it was convenient for him, and he would leave half the time if he had an offer of sex.

'What's happening at work?' I asked.

'My boss, the one I told you was super uptight, definitely not getting any sex, and a little bit racist, anyway, she's been really on my back about my deliverables—'

I tuned out, Jerome didn't need much from me once he was on a roll, the occasional nod, or sound effect to show I was listening; a strategically placed 'aw' or 'hmm' was enough. I've known this about him for years, perhaps ever since I've met him, and yet it's only when I'm laid up in hospital and I can't get away it feels like a problem.

I shifted, pushing myself a little further up the bed, sending a jolt of pain through my hip and side where the bruises were. The leg in the plaster was protected and I hardly felt it. I waited to see if Jerome registered my discomfort, but he made no mention of it, and didn't slow his monologue.

Now I'd noticed these bad behaviours in my friend I could no longer ignore them. Every time he started a sentence with 'I' it grated. There must be something about being in a lot of pain that ruins the patience.

'I need to have a rest, sorry,' I said, cutting him off mid-sentence.

'Oh.' He stared for a moment, as though not sure how to respond. 'I'd better go anyway. I'm meeting Anton for a drink in the city.' He wriggled his eyebrows suggestively, I'm sure he wanted me to ask about Anton.

'Thanks for visiting. It's been so lovely to see you.' The words felt wrong in my mouth, I hoped my impatience wasn't showing on my face.

The Tarot Reading

'Love you, talk soon yeah?' Jerome stood to give me a kiss on each cheek. 'Be good.'

'I will.' Not that I'd have much opportunity for anything the least bit rebellious from the hospital bed. I watched Jerome walking out of the room before laying back against the pillows. I exhaled, letting go of the tension I had been holding in my belly, and shoulders.

3.

I was allowed home after six days in the hospital, on the proviso that Bekky was going to help me with putting a bag over my cast to shower, to cook, and whatever else needed doing until I was able to put weight on the leg. She wasn't impressed if the expression on her face was to be believed, but she agreed.

The first three days I was exhausted after the most basic tasks, I hadn't moved around much in hospital, and now I had to get up to the toilet and kitchen several times a day.

At some point during a sunny afternoon, sitting on the couch with my leg propped on some cushions, I fell asleep. I found myself dreaming vividly; the colours were too bright, the sounds too loud, it was almost painful. I blinked and tried to orient myself, and when I opened my eyes, I saw the doll. Except now it was bigger, nearly a metre tall, and looked like she was made of porcelain instead of being fabric. She was walking towards me, down the hallway from my bedroom. Her eyes moved around in her porcelain face, her arms and legs working on their own to bring her closer and closer to me. Her gait was odd, slightly lopsided, but then she was a doll brought to life in a dream, so it seemed natural for her to walk a little strangely.

I should have been terrified, every waking encounter with her had been scary, and her reappearance in the dream world could easily have resulted in the same existential terror, yet I was calm. I sat up on the couch, I'd been lying down to nap, and my leg was no longer in the cast. I swung my legs around to the floor and waited for the doll to arrive.

'Anya.' Her painted porcelain lips didn't move, but I knew it was her voice. 'My name is Joan. I'm the high priestess. I've been sent to protect and guide you, but you've rejected my aid, so I have to visit in your dreams where we can talk freely.'

'No way. You're a talking doll. This is a dream. I'll wake up in a minute.'

Joan sighed heavily, it was a weird sound given she had no mouth or lungs with which to make it. Maybe it was more of a telepathic understanding equivalent to a sigh. 'You have not heeded the guidance of the tarot reading. We worked through Raven to show you the way to spiritual fulfilment and a joyful life, but you have sent me away, many times, and now you are catastrophically injured.'

'That's a bit strong, I've just broken my leg, I'll be fine in a few weeks.' I laughed, a manic, high-pitched laugh of disbelief.

'If you will not accept our gifts, our love, our time, we will leave you to your fate. Remember the omens Raven pointed to, the Devil in your life, the unforeseen tragedy. Your life is in the balance, but we cannot force you to change.' She held her porcelain doll hands facing the ceiling in exasperation.

'No, wait. What do you mean my life is in the balance?'

'This is not the only bad event we foresee on this path. Your accident with the motorcycle, it is merely the first of a series of disasters. Each worse than the last.'

'What's worse that being hit with a bike?' I said, mostly to myself.

'Some of my kindred think it unwise to tell you . . . the Devil is causing your body to decay. Your insides are festering, if you act now, they can be saved. If you withdraw from his presence and take heed of our warnings. If you change your ways in time, you will be saved.'

'Saved. You sound like the bible bashers yelling in Bourke Street.' I didn't feel sick, but I had already started to pull away from Jerome. I assume that's who she meant by the devil.

'You know of whom we speak,' Joan said, as though reading my mind. 'His ways are corrupting you. Diverting your true path. I can help you, but you must keep me by your side. Even when you wake. Do you swear to undertake this task?'

'What task?'

'Do you swear?' Joan said, her voice somehow louder and more insistent as though she was yelling.

The Tarot Reading

'Okay, I swear I'll stop hanging out with Jerome. And I won't put the doll in the bin next time.'

I woke up with a start, my brain still ringing form the magical voice of the doll in my head. My left leg tingled inside the cast, and my eyes were bleary from sleep. I sat up and saw the fabric doll sitting on the coffee table. In her hand this time was a tiny fabric book, and in the other a small round object.

In the tarot, the high priestess is aligned with the moon, I thought, although I wasn't sure how I knew that. My phone vibrated on the coffee table; I picked it up to see a message from Jerome.

Anton and I are having dinner in Carlton, do you want me to come visit before that? I'm so bored without my bestie to talk to.

Of course, he makes it about him, and nothing to do with my being caged up in the house with a broken leg. A twinge of pain ran down my side, as I tossed the phone back onto the table without replying. I hoped he would know I didn't want company by my silence, and not come anyway.

How am I supposed to get rid of him? I can't tell him I don't want to hang out anymore, can I? The doll sat on the table staring at me with her embroidered eyes.

'Do you realise what a crappy position this puts me in? I don't have many friends and now you want me to cold shoulder my best friend?' I flopped back on the couch and threw my arm over my eyes.

A crushing urge to cry rolled over me; my eyes stung, my throat tightened, and my breathing became all shallow. What sort of life was I living to realise my best friend used me as a rubber duck? I didn't need a personality, or any opinions, he needed an audience for his grandiose monologues, and when there were no men waiting to fuck him, I formed his own private auditorium.

Hot tears streamed down my cheeks, landing in my ears. I shook my head dislodging them to run into my hairline. What a mess I was. Maybe it was for the best that the—I didn't even know who, the powers that be, had stepped in and stopped me from following Jerome around until he, well, I wasn't clear, but somehow, he seemed to be poisoning me over repeated exposures.

I guess his bed partners saw him once, maybe twice if they were lucky, and he moved on, they wouldn't have his toxicity seeping into them over years and years like I did.

'What am I supposed to do then, Joan?' I said to the doll. She sat on the coffee table staring at me, inanimate.

'Are you talking to the doll?' Bekky had come home at some point during my nap.

'Yeah. Her name is Joan. It's a long story.'

'Tell me.' Bekky sat on the floor next to the couch.

'What do you mean?'

'You were asking the doll for advice; do you think a human person might be better to ask?'

I bit my lip, what would she think of me if I told her the doll spoke to me in my dreams?

'I think I should stop spending time with Jerome.'

Bekky's head jerked back as though she were shocked. 'Isn't he your best friend?'

I looked away. 'I used to think so. He says I'm his best friend, but I don't think he knows the first thing about me—when we hang out, he never asks about me, we always do what he wants to do, and if he gets a text from a hook-up, he ditches me. I just…'

'You just?'

'I wonder what I get out of the relationship. If I might be better off trying to find a new friendship group, expand my horizons. There's no chance Jerome will introduce me to a nice man to settle down with, and he's quite insulting.'

'Mmm.' Bekky ran her finger back and forth over her lower lip. 'I didn't want to say anything, because I thought you two were so close, but I've never liked him.'

'Never?'

'No, he's . . . well you know what he's like. He'll take what he can get from a person, use them up and move on.'

'Is that why you don't come out with us?'

Bekky nodded. 'I enjoy your company, Anya, but Jerome is like a black hole. Take, take, take and I don't want that energy around me.'

I didn't know what to say. I had lived with Bekky for years, and Jerome had been a part of my life the whole time, popping in on the way to meet someone or other, or standing me up at the last minute, and all along Bekky didn't like him.

'I probably wouldn't have appreciated you saying so before. Thank you.'

Bekky put her hand on my good knee. 'Of course. You deserve people around you who love you and lift you up. He doesn't.'

'So how do I . . . extricate myself?' My phone buzzed again on the coffee table. I picked it up to read the message.

I'll be at yours in about 15minutes. Can't stay long, you better be awake, haha.

My face went slack, my eyes stared straight ahead.

'Show me?' Bekky put her hand out to take the phone, I let her. 'Wow. He doesn't even wait for you to reply to say it's okay. He's a real piece of work.'

'How do I—what do I say to him?' My throat felt tight with rising panic.

'Let him come. You can tell him you need some space in person, he might be more likely to hear you face to face?' Bekky's voice rose in tone as though it were a question, not a statement.

'I don't want to see him. I wish I could . . . close my eyes and have him gone.' My eyes flicked to the doll, it hadn't moved, of course it couldn't move but its posture seemed more friendly, protective, as though now I'd made the decision to cut ties with the man who was draining me there were two strong women in my corner to support me.

'You'll have to tell him more than once. He'll probably think you're joking, or high on painkillers, but if he comes around and you tell him he can't visit, that will be one less time he's walked over your needs to satisfy his own desires.'

'You're right.' I looked down at myself, in tracksuit pants with one leg cut off for my cast, and one of the T-shirts I slept in. I couldn't spar with Jerome looking like this. 'Can you help me change my top?'

'Of course.'

With as much energy as I could gather, I hurried to the bedroom, with Bekky in toe to help. We found a clean T-shirt, and I even put on a bra. I felt presentable, or at least not ashamed to be seen, that would have to do.

As I was navigating the hallway back to my spot on the couch, the doorbell rang. Bekky and I locked eyes, she nodded and stood behind me as I turned to open the door.

'You're not dead. Good,' Jerome said as I swung the door open. He started to step forward, and I put my hand out.

'It's not a good time for a visit.'

He hesitated, foot raised in mid-air. 'You're such a kidder, move out of the way, hoppy.'

'I'm serious. I don't want you to come in.'

His eyes narrowed, placing his foot down on the door mat. 'This isn't funny. I said I was coming to visit. Where's your sense of hospitality?'

'I said no. I've got a broken leg; I don't want to entertain you. Please, come back another time.'

'Why are you being such a bitch? You never say no to me.'

'You're right, I haven't said no before, but I'm saying no today.'

'Well.' He drew himself up to his full height and looked down his beautiful patrician nose at me. 'I don't know why I should put up with this treatment. I suppose you're taking a lot of painkillers, so I'll let you off this once, but don't think I'm not keeping track.'

'Goodbye, Jerome.' I pushed the front door closed and sagged against it.

'Well done.' Bekky's voice was small but comforting.

'I've never seen him so furious.' I pushed myself upright and started to wobble back to the couch. 'My legs are jelly.'

'Sit down, I'll make a nice cup of tea, and then you can let the adrenaline wear off. What a freak to be demanding to come visit when you're the one with a broken leg.'

'He does what he wants when he wants. I'm surprised I've been his friend so long.'

Bekky clanked around the kitchen making the tea. My legs weren't the only part of me that had reacted—my arms were weak, and my heart still pounded in my ears.

The doll on the coffee table had a slight smile, as though she was pleased to see me taking her advice.

'I hope you saw that. This better not make things worse,' I said to the doll.

Twenty minutes later when the initial shock had worn off, I was quite pleased with myself. I was wrung out, and while the cup of tea was comforting, I couldn't help feeling a little lonely. I still had Bekky, we'd been friends before we moved in, but I had let Jerome be most of my social network for far too long.

'I need a hobby,' I announced to the empty room.

'You talking to me?' Bekky's head popped around the kitchen doorway.

'I think I need a hobby. Something to keep me from going back to Jerome when I'm back moving around.'

'That sounds good. What sort of hobby?'

'Uhh . . .' I hadn't thought that far. I didn't do much—walked for exercise with the occasional yoga class, never been much into music or singing, and crafts seemed a bit old-lady-like.

'Maybe dancing?' I said after a while. 'Though it might be a while before I'm up to it.'

'I have a friend who does pole dancing, she really enjoys it, part exercise, part fun. Really good for the core and easier on your feet that some other stuff.'

I made an unenthusiastic face.

'Or not . . . I used to draw you could join a drawing club? Or a book club?'

'That sounds a bit more my speed.' I smiled, trying to be reassuring, Bekky was doing her best, but I felt adrift. Without Jerome I had no idea who I was. I supposed that was part of the lesson the doll wanted me to learn. Damn it if she wasn't right.

'You could go to a psychic; they might know what sort of thing you should get into.' Bekky spoke from the kitchen where she was preparing dinner.

'I think I've done my dash with psychics after that tarot reading.'

Although she might be onto something. I pulled out my phone and looked for Raven the tarot reader, I figured he might have more to tell me since I'd kicked the devil out of my life.

Now make sure you don't let him back in, I thought to myself.

4.

Raven had a little shop in a strip mall in Footscray. The night markets were finished for the year, and I wasn't up to navigating a crowd. It had been a couple of weeks since my confrontation with Jerome, and he had tried to visit a couple more times; I brushed him off with excuses about being tired with the leg, and thankfully he never turned up on my doorstep again. As time went by his texts were less frequent, though he hadn't given up yet.

I took a taxi to Footscray to the storefront where Raven's website said he worked. I had made any appointment online but used Bekky's name for the booking in case he refused to see me.

If he was truly psychic, he'd know I was coming but it seemed like he needed the cards to help him. Not that I believed he was a proper psychic, although I had a doll whose face changed and visited my dreams, so perhaps I should be more open minded.

I hobbled in with my crutches, the bell over the door chimed as I entered.

'Be right with you,' a deep male voice said from somewhere at the back of the shop. The products for sale were mostly crystals and New Age stuff: dreamcatchers hung from the walls, brightly-coloured paintings of unicorns and other mythical creatures to the left, and an array of books to the right proclaimed all sorts of ways to better your life.

'Right, I'm here—it's you.' Raven stepped out from behind a black velvet curtain screening off another room.

'Yes.'

'Your leg?'

'Hit by a motorbike.'

'I . . . uh I didn't realise it was you I was seeing. I'm not sure I can do a reading.'

'I've started separating from the bad influence. At least, I'm trying. A doll, or possibly a spirit, called Joan has been guiding me, but she's . . . cryptic to say the least. I wondered if you had any more useful suggestions.'

'I have never given a reading like yours. Scared me. Whoever that person is, they were a blight on your spiritual wellbeing. I'm glad to hear you're making changes, but I'm afraid I'm still not comfortable with another reading.'

'Please? I've come all this way, and on a broken leg.' I laid it on thick. I didn't want to go home without what I came for.

'It took me a week to calm down last time. The cards are never so black, but you . . . I'm not even sure if getting rid of one person would be enough.'

'I'm here to learn. You turned my life upside down last time. I thought I was doing alright but since that day everything has fallen apart. I need help to rebuild, or at least a few pointers in the right direction.'

Raven's pale skin was blotched with red, whether it was stress or embarrassment or something else I couldn't tell. He rubbed the back of his neck, mumbling to himself.

'Alright,' he said after a while. 'Give me a minute to compose myself, and we'll have to do a bit of a cleanse of you too. Sit down here,' he pointed to a chair behind the counter, 'and I'll make us some ginger tea and then you can come out the back where I do the readings. What is your name?'

'Anya, and thank you.'

'I'll take the payment in advance. Fifty dollars cash, please.'

Perhaps commerce is guiding his decision more than he would like to admit, I thought as I pulled my money out to pay him before he disappeared into the back of the shop again.

I sat in the chair for at least ten minutes while he bustled around behind the curtain, I caught snippets of him talking to himself, possibly talking himself into the reading. My leg had started to ache, the taxi ride, standing in the shop and this uncomfortable chair all contributed to a throbbing leg inside the moonboot.

Eventually the muttering subsided, and he came back through the curtain with an air of calm certainty, if a little undermined by the remnants of blotchy redness on his thin neck and upper chest visible through the open buttons of his black shirt.

'Come through, please,' he said, holding the curtain back for me as I walked through. Behind the curtain was a narrow passage, a battered-looking white painted door opened onto a tiny kitchen—just large enough for a kettle, a microwave, a minifridge, a sink, and a row of cups hanging from hooks on the wall. Further down the hall, we stepped onto a covered concrete balcony, I paused to step down the small step onto the patio and then again to step up into the small weatherboard outbuilding. The room was a little larger than the average closet, perhaps a converted garden shed. The carpet was faded deep red, on which were placed the same folding table and chairs that Raven had at the market, complete with the large crystal ball in the centre. The walls were unadorned fibreglass cladding and there were no windows.

I manoeuvred my way into the small space and sat heavily on the closer of the two chairs, propping my crutches against the wall beside me. Raven followed me in and arranged himself opposite. He pulled out a large deck of tarot cards from some hidden pocket and started to shuffle them.

'While you were waiting, I did a little cleansing of the space, and preparing myself for anything that might come up during your reading. Last time, as I say, it was rather disconcerting, however your aura is much clearer today.' He took a deep breath, closed his eyes, hands still shuffling the cards.

'I want you to picture in your mind the question you would like answered. It can help if you close your eyes,' he said, his voice taking on the soothing drone of a mediation teacher or yogi.

I let my eyes drift closed.

'Deep breaths, in and out, through the nose. We're here to help guide Anya to a new, light-filled life of spiritual service.'

I cracked my eyelid a little to see if he was mocking me, but Raven's eyes remained closed, his expression impassive, a little over the top, but sincere.

'Open your eyes.' Raven put the cards face down on the table to his right. 'Take the cards and give them a shuffle. Hold in your mind the question you wish to answer. Think about your plans and desires for the future.'

I took the cards; my fingers were clumsy with them the same as last time. I held in mind my home, being happy there, surrounded by friends, Jerome safely and completely out of my life. Maybe even a romantic interest if I was so lucky. Joan came into my mind, her bland doll-face flashed across my inner vision before fading again, maybe she wouldn't stay once I was on the right path. When it felt right, I put the cards back on the table.

'We're going to start with a simple three card spread. I will ask the cards to guide us to see the current situation, any remaining obstacles, and to offer some advice.' Raven took the cards in his left hand. 'If this short reading is—goes well, we can spend a little more time and perhaps consult the crystal ball.'

I nodded, more because he seemed to require a response than anything else.

'Two of pentacles. A difficult situation but perhaps not as bad as you thought. You must make some adjustments to your path to achieve what you need to.'

He flipped over another card. 'The obstacle, eight of swords. You're in conflict, crisis and perhaps people are talking about you behind your back. Sounds about right, but this is not a disastrous card, there is hope in it. Difficult to get out of need not mean impossible.'

I was barely breathing. The last reading Raven had given me seemed comical at the time but had resulted in a broken leg and the dissolution of a relationship I had come to rely on. At least this time he seemed to be taking the cards in his stride, his skin was almost blotch-free.

'Finally, three of pentacles, another pentacle. This suit represents earth, grounding, stability, sometimes manifestation. Perhaps we can interpret this as suggesting both the obstacle and the solution are in possessions, in money. Three is the card for mastery, for learning a skill, for renown or nobility. The solution then may lie with making a change in your skills, surrounding yourself with others and prospering in a new field.' Raven looked at me expectantly.

'I'm not sure what that means.'

'Not yet maybe. Are you happy at work? Now that you've moved out of the orbit of the devil, I see he has not appeared again, perhaps you have room in your life for more fulfilling work, or hobbies.'

'I do have more time on my hands without Jerome. He was very demanding, and flaky.'

'Consider what you need to do to set your path clearly. It will be very easy to be drawn back into this man's sphere of influence. People like that love to target someone vulnerable, lost, in any way unsure.'

'Thanks.' I wasn't sure how this helped me and didn't like the insinuation that I was weak.

Raven cleared the cards back into his left hand and secreted them away to wherever he'd taken them from, I didn't see it even though I was looking for it this time.

'Take my hand,' he said, laying his right hand, palm-up, on the black tablecloth. I did as he asked.

'We're going to consult the crystal ball for further guidance.' Raven stared at the ball in the centre of the table in silence.

For a while I wondered if he was going to say anything but then his eyelids flared a little, a small frown creased his brow, before his face returned to its slack open stare.

Must be a slow process, I thought.

'There are so many images floating around you. Your past, your friends, your contacts, your spirit guides, Joan the high priestess, watching over you. It's hard to make out what is advice for the future.' Raven breathed deeply and continued to stare at the ball.

'You're on the right path, but you will have to fight to stay on it. There are many distractions, shiny objects beside the path to draw you away, not least of which is this ex-friend of yours. He won't let you go easily, but in the end, he will move on to another easier target if you stay strong.'

'Okay,' I said.

'I see some shadowy images ahead, they feel like positive influences, perhaps new friends, or lovers, perhaps they're children, it's hard to tell. They are waiting for you to find your way to them.'

'I was really hoping for something a bit more specific.'

The frown crossed over Raven's brow again, but his eyes remained fixed on the ball. 'You and everyone else who comes in here. I'm not a mind-reader, I can see the patterns around you, but the future is never fixed. It's up to you to create a life that brings you these positive influences, that creates joy and energy.'

I was silent, in case there was anything else to be gained.

'That's all I have.' Raven raised his eyes to mine, let out a sigh and pulled his hand away. 'You'll be thinking it was a waste of time and money to come here, but I promise you have the strength to do this; you will be better off as long as you can stay true to yourself.'

The Tarot Reading

I sat back against the chair, letting my head hang back to gaze at the ceiling. I don't know what I expected, but after the first reading I was disappointed. I hadn't come in hoping for drama, but now in the face of its complete absence, I was almost angry.

'Drama is not what gives life meaning. It doesn't serve you. You need to let it go with your old friend.'

I frowned slightly and looked back to Raven. 'What?'

'It's not hard to read you, your face and body language are very open. I see you wanted something juicier, but the universe wants you to learn to be humble, get in touch with yourself, be authentic.'

'Mmm.' The same stuff they say to people who want to lose weight, don't eat so much and you'll drop down. 'Easier said than done.'

'I believe in you. The energy around you will help keep you on the right track. Your main task will be to listen to the right people, or spirits as the case may be, and you'll be fine. The universe has smiled on you. Not everyone who had made it so far down the dark path would be able to get out so easily.'

'Sure.' I couldn't keep the scorn out of my voice, a major traumatic injury was a pretty steep price to pay for a new lease on life, but I had to admit I could have been killed in that accident. 'Thanks for your time.'

'Of course. You're welcome back any time, providing you don't fall back with certain people.'

'I'll do my best.' Now the reading was over the throbbing in my leg had started up again and I was desperate to get home. I struggled to stand and hobble back over the patio, through the narrow corridor and out of the shop. Raven was quiet as I exited, and I didn't have the strength for any more conversation.

The taxi ride home was unremarkable, save the few potholes and uneven road surfaces that jolted my jangled leg. By the time I got home, a little after five, I was ready for bed. I lay down, my left leg propped up on a pillow so some of the swelling could go down.

I looked over to my desk to see Joan, the doll, looking down at me with a half-smile.

'I'm doing my best,' I said aloud.

It's a long journey but we believe in you, you'll be fine now, Joan's voice echoed inside my mind. I'm fairly sure I was awake for that bit, but I fell asleep quickly afterwards, hopeful I was on the right path.

*

The next morning, I couldn't find Joan. I looked around the bedroom, in the lounge, in the bathroom (just in case), in the cupboards, but she wasn't anywhere.

My leg was still sore after all the excitement of seeing Raven the day before, so spent the day with it up.

'You okay?' Bekky said as she came into the lounge.

'Yeah, why?'

'Dunno, you look awkward.'

'Broken leg will do that.'

'True.' She walked past into the kitchen and turned the kettle on.

'Have you seen that doll?'

'Joan?'

'Yeah.'

'Not lately. You want a cuppa?'

'Yes please.' Should I be worried that I couldn't find Joan? I'd been trying to get rid of her for so long, and now she was gone, the uneasy feeling I had when I looked at her was now when I wasn't looking at her. Not knowing where she was, if she might pop up at any time, it was somehow more chilling than her constant presence.

Bekky came in with the tea and sat on the other couch. We watched a British comedy panel show, they were her favourite thing, and since I had no strong opinion about it, we sat through three half-hour episodes before I had to get up to pee.

As I was coming back into the lounge, I stood at the door. 'Are you heading to the supermarket today? I need a couple of things and thought I'd tag along if you don't mind.'

'Sure. Wanna go now?'

I nodded. 'Whenever.'

'I'll get the keys.' Bekky pushed herself out of the squishy couch and headed to her room to grab something.

I followed her down to the carpark, and I saw a familiar cardboard box in the storage cage; the box I'd put Joan in when I was trying to hide her.

'One second, I need to check something' I said to Bekky. I unlocked the cage and pulled the box toward me. When I opened it, it was empty, Joan wasn't in there either.

I guess she's gone. She turned up on my doorstep all on her own, and now she was gone just as suddenly. Maybe she'd done what she came for, I was rid of Jerome, I'd listened to her advice and now she was on her own again.

She knows where I am, if she needs to tell me something.

Bekky beeped the horn, a short sound to remind she was still waiting.

'Coming,' I said. I locked the cage and turned my back to it and the empty box.

Footprints

1.

In the beginning there was the void. The void was vast and empty. The void coalesced the first gods, elemental spirits of air, earth, fire, water, and psyche. They created the worlds from these five elements, but no growing things yet formed.

The first gods had no gender and would come together in all combinations to produce the next generation of gods.

The second generation were more powerful and complex than the first. Their minds were quicker and more nuanced, but they would still have been called stupid by our standards. They created living things; amoebas, plants, and small, simple things which they tended to and ate for sustenance and pleasure.

In the second generation was born a womb goddess, she had many names, but they're all forgotten now.

'Sister Womb,' said her brother, Wisdom.

'Yes?' she answered, looking up from a basket she was weaving with her sister, Night.

'We want you to create a creature to do the work for us. We are tired of having to tend crops. We want to take our leisure when we feel like it,' Grain interrupted.

'What makes you think I can help you with this?' Womb asked.

'You can create anything, sister. You are the Womb, the mother of all things. Surely you can create us some creatures that will be clever enough to plant the fields, and maybe raise other beings to eat,' Wisdom said.

'I cannot create something from nothing. The elementals, our parents, could do so, but I need something to work with. What will you bring me?'

Night said nothing, merely looked on.

'I could make you some shapes in mud, then you would only need to give them life,' Grain said.

'I can give them life, but their minds would be mud. I need more.'

'You could use the blood of brother, Wisdom,' said Night.

'Come now, this was my idea. I'm not going to be sacrificed into the mix.' Wisdom took a step back from Night, afraid of what the glint in her eye meant.

'Wisdom need not to die, I don't think. I need only a pound of flesh to feed the mud creatures,' said Womb.

After it was decided, Grain went to find mud from the finest, deep brown soil, to make these new creatures. He fashioned fourteen figures, each with two legs, two arms and one head just as he had. He laid them in two lines.

'They are almost right,' said Womb, when she saw the mud figures. 'I will make two types, as there are brothers and sisters among us, so should there be in these new creatures.' She made some changes to each of the figures before nodding to herself.

'Give me your arm,' Womb said to Wisdom. 'I will take the flesh from it to bestow intelligence and thought on these new beings. I will take flesh from myself and add it to allow them to create more of themselves.'

Into the heads of each mud figure, Womb placed a part of Wisdom's flesh. Then she took a long, ornate dagger, a gift she's been given by her brother Time, and cut her forearm. Over the lower torso of seven mud creatures, she placed seven drops of her blood.

'They are almost ready. We will leave them here for seven nights and seven days. At the end of this time, our brother, Storm, will bring down lightning and the fourteen will rise, animated of their own accord. Once they are alive, Wisdom and Grain, you may use them to tend your fields or whatever else you could need.'

After seven days and nights passed, Storm conjured a great tempest, rain, wind, thunder, and lightning lashed all around the fourteen figures. At first, Womb was worried she hadn't imbued them correctly, and they would not rise, but as the clouds cleared and the dawn broke over the mountains, the figures had been transformed from mud to flesh and bone.

The new humans were confused. Why had they been born? Who were they? But the gods taught them to speak, and tend to the crops, to breed, to sing, to lament, and to worship them. For many seasons, the humans were in awe of their creators, and did their bidding without question. As more and more humans were created, the gods guided them less, allowing the older humans pass on the lessons.

After many hundreds of generations, the humans were plentiful and prospering.

'Your children disturb our rest, Womb, you must make them stop,' complained Grain.

'You wanted them to tend the fields, so you did not have to. I did what you asked, and now you complain that my children are noisy?' Womb shook her head.

'There are too many. They are everywhere. I cannot get away from them even if I wanted to. They are blanketing the world. You must destroy them,' said Wisdom.

'I would sooner destroy myself as destroy my children. If you want fewer humans, you deal with them yourself.' Womb was angered and saddened by her brother's disregard.

'What if you made it harder for them to procreate? Perhaps only one in ten couplings would create a new human? That might help to quiet them, and slow their spread,' said Day.

'Maybe if we made it so they slept while it was my turn in the sky, that would quiet them for almost half the time,' said Night.

Womb nodded. 'I will not allow my creations to be destroyed, but I will allow these changes.' She muttered words of ritual, drawing her fingers in the sand in front of her into intricate patterns. The ritual took all day and all night. When it was done the humans all fell to the ground asleep for the first time and the gods were pleased.

2.

Melanie woke with a start; it was still dark. She'd been having an intense dream about the beginning of the world. She shook her head; must have been that podcast she was listening to last night filling her head with mud people and creator gods.

She rolled over, it was cold in her Melbourne apartment. Winter chill crept into her room overnight, the windows had a layer of condensation from her breath. Mel liked to sleep with the curtains open a little, she's read somewhere it was good for biorhythms to wake with the dawn, although in summer she usually slept through.

When she walked into the kitchen, the tiles were freezing under her bare feet.

Should've put on socks, she thought to herself as she flicked on her coffee machine ready to make her first cup of the day.

If there were gods these days, she suspected they would be called Coffee, and Wi-Fi. Perhaps even social media would have a deity, given how much time the average person worshipped it. We were no longer awed by the passage of the sun across the sky, or the cycle of grain from planting to harvest. That stuff had all been explained by science; quantified and categorised to the point where it had lost all sense of mystery.

Mel showered while the coffee machine did its thing; it would be ready to brew when she was dressed. She put her favourite navy-blue insulated metal travel cup under the coffee machine's spout and was ready to face the day.

Her mind was still a little foggy from sleep, but when she stepped out of her apartment building onto the road towards the train station, she saw muddy footprints. They led all the way up to her building's front door before stopping. They were not shoe prints, these were muddy prints of bare feet; enormous, with wide-splayed toes, something Mel thought was ill-advised in Melbourne winter.

The footprints came from the direction of the park, and the river beyond a couple of minutes' walk from her building. She shared the track with them for a little way before turning off to the train station to the north.

Perhaps someone fell in the river and had to walk back to their apartment dripping mud after them, she thought.

At work, Mel didn't think about her dream or the footprints, her mind was focused on the everyday tasks in front of her; emails about this project or that, a couple of meetings that were frustratingly circular in their conversation, and a catch-up with her boss about priorities for the week. It was only when she walked up to the huge plate glass door at the entrance of her building on her way home she remembered the footprints, but when she looked for them, they were gone.

It hasn't rained today, whoever they were must have cleaned up after themselves, very community-minded, she thought.

Mel waved her fob next to the little black rectangle on the wall and let herself in. As she entered the small foyer, a wave of cold swept over her. She made a mental note to have a word with the building manager about having the air con set too cold.

Cooking was not Mel's favourite thing, she had never really gotten the hang of it, and burned or otherwise messed up the recipe more often than not. For dinner that night she ate a frozen beef korma, it was one of the better options from her meal delivery subscription service.

After eating, Mel's eyes were heavy, but it was too early to go to bed. She sat on the couch and turned the TV on, selecting the next episode of a crime procedural show she'd seen several times already. She laid her head back, and let her eyes drift closed, just for a moment.

When she opened her eyes, she wasn't sure where she was. Her apartment was dark, and the TV had turned itself off. Mel reached for her phone to check the time but couldn't find it on the coffee table. She stood and shuffled, arms outstretched to the wall, fumbling for the light switch. When she flicked it, nothing happened.

Must be a blackout, she thought. Or maybe the fuses had flicked off. Trailing her hand along the wall, Mel made her way to the front door of her apartment, where the switchboard was set into the wall. She opened the front door to check for light in the corridor, and the red emergency lighting was on, dimly illuminating the passages and stairs.

The keys hung on a hook next to the front door, directly below the fuse box, so she grabbed them and went out into the dimly lit red corridor. Mel's apartment was on the third floor, the stairs were straight ahead when she exited. Her feet knew the way at least in the dim light she should be able to avoid falling down the stairs.

The power was out on the second floor, on the first and the ground floor. She hadn't thought to grab any shoes, she hoped she wouldn't have to stand outside for too long while they fixed the problem, whatever it was. There was no alarm going off, maybe she could have stayed in her apartment but that had seemed like a bad idea.

Outside the building, several other residents were gathered. An ambulance with the lights flashing had parked in front of the building. Two paramedics were huddled over a small figure on a trolley, she couldn't make out who from that distance.

'What happened?' Mel asked a woman she recognised from the second floor. Her name might have been Sue, or possibly Sally.

'I don't know. I didn't hear anything. I came out because the power's gone and there was Julia being carted off,' the woman replied.

'Julia?'

'Yes, you know from your floor. She keeps trying to organise activities?' Steve, another neighbour piped up. Mel knew him as he would do small handy jobs around the building sometimes.

'I remember.' Mel's memory was vague, Julia was a small, elderly woman, with dyed deep-red hair, who always had time for a chat. Mel knew enough to have an excuse ready to escape her if the conversation went on too long. In spite of the tendency to chat, usually gossip about the neighbours, Julia was a nice older lady who had a lot of life left in her. 'Did they say what's wrong with her?'

'No,' Sue replied. 'She hasn't moved for a while, they don't seem in any hurry to get her out of here so either she's basically fine, or there's nothing more they can do.'

Then the paramedics pulled the sheet up over Julia's face.

Mel shuddered and woke with a start. Her TV was still on, though the show had moved on several episodes from where she had started. A cold thread of fear lay in her belly.

I know it was a dream, but I'd feel better if I could check on Julia, Mel thought. It was a little after midnight, not a sociable time for a visit; it would have to wait till the morning.

Footprints

A yawn rippled through her jaw and Mel decided it was time to go to bed for real. Even with the uncharacteristic evening nap, she fell asleep within a minute of her head hitting the pillow.

The night passed without any more eerily realistic dreams, though Mel woke up feeling not the least bit refreshed. With an effort she pushed herself out of bed, did her morning routine; shower, dress, coffee, and head out the door.

Julia's apartment, number 307, was across the hall and down a few doors. It wasn't yet eight o'clock, but the urge to check on her was as strong as it had been last night.

I won't tell her that I had a dream, I'll pop in and ask if she needs anything, no use worrying her over nothing.

Mel knocked four times on Julia's door, loudly in case she was hard of hearing. She stood for a while, uncertain, before knocking again, this time very forcefully.

'Julia? It's Mel from across the way,' she said aloud, in case the older woman was afraid to open the door. Minutes passed, and the uneasiness in Mel's belly didn't abate. She knocked a third time, banging her hand on the door hard and calling out again.

Still there was no answer. Perhaps she was out, or a heavy sleeper, there were lots of reasons she might not answer. Mel shook her head; she was being silly. Still, it wouldn't hurt to try the door to make sure it was secure.

Mel laid her hand on the door handle and pushed down. To her surprise it was unlocked and with a push, the front door opened.

'Julia? Are you home? It's Mel, your neighbour. Your front door was unlocked.' Mel stuck her head into the apartment, it was dark, cold. 'I came to check you were alright, the door was open. I'm coming in, okay?'

The apartment was silent, and an earthy, compost-type smell pervaded it. Mel had never been into Julia's apartment but given how much perfume the older lady wore, moist earthy rotting wasn't the smell she expected.

Mel walked down a short corridor into the kitchen dining area. Dishes from a meal for one lay on the table; a plate with few morsels left on it, and half a glass of red wine.

'Julia, are you alright?' The tightness in her belly grew worse as Mel went further into the apartment. She stepped forward and almost slipped on something on the floor. Looking down, in the gloom, it looked black, and sticky.

Mel's heart raced in her chest, what if it was blood? Steadying herself with one hand on the wall, she searched for a light switch, though it wasn't easy as the layout was different to her own apartment.

When her hand came across the light switch, Mel flicked it on, and was momentarily blinded by the sudden light. She looked back to where the slippery patch was and saw it was pale brown mud, not blood, smeared a little where she'd stood in it. She let out the breath she'd been holding, Julia must have left the apartment unlocked by accident. Mel's gaze was drawn back to the mud, it was a huge bare footprint, as she'd seen outside the building yesterday, but this one was wetter and fresher. She looked around the room, there were no more footprints just that one behind the chair where Julia must have been eating her dinner.

I'll check the other rooms, to make sure Julia isn't home, and then I'll call the building manager to get them to lock up the apartment.

Mel tried to convince herself it wasn't snooping. As she moved through the apartment the earthy smell became stronger, almost unbearable. The first room off the kitchen was the study, with a desk, chair, bookshelves and other bits and pieces, but no sign of Julia. The next door was the bathroom, sparkling clean, though Mel wouldn't have expected anything less. The third door as she headed towards the balcony was the master bedroom, and lying on top of the bed was Julia's small frame. The earthy smell was so strong Mel could barely breathe, there was more mud on the carpet, a lot of it, on the bedspread, and all over Julia.

Careful not to step in it again this time, Mel hurried to the figure on the bed.

'Julia, are you alright?'

Stupid question really, she was covered in mud face down on her bed, it didn't bode well. There was no reply, so Mel put her hand on Julia's throat. It was cold, and clammy, and Mel flinched away.

She took a deep breath and tried again, putting her fingers on the spot where a pulse should be, but felt nothing. Her neighbour was dead, and somehow had become covered in mud in the process. It didn't make sense.

The only thing Mel could think to do was call the emergency number, triple-oh. An ambulance would be able to sort it out.

'Hello, what service do you require?' the operator, a young male voice, answered the phone after a couple of rings.

'Um,' Mel hesitated. 'My neighbour, I think she's died. Do I need police or ambulance?'

'We'll send both, but I'll start with ambulance. Please hold.'

There was a short metallic click, then the phone rang again.

'Ambulance. What's the nature of the problem?' another operator said, this time an older woman Mel thought.

'My neighbour's died.'

'Are you sure they're dead?'

'I think so. She's cold to the touch, no pulse or breathing.'

'What's the address? I'll send someone to you.'

Mel gave the address.

'You'll need to stay until the ambulance arrives. How old would you say your neighbour was?'

'Late seventies at least. She's always been very active but she's elderly.'

'I see. Any history of illness?' the operator asked.

'I'm not sure. We weren't close.'

'Okay, thanks. I need to get onto another call. If the paramedics can't find you, can I give them your number?' The operator read Mel's number back to her.

'Yes, that's right.'

'Good luck.' The operator hung up and the line went dead. Mel heard a high-pitched whine, felt a little faint, and had to steady herself against the head of the bed.

3.

The ambulance arrived ten minutes later, the paramedics were efficient in their work, having established that Julia was beyond their help, they had to hand over to police. Mel gave her statement to the tall, slender, serious constable who came to watch over the body until the someone could collect it.

'So, can I go now? I mean, I should get to work at some stage.' She had texted her boss while the paramedics were working on Julia.

'Yes, I think we have all we need from you at the moment,' the constable said.

Mel walked to the train station only half aware of the movement of her feet in front of her. The footprints were back. She hadn't noticed any mud between Julia's house and the front of the building, perhaps it was a coincidence there was mud in the house and outside, though it hadn't been raining lately.

Her brain didn't seem to work at all that day, the second day in a row she'd been distracted at work, though she had a better excuse today.

'Why did you come in?' her boss, Andrew, asked at the lunch table.

'I thought I should,' she replied.

Footprints

'You could have had the rest of the day off. Finding a corpse is good enough reason, even for a tyrant like me.' He smiled to emphasise that last part was a joke.

'You're probably right. Although I didn't really want to be in the building with the police and everyone floating around. I thought work might be a good distraction, but I seem to have failed at distracting myself.' She stared out the window at the bright sky, it was as though the weather was entirely unaffected by her mood, or the death of her neighbour. Mel got up from the lunch table, put the uneaten half of her salad in the bin and went back to her desk.

A few emails had come in through the morning, but she hadn't yet looked at them. A quick scan reassured her they would wait until tomorrow. Her meeting at half past three had been pushed to later in the week, and her afternoon was now free.

It would be a great opportunity to knock over some of the work she'd been trying to get to over the last few weeks, but that didn't seem likely. Mel's mind kept replaying the scene in Julia's apartment.

The earthy smell. Face down on the bed as she knelt beside it. So much mud, all over the room. Sprayed on the walls as though someone had been throwing it. What could have made that mess? And how did Julia die?

Mel opened a new internet browser and typed in "mud related death", which yielded a lot of unhelpful results including a landslide in Bangladesh, and a weird bacterial infection in Cairns. Next, she tried "suspicious mud death" but the results veered off into other types of suspicious deaths very quickly. The footprints had to mean something, and the amount of mud in the apartment wasn't just a bit of wet dirt.

Something tickled in the back of her mind, an urban legend or ghost story she'd heard somewhere about a mud monster, so she tried "mud monster legend". This brought up lots of stories of mud monsters, creatures born from swamps or bogs that rose up to kill townsfolk, or the golem from Jewish mythology, which was an animated being of dust or earth. In Norse mythology they had the clay giants, even in Bible, Adam was made from mud animated by God's breath.

Despite being plenty of folk stories and myths about creating people from mud, the outcomes were variable. On the one hand the Jewish golems were protectors, and Adam was the originator of all humankind, on the other hand, fairy tales and creepy pastas usually made mud monsters the bad guys, or the tool of the bad guy.

Mel shook her head. *Get a grip, there is no mud monster going around killing little old ladies,* she told herself. Closing the laptop, she packed up and went home.

*

Every day Mel looked for footprints outside her apartment but saw nothing. After a week or so she was convinced she'd imagined the whole thing. Then on Saturday morning on the way out to get a coffee from her local café she saw them again. Large feet with splayed toes left in mud, they had dried by the time she saw them, and they went right to the front door of her apartment building.

Determined to prove to herself they were real, Mel decided to skip the coffee and follow the tracks. Her apartment was not far from a river, with verdant parkland all around it. The tracks went along the footbath towards the playground.

Mel walked along, following the prints backwards away from her building. A couple of times, they were lighter, even vanishing entirely over some grass at the entrance to the park, but she picked them up again.

After ten minutes of walking the tracks disappeared into the river. Where they had emerged from the riverbed, the banks were low and swampy. The bank was messy and torn up as though a great scuffle had occurred. The large footprints started here, but Mel thought she saw another set of shoe prints in the sludge as well.

A chill wind blew across the surface of the river and caused Mel to shiver.

Who else had been here? What happened to create such a mess? Why did I come here?

She looked up the track both the way she had come and the opposite way, further towards the city; there were no other people to be seen, yet a prickle on the back of her neck made her think she was being watched.

Don't be silly, she thought, turning around and marching back up the track towards the street, and the café. *I must be in dire need of caffeine to be inventing phantoms watching me. This mess was probably some dumbarse teenagers getting drunk and skinny dipping.*

Once she was back at the road, the prickling on the back of her neck eased. Perhaps she was a city slicker who got creeped out in quiet places of nature.

The café was about five minutes' walk back towards home, off the main road a little. Woven cane seating and small circular tables were lined up along the front window of the shop giving that distinct Parisienne feel. Most of the tables were full of locals sipping coffee and chatting, unaware of the creepy morning she'd been having.

'Latte with one today?' the barista asked as Mel walked up. Her favourite barista was Geoffrey, the painfully-French owner and operator, but he didn't work on weekends. This barista was a swarthy South American with a moustache like a caterpillar over his top lip. His accent was thick, but he understood well enough.

'Yes, thanks, Tomás. I really need it, the morning I've had.' Mel laughed, a nervous, high-pitched laugh, and hoped he didn't ask any further questions.

'That's not good. What has happened this morning?'

'Nothing, I went down to the river and got a bit freaked out. My fault entirely, I'm sure.'

'I've been down there a couple of times after work, it's very peaceful, but sometimes people are…' He thought for a moment, perhaps trying to find the word, 'people are doing strange things down there.'

'What are they doing?' she asked, her curiosity piqued.

'The other day, maybe a week ago? There was a man dressed all in black, but he was looking like, a wizard or something, maybe a dress up party, and he was standing in the water, up to his knees, saying words I didn't understand.'

'How weird. What was he saying?'

'As I say, it was not something I could understand. Not English I think, and definitely not Spanish. I looked around for a camera, you know in case it was video for the internet, but no, he was there by himself.'

'That is strange.' Mel chewed the inside of her lip and wondered what the man had been doing. Perhaps having a mental health episode, but given the muddy footprints and Julie's death, it could be something more sinister.

'Here you are, latte with one.' Tomás handed her the coffee with a grin.

'Thanks.' Mel took her takeaway cup and walked back onto the street, putting one foot in front of the other as though in a trance.

Looking up Mel realised she'd made it all the way home without noticing anything. The footsteps ended at the glass door just as they had earlier that morning. She shivered; the feeling of being watched was back.

Without having a good reason to do so, Mel decided to use the stairs up to her apartment, and to walk around each floor looking for any tell-tale muddy stains or earthy smells. She lived on the third floor, the building had six floors in all.

Each floor was about twenty apartments, laid out similar to a hotel: two arms around a central courtyard space. Mel walked slowly, lowering her eyes, focusing on the floor and the smells around her.

On the first floor she smelled incense, probably *nag champa*, it reminded her of the time she'd done yoga for several months because the instructor was hot. It came from one apartment near the lift. From another she caught a faint smell of burned toast. On the second floor, the only scent she encountered was a sickly fruit smell, as though perhaps someone was away on holiday and had left bananas out. The third floor smelled more familiar, her neighbours a couple of doors down were smoking marijuana again, masking most other smells, though the earthy scent lingered when she passed Julia's door.

She'd never been up to the floors above hers; there was no roof access, and she didn't have any friends on the upper floors. On the fourth floor she went past one apartment with an overwhelming bleach smell, hopefully it meant someone was being overzealous with their cleaning, and not trying to cover something else.

As soon as she stepped out of the stair well onto the fifth floor Mel tensed, the hairs on the back of her neck and forearms standing on end. A hint at first, then as she went down the left-hand corridor the smell grew steadily stronger. After Julia's apartment and her excursion to the riverbed, she was more attuned to the scents of the different layers; mud, rotting leaves, and wet earth that made up the smell. It seemed dead somehow, a smell of decay and death. Nothing like the fresh smell of hot earth after a little rain, that seemed happy, joyful, hopeful; this boded ill.

Fighting her urge to turn away, Mel approached the door where the smell was strongest.

Apartment 507.

She didn't know the people who lived there; she tried to be neighbourly, though there were a lot of people she encountered in the halls she vaguely recognised but couldn't have named.

Mel knocked on the door. She wasn't sure what she expected to happen, but a knock seemed like a good start. She counted to thirty in her head, then knocked again more forcefully.

Still no response. She put her ear to the door, in case there were footsteps of someone approaching or sounds of distress, but there weren't any. In her bag she always carried a small notepad and pen, in case, today she was very glad of it.

Hi, it's Mel from number 304. I think I might have a package that was meant for you. Can you give me a ring, or drop in, to my apartment? Thank you.

She added her phone number to the bottom of the note, folded it once, and pushed it under the door. There was no way writing the real reason would work, she had to think of something that would entice the resident to come to her, but not be so alarming they called the police instead.

For completeness, she continued around the fifth and sixth floors, but found no more earthy smells. Three in one building would be very unlikely and at least now she was sure nothing else was going on. Nothing she could smell anyway.

Mel returned to her apartment, walked in her front door, put down her bag and stopped still. Now she had found another apartment where the mud seemed to be present what did it mean? Was the resident in danger? Were they the person who had brought the mud into the building? If they were in danger, she should help them, but what if they were the one doing the weird stuff in the river?

Then again, why would the person controlling the mud monster have been followed? If she were in control of the thing, it would definitely not be making an appearance in her apartment. Safer than to assume that the resident of number 507 was the next target.

Mel sat at the dining table, mind still whirring, and stared blankly ahead of her. With Julia, there had been footprints two days in a row. That could mean that the first day was an opportunity to scope out the place, and the second day was when she'd died.

Footprints

She had so many questions and no answers. The only thing she could do was wait, hoping the person got her note and came down to collect their non-existent parcel. It was lunchtime, but her mind was too busy worrying over the meaning of these new footprints to eat.

Mel spent most of the rest of the day worrying over what to do about her neighbour on the fifth floor. A little before midnight, she had been staring in the direction of the TV without taking anything in for a couple of hours when she shivered like someone had walked over her grave. It was as though she was wide awake and jittery all of a sudden. She decided to check on apartment 507 to soothe her nerves. She felt stupid, it was an over-reaction, but what if the resident was in danger?

Her mind wouldn't let her settle, so on the off chance something was happening right at that moment, she took the lift up to level five to investigate. When she exited the lift, the scent of mud, wet leaves, and decay was overwhelming. There were no footprints on the carpet, and she went straight to number 507.

Even from several metres away, Mel saw the front door was ajar.

Fuck, why didn't I come back earlier, perhaps I could have done something before it was too late, she thought, berating herself. But even if they had been home, what could she have said to them that would have made them understand the danger. She barely knew what was going on herself.

Fleur Blüm

Inside the apartment was dark, she stood on the threshold, pushing open the front door with two fingers. The lights from the corridor illuminated a long triangle into the home, showing the wet muddy footprints; both going in and coming out. They stopped at the carpet, as though the mud had somehow not touched the ground outside. Mel shivered.

'Hello?' she called into the dark apartment, straining to hear a reply. She took a couple of steps inside, careful to avoid stepping in the mud. Switching on the light on the wall just inside the door she called out again.

'Hello? It's Mel, from downstairs. Your door was open, are you okay in here?'

The footprints lead straight towards the sofa, sitting in the half-dark further into the house. Mel approached, switching on another light as she came through, and stumbled when she caught sight of the full scene in front of her.

On the back of the couch were vast smears of brown mud. A lamp was knocked onto the floor, the glass shade smashed. Muddy footprints were laid on top of each other all over the rug in front of the couch, perhaps there was a struggle. And there, partly draped over the footstool, was the unmoving body of a man in blue jeans and a green polo shirt.

A thread of recognition pulled at Mel's brain, perhaps they'd crossed paths in the hall, but she didn't know his name.

She approached the man, he was in his forties, brown hair with flecks of silver, and the start of wrinkles around his eyes. His mouth was covered in mud, as were his clothes, hands, and neck. His blue eyes were open wide and staring.

Mel put two fingers against his throat to feel for a pulse, she felt nothing, he was tepid, perhaps not dead long, but certainly not revivable. The smell of mud and dirt in her nostrils started to feel claustrophobic, as though she couldn't get enough oxygen because everything was covered in mud, including her nose. She withdrew her hand, her fingers now coated in wet mud.

The violent urge to get her fingers clean came over her in a rush. She wanted more than anything to get out of the apartment, to run back home, lock the door and pray whatever was happening would stop of its own accord. Wiping her fingers on a portion of the man's polo shirt that seemed to be the least dirty, she backed away, retracing her steps toward the front door. Déjà vu and panic vied for primacy inside her.

Almost without thinking, Mel pulled out her mobile phone and called the emergency services to report a body for the second time in as many weeks.

'Hello, what service do you require?' the operator, a woman this time, asked.

'My neighbour's dead, I think I need the police.'

4.

The police arrived about fifteen minutes later. Mel had been standing in the hallway, not wanting to wait in the apartment with the body. The smell of mud and decay was so strong she wanted to gag.

She'd had to rush back inside to open the door of the building when they had buzzed over the intercom but had quickly gone back to the hallway afterwards.

'Hello, are you Mel? The person who called triple-zero?' asked a squat-looking police officer as they approached from the lifts.

'Yes.'

'You didn't want to wait inside?' asked the other police officer, a woman the same size and shape as her partner.

'It smells bad, and it's creepy.'

A ghost of a smile crossed the female officer's face. 'Doesn't that describe every death we've had to attend Ed?' she asked her colleague.

'I reckon. I'll go in, you stay here with Mel…' he raised his eyebrows at Mel in a question.

'Melanie Green.'

'Alright Mel, I'm Senior Constable Stacey Hart, let's start with the name of the deceased.'

Mel opened her mouth, then closed it again.

'The name?' Hart prompted gently.

'I, uh, don't know his name.'

Hart blinked twice, before continuing. 'I see. What was the nature of your relationship with the deceased?'

'I live in the building. Apartment 304. Earlier today I thought I noticed . . . something suspicious so I was doing a quick check of the floors, I know it sounds psychotic, but I saw the door ajar and I was worried something had happened.'

'What did you see that made you suspicious?' Hart was holding a small notebook in one hand, her other held a pen ready to take down notes, though she hadn't written anything yet.

'It sounds crazy.'

'I'd like to hear it, even if it does sound a bit silly.'

'I found a neighbour, Julia, last week, dead in her apartment, and there was all this mud everywhere, the stench was in my nostrils all day. Anyway, I smelled it on this floor earlier today, but wasn't sure, so I came back to double check if something hinky was going on.'

'Another death in the building?'

Mel looked at her fingernails and started picking at the cuticle on her left ring finger. 'Yeah, Julia, on the third floor. I found her kneeling at her bedside but there was mud everywhere, and her door had been left unlocked in the morning so I went in to check on her. She was in her eighties and could have left it open in a moment of forgetfulness, but—'

'Base, can you look into another suspicious death at my location in the last couple of weeks please?' Hart spoke into her radio. 'I'll have the station send over the details. It's possible they're unrelated but in this sort of situation it pays to be thorough.'

Mel nodded. She couldn't tell the cop that she suspected someone had made a golem and was using it to kill people in her building. Perhaps it wasn't a bad thing that the police were getting curious. 'Is it weird that I found both of them? I mean, are you going to be looking into me?'

Hart's smile faded. 'We look into everyone who finds a body. Especially a potentially violent death, and doubly so if it's their second body in quick succession.' Her smile reappeared. 'Usually, we find they're not involved though, I can't imagine you managed to kill two people while covered in mud, apparently, and clean up in time to call us. I think you're pretty safe.'

'Speaking of, what do you think the mud is about? Does it smell weird to you?'

'Now you mention it, it does smell a bit funky. Like rotten? Most of the mud I've come across doesn't really smell, but then again, I don't come across so much mud very often.' Hart wrote something on her little pad. 'We'd better get your details down, and your statement, so let's start with full name and address?'

It took another twenty minutes standing in the hallway to get everything down to Hart's satisfaction. In the meantime, the other police officer had finished looking around inside the apartment and came to stand quietly beside them as Hart finished going through the basic questions.

'I think that's everything I need. I'll type up the formal statement and you'll need to come down to the station to sign it sometime this week, same as you did for the other body no doubt. We'll call you.'

Mel nodded.

'You can head back to your apartment, but we may need to be in touch to follow up.'

'Okay, thank you.' Mel lingered, half wanting to go back into the apartment for one last look. 'How did he die?'

Hart looked at Ed, after a brief unspoken exchange, Ed answered. 'It's hard to tell, there's a lot going on in there and obviously I didn't touch anything, but if I was going to guess; strangled. But we'll have to wait for the coroner to make a determination.'

'Of course. Thank you.'

When Mel got back to her apartment it was after one in the morning. A wave of fatigue washed over her, she felt lightheaded and her eyes drooped heavily. Mel made it back to her bed where she flopped onto it, facedown.

She woke a few hours later, fully dressed on top of her bed. Mel pushed herself up, did her nightly routine and climbed back into bed.

I might have the day off tomorrow, she thought as her eyes closed again.

*

The next time she went into work was a Friday. Her boss had seemed happy enough to accept that she'd slept badly the morning after she found the second body.

'I see you've deigned to join us this morning,' he said, coming by her desk about nine thirty.

'Good morning. I wanted to tell you more yesterday, but it wasn't something I could discuss over text.'

Rowan was a slim man in his late forties, completely bald and cleanshaven, with clear, rimmed glasses. He was the head of her team and while he was fair and got his work done, he was not well liked around the office, people found him abrasive; especially in emails.

'Maybe I can come into your office and give you the run down?'

His eyebrows rose up. 'That's a good idea,' was all he said.

His office was on the other side of the building from where Mel sat in the open plan section. 'What's the real story?'

Mel took a deep breath. 'Do you remember a while ago I found my neighbour; she'd died?'

'Yes, that was weird.'

'It gets worse. I found another neighbour on Wednesday night. It looks like foul play. The police were called, I had to give a statement, the works. As a result, I didn't sleep well.'

'I'll bet you didn't. What do you mean you found them though? How many people die in your building that you're constantly finding corpses?'

'I've lived there for three years and no one else has died, and now two in two weeks. And I discovered both, it seems unlikely. I did notice signs of something weird and went to investigate both, maybe I'm too curious. Anyway, I don't plan on finding any more corpses. The police might think I was making them.'

Rowan didn't laugh. 'I'm concerned. Do you need to use the employee assistance program? Perhaps a session with a counsellor to go over what you've been through.'

Despite being what a textbook might suggest was the right thing to say in this situation, Rowan's tone was robotic, and distant, and Mel felt dismissed.

'I'll look into that. I thought I should let you know the full story of why I needed the day off.'

'Of course. You don't have to justify taking sick leave to me you know. Unless you need a doctor's certificate, which you don't for one day.' He shifted in his chair, looking away towards the door.

'I'll let you get back to it, thanks for listening.' Mel stood up, and Rowan looked relieved not to have to continue the strange conversation.

He really isn't much good with people, Mel thought as she walked back to her desk, *I guess he tries, which is halfway there.* The rest of the day crawled by; her mind was still filled with the images of the two dead people she'd encountered. It occurred to her she didn't even know the second one's name; she pulled out the business card Hart had given her.

'Hello?' Hart's voice sounded harried over the phone.

'Hi, um, it's Mel Green, I found a body on Wednesday night, and you came to take my statement.'

'Yeah, with all the mud. That was a weird one. Is there something you wanted to add?'

'Not exactly. I—well I don't know the deceased's name and I thought you might be able to tell me.'

'It's not standard procedure.'

'I know, but I would like to pay my respects to the family. I can probably find out from one of the other neighbours, I thought asking you might be less intrusive.'

Hart was quiet on the phone for a moment. 'You're right, it's not going to be hard to find out, so I'm not really giving you anything you can't get pretty easily. Hold on a second.' There was a rustling of paper down the line while Hart presumably looked for the name in her notebook. 'Darius Todd.'

'Thank you, that's so helpful. I really appreciate it.'

'Don't tell anyone you got it from me, I'm not allowed to give out information like that.'

'Of course. I heard it from someone else. Thank you again.'

'Okay, bye.' Hart finished up the call, perhaps she was out at another scene or wanted to end the conversation after doing something a little dodgy. Either way Mel had what she needed.

Mel needed to concentrate on her work for the rest of the day, after the awkward conversation with Rowan she didn't want to give him any reason to be suspicious by doing work outside of her job.

Footprints

Back at home that night she went straight to her
laptop and started looking for information about her
neighbour, Darius. He had a Facebook profile with a few
photos and invitations to donate money to various
causes. Perhaps the rest of his profile was locked down
and given he was dead it wouldn't be any use sending a
friend request.

A sadness started in her belly, this person had died,
just like Julia, and she didn't know why or what
connected them. The only obvious connection was they
lived in the same building and had died in much the same
way but that didn't tell her much.

Why had the mud monster chosen them to kill? What
was the purpose? A golem, in most of the mythology
she'd come across, was built to carry out the will of its
creator and didn't have intelligence or will of its own.

It would have been powerful magic to raise a mud
monster like that. Three weeks ago, Mel would have said
it wasn't possible, but here she was trying to justify her
hunch. There were no footprints that morning, or when
she came home. Perhaps the spree had ended, and she
could go back to pretending the world was a sensible
place.

Turning her attention back to the search for Darius,
she looked through his friends list, a couple of names
seemed familiar, perhaps others in the building. Then she
remembered the building had a Facebook group which
they mostly used for griping about the bins, giving away

unwanted items and sometimes to say the doors weren't working.

Mel browsed the entries in the group. Darius hadn't been especially vocal, though he had made a few posts; a complaint about noise levels on his floor, or a mess left by a dog in the lift. He was a little abrasive, there were a few back and forth exchanges that could almost be called heated between him and some of the other residents. Mel's eyebrows rose in surprise when she saw that Julia was also complaining on the same posts, about the same things. Could it be as petty as that? A person in the building who didn't like the arrangement of bins or keeping the building clean. Mel shook her head, *that's not a reason to kill someone.*

A few people had posted negative comments in response, but never the same person repeatedly, so that didn't seem a useful avenue to pursue. The moderator of the group, Helen, was also the volunteer in charge of managing the building. Since it was only a small building of fifty or so apartments, they didn't have a building manager on staff, and the owners committee did most of the work. Mel decided to have a chat with her.

Helen lived on the second floor, Mel took one set of stairs down and knocked on apartment 201.

'Coming,' Helen yelled from behind the door. There was a considerable pause as she made her way to the door. Helen was an older woman, very energetic despite using a walker to get around. She might have been in her late seventies, with her white hair tied back in a severe bun, and her doughy figure hidden under layers of wafty garments in various shade of aqua.

'Melanie,' she said a little breathless. 'What can I do for you at this hour?'

It was a little after seven, perhaps late for an older person, but still a polite time to call Mel had thought. 'I wanted to ask you about the deaths in the building lately.'

Helen's face pinched, her mouth tightening into a tiny circle. 'Very unfortunate business. Come in, I can't be standing around here all day.' Without looking back, Helen turned and walked back into the apartment. She had hung dozens of family portraits all along one wall; Mel assumed they were family, given they all had variations of the same round face and plump bodies. On the back and arms of the couch and armchair were several doilies, perhaps to keep them clean, and on the wall behind the television was an enormous image of Jesus Christ on the cross. Mel was shocked at how gory it was for a religious icon, and compared to the soft, plush, frilly décor it stood out.

'Sit down,' Helen ordered, waving her hand at one of the dining chairs as she settled herself in the nearest armchair. 'Now, what do you want to know about these deaths?'

Mel took a breath. 'I'm not sure. You'll be aware it was me who discovered both, and that they seemed to be unnatural passings, for Darius more so than Julia. I wondered if you'd heard anything? About enemies or arguments, they might have had, or funeral arrangements.'

Helen squinted her eyes; her demeanour always much more like a military drill sergeant than her grandmotherly appearance might have suggested. Somewhere in the back of her mind Mel recalled she had been a school principal before she retired.

'Julia was a lovely soul, couldn't have had an enemy in the world. I'm sure you know we were quite the bosom buddies.' Helen's eyes became wet with unshed tears before she brought her emotions back under tight control. 'The last I heard was she'd had some sort of heart attack while praying. I don't see how that would be suspicious.'

'What about the mud?'

'Mud?'

'Yes, it was all over the floor and on her body.'

'Mud? You're sure?'

'I was there. It was clearly mud. Footprints leading into the bedroom and smears all over the bedspread and on Julia. The police can't be thinking it was natural causes with all that.'

Helen's eyebrow twitched upward. 'And you found Darius? In the same arrangement?'

'No, he was—there had been a scuffle of some sort. The police at the scene thought he might have been choked. The same mud, footprints, smears all over the place, but nothing in the corridor or lift.'

'Hmm.'

Footprints

Mel waited in case Helen was going to say more, but she did not elaborate. 'Is there anything you know that might explain it? I'm at a loss.' It wasn't quite true, but she was certainly at a loss to explain it any way other than with a wizard controlling a mud monster, something no-nonsense-Helen would hardly be inclined to believe.

'I don't know what to tell you. Julia and Darius weren't what you might call close. He seemed a good egg, always on time with his fees, handy around the building, reliable with keeping his mess in order. And Julia, of course, was a blessing. I can't imagine anyone wanting to hurt either of them.'

'And they weren't connected somehow?'

'Not that I know of. Not distant family or anything like that. Though I suppose they did have two of the nicest apartments in the building, good views, excellent floor plans. They would be worth a bit now.'

Mel shivered; it couldn't be that—killing someone for their apartment? Surely not. Though perhaps it was as valid as killing someone for complaining about how the rubbish was taken out or how much noise the neighbours made.

'They were both owners then. Not renting?'

'No, dear, both owners. Julia had hers outright, no mortgage, and Darius, I don't know, but I should think he had a mortgage.'

'You're probably right.'

'I saw the two of them at the Christmas picnic, they were both social types. Julia was lovely, always brought so much delicious food, and Darius brought sausage rolls—homemade. I think it was the only thing he knew how to make.'

'They were good though.' Mel remembered the picnics she'd been to over the years, they were a little awkward, neighbours gathering who otherwise had very little to do with one another. She felt a little left out, some of the neighbours were very friendly, Mel would see them going for walks together. And the families with kids would babysit and do activities together.

Mel often felt strange in social settings. As though she was an alien studying human interactions, rather than knowing what to do. It had been much worse in high school, but then again, most things were worse in high school. She'd learned a few tricks, remembering people's names, their jobs, kids, and hobbies usually gave her enough material to keep the conversation going without having to say too much herself. She realised Helen was still talking about Darius's sausage rolls and tried to concentrate.

'It's such a shame he's gone, what a bright young man, talent in the kitchen notwithstanding,' Helen said.

'I thought you liked the sausage rolls?'

'I did, dear, but it says something if you can only make one dish. That's all I meant.'

Mel laughed nervously. 'I can do half a dozen, so I'm not much better.'

'I'm sure that's not true. I can give you the recipes for a few foolproof things to add to your repertoire.'

It was a struggle to keep her mind in the conversation, clearly Helen wanted to talk about food, but all Mel could think of were the muddy faces of the two neighbours she'd found dead. 'I'll have to get going, thank you for the chat.'

'So soon? Well, I suppose you've got plenty to be getting on with.' Helen's face drooped in sadness at the suggestion of leaving. Perhaps she was lonely, Mel made a mental note to drop by for a cup of tea some time, especially with Julia gone.

Heading back to her own apartment, Mel wondered if she had gained anything from the conversation. She still didn't understand how the two deaths were connected except for the obvious; similarities in the scenes, their apartment numbers—307 and 507—and her finding the corpses. She felt helpless, lost, and deflated.

5.

Mel waited for something else to happen, but nothing did. She had resigned herself to never knowing the truth about the deaths. She decided not to attend Darius's funeral, she had barely known him after all.

One Saturday about three weeks after her chat with Helen, Mel was leaving to get a coffee when she ran into someone letting themselves into Julia's apartment.

'Um, hello, can I help you?' Mel said, approaching the man standing in front of apartment 307.

'I'm Tony, Julia's nephew. The family has asked me to start sorting out her estate. And you are?'

'Mel, I live in 304, obviously.' Mel's cheeks started to heat, of course she lived there, she'd just left it. 'It's nice you're doing that for the family. Did you, uh, get a briefing on the state of things?'

Tony frowned. He was in his late forties, a little bit on the tubby side, with broad shoulders and a bulky frame, solid and strong. His button down blue and white checked shirt was straining a little around the tummy, perhaps put on a little weight recently. Below the shirt, he wore dark blue jeans and leather sandals reminiscent of a Roman gladiator with their multitude of straps. 'The state of things?'

'There's umm, mud all over the interior.'

'Mud? Why on earth is there mud? How do *you* know?' His frown deepened.

'I found her body.' Mel swallowed; her mouth suddenly dry as the image of Julia's body flashed through her mind.

'I had no idea. I'm sorry you had to find her like that.'

There was a lengthy pause in which neither of them said anything more.

'Do you think you'll need a hand? I can help out a little,' Mel said.

'No, that's probably not necessary.' Tony waved his hand at the idea.

'If you change your mind, I'm just across the way here.' Mel paused. 'I'm going for a coffee; do you want me to bring you anything back?'

'I'm fine, really. It's kind of you to offer. I'd better get cracking, especially if there's cleaning that I wasn't warned about that needs to be done first.'

'I'm sorry for your loss. Julia was a lovely person.'

Tony looked down for a moment, before looking back to her. 'She was.'

'Have a good day.'

'You too.'

Mel lingered as he pushed open the door and stepped into the empty apartment. The smell of wet, rotting earth had mostly dissipated and Mel was surprised to find herself relieved not to smell that again.

*

When she arrived home after grabbing her coffee and taking a relaxed stroll around the neighbourhood, she found a piece of paper had been slipped under her door. She picked it up and walked to the kitchen before opening the folded sheet.

You need to keep your nose out of other people's business. Do that and maybe we'll let you live.

Mel staggered back, catching herself on the fridge to stop from collapsing onto the floor. The note slipped from her fingers and fluttered down. She slid her back down the fridge and sat on the hard wood floor, looking sideways at the note.

Maybe we'll let you live.

It was the sort of thing that happened in movies. Who would have sent her such a violent note? Just as she was about to give up on the mud monster theory in favour of some other, less sinister sequence of events, receiving a threatening letter may have had the opposite effect than its author intended.

After a few minutes trying to get her breathing and heart rate back to a normal pace, Mel leaned forward to look at the note more carefully. Typed, so she couldn't compare handwriting. Delivered to her door, and not her letterbox, so the sender must be able to get into the building. It didn't use her name anywhere, but she assumed they knew who she was. Even if they didn't know her name, they knew where she lived so any safety in anonymity was moot.

Apart from the typed text on the front, there was a brownish red smudge. She sniffed it gingerly, and was relieved it didn't have the distinct smell of the mud creature. She thought it might have had a slightly metallic undertone, and she wondered if the smear was blood, but she dismissed that idea.

She turned it over, a normal sheet of printer paper by the look. Nothing on the reverse side. Folded into four very neatly, with the typed message sitting squarely in the middle of the page.

Would the police want to see it? She wondered. It was technically a death threat, but was receiving a note like this a police matter? Mel turned the paper over and over in her hand as she pondered what to do about it.

Finally, she decided to call for help.

'Hello, Constable Hart speaking.'

'Hi, um, it's Melanie Green. I don't know if you remember you came to my building recently when I found a dead neighbour.'

There as a small sigh on the other end of the phone, Mel knew that Hart was not especially keen on her, but she needed an answer. 'Yes, I remember.'

'I . . . well, I wasn't sure what to do but I had an ominous note slipped under my door. Is that a police matter?'

'What do you mean by ominous?'

Mel read the note aloud to Hart, then added. 'I think they're for real. It scared the crap out of me when I read it.'

'Mmm,' Hart said, before a lengthy pause. 'It's certainly a concern. It's up to you whether you want to report it formally. It could be nothing, but there have been two suspicious deaths in your building, so maybe it's not nothing.' She seemed to be talking to herself as much as to Mel.

'What should I do?'

'Does your building have cameras?'

'Yes, but I think they're only on the entry points, not in the corridors. I can ask.'

'That would be a good start. If you have footage of the person putting the letter under your door that'll be a great help. Once you've worked out if there's a video, you can come in and I'll take your statement.'

'Right. Okay.' Mel's belly was still curdling inside her. 'Should I be worried?'

'It's not nice to receive a letter of that nature. Have you been doing anything unusual? Can you think of anyone who would want to harm you?'

'The only things that come to mind are the deaths. Darius's death was suspicious and given the similarities to Julia's, that makes her death seem concerning too. I guess I've been making some discreet enquiries. At least, I thought they were discreet.'

'It's best if you leave the sleuthing to the police. If there is someone targeting people in your building, you don't need to give them any more reason to look at you. Go about your usual routine.'

'Okay.' Mel agreed but wasn't sure how she would convince someone she had stopped snooping. Now she thought about it, the note had only appeared after the chat with Tony. Maybe someone had seen her talking to him.

'I'm going to have to get going, unless there's something else?' Hart said.

'Should I . . . put it into a plastic bag or something for evidence?'

'If you like. Call me back when you've reviewed the video footage. Bye, Melanie.' Hart hurried to hang up the phone and Mel felt a little hurt. The more she thought about it, the more she was convinced whoever was responsible for the mud monster knew she was interested. She wouldn't be bullied into letting this go. If someone was killing people in her building, she wanted to find out why, and stop them.

Mel looked at the kitchen clock, after all that excitement she'd been sitting on the floor in her kitchen for over an hour. It was nearly two o'clock, her stomach grumbled that she hadn't eaten for a while and her bottom had gone to sleep.

I'll visit Helen after I've had some lunch, Mel thought. Helen knew how to access to the security videos.

*

Helen looked surprised when she opened the door to Mel a bit over an hour later.

'I didn't expect to see you today, dear,' Helen wandered back into the apartment leaving Mel to follow and close the front door behind them.

'Yeah, I actually had a question about the CCTV.'

Helen had settled herself into a lazy boy style recliner and pointed to a dining chair where Mel could sit.

'CCTV, eh?'

'I had an unpleasant note put under my door and I wondered if I could see on the cameras who had put it there. They didn't sign it.'

'What kind of unpleasant?' Helen sat forward in her chair as though eager to hear more juicy details.

'Warning me to stay out of their business or else. But it really rattled me, and to be honest, I'm not sure how I can stay out of someone's business if I don't know who it is.'

'That is a conundrum. The cameras are only on the garage doors and in the entry way. We don't have them on each floor. Possibly it's something we could look at putting in, but it's never been needed.'

'Until now,' Mel muttered.

'That's very true. Two deaths and a nasty note. Perhaps we do need to have better surveillance.'

'What do you mean? Has someone asked you for footage?'

'Oh yes, dear, the police were after the footage after Julia's death, and of course they were back again when

Darius was found. They seemed quite miffed when I explained I didn't have any.' Helen stared into middle distance as though contemplating saying more, but she didn't.

'I guess that answers my question then. I'll leave you to it.' Mel wasn't sure what the old woman had been up to before she arrived, but she was lost in thought now, and Mel didn't fancy sitting around waiting for her to be lucid enough for conversation.

'I'm sorry I couldn't help. I do hope you can manage not to snoop too much and avoid another note under your door.'

Mel stood up, readying herself to leave. The comment struck her as harsh, Mel's throat tightened in sadness and rage. How dare Helen imply she deserved such a note by snooping? If she didn't do some poking around there would be nothing happening after Julia and Darius's deaths.

'Thanks for your help,' Mel said, trying to keep her feelings out of her voice.

So much for the video surveillance, she thought. Instead of going back up the stairs to her apartment, Mel went to the front of the building. She hadn't noticed whether there were any muddy footprints when she went for coffee, she'd stopped looking for them.

As she approached the glass front door, she saw the footprints clearly. How could I have missed them? After collapsing when she read the note, and her drop in to visit Helen, the mud had dried. It wasn't worth following them back to the riverbed again, she doubted there would be anything more to learn from it, but perhaps a walkthrough of the building was needed.

Mel hoped the mud monster had delivered her note, and that was its only reason for being in the building, but something in the pit of her stomach told her she couldn't go home without checking the other floors.

This time she took the lift to the sixth floor and worked her way down. There was no smell on level six, nor on five, but as she descended the stairs to level four her nose tingled. The wet, rotten mud smell was faint, but definitely there. She walked down the north side of the U-shaped floor, and sensed very little, but when she returned and when into the south side, the smell became stronger. It was a little hard to pinpoint at first, but after a couple of passes she was sure the source was apartment 407.

Why is it always the zero-seven apartments? Mel thought as she knocked on the door. There was no response, she put her ear against the door to listen more closely. Mel stood and knocked again, harder this time. 'Hello, it's your neighbour, Mel. Are you home?' she yelled, hoping to entice the occupant to open the door if they were merely ignoring her knocks.

She waited for a full minute, pondering her options. The mud thing was in the building, or had been at some point that day. She could smell the dirt, mud, and decay, what if she was too late? Or the occupant was out on an errand? She sighed, and turned to leave, but turned back just in case. Mel put her hand on the door handle and pushed down; it wasn't locked, and she pushed the door open a little. The compost decay smell hit her as she opened the door to a dark room.

'Hello? I'm coming in,' she said loudly, though she already knew the neighbour who lived here wouldn't answer. Mel felt along the wall for the light switch and gagged as her fingers ran across cold, wet, sticky patch in her search. A moment later she found the light and flicked it on. The scene was exactly as she'd imagined, mud everywhere, on the floors, the walls, the carpet, the furniture. Not quite as much as in Darius's house but more than Julia's. The coffee table had one leg smashed under it and was sitting tipped onto one corner. The kitchen seemed clean, perhaps the fight had missed it. Mel stepped closer, the smell of the mud searing her nostrils as she approached the bedroom.

The damage in this room was extensive, mud all over the bed, on two of the walls, including a muddy stain over a fresh hole in the plasterboard. The size and shape were of a large person, perhaps the occupant of the apartment had pushed the monster against the wall hard enough to break it. Mel's eyes travelled down to the floor beside the bed, and it was then she registered the brown and red streaked shape there; another neighbour taken violently by this mud creature rampaging through her building.

Fleur Blüm

The room spun around her, and she steadied herself placing a hand on the wall beside her, looking away from the corpse to catch her breath.

Finding two dead people might be a coincidence to the police, but three made her a suspect. Mel backed out of the bedroom, trying not to touch anything else. There was no need to check whether the neighbour was dead, her head was almost completely turned around. She couldn't have survived that.

Mel found herself in the corridor outside the apartment and took a moment to catch her breath. She needed to notify someone, the police, but she didn't want to call the emergency number again. Pulling out her mobile, she pressed redial to call Hart.

'Is this about that letter again?' Hart didn't even say hello this time.

'No, something else.'

Hart sighed loudly. 'Okay, well spit it out, I'm working on something right now.'

'I found another body.'

'It's not appropriate to joke about that.'

'I wish I was joking. I . . . wanted to check the building before I settled in for the afternoon, and—' and what? She couldn't tell Hart she smelled mud and tried the door.

'And you happened to stumble on a body?'

'I thought I heard something in number 407, so I knocked, and when no one answered, I tried the door, which wasn't locked, so I went in and—'

'You're serious? Fuck.' There was a muffled sound as though Hart had covered microphone. After thirty seconds or so, she was back. 'Are you there now?'

'I'm in the corridor outside the apartment.'

'Okay, stay there. I'm coming now. Don't touch anything and don't go anywhere.'

'I'll be right here.' Mel felt numb, again waiting for the police to take charge of a dead neighbour. What the hell is going on?

Hart was there within twenty minutes, a relatively short time, though Mel had become more and more upset, convinced they would believe she had done this.

'I had hoped not to see you again,' Constable Hart said as she approached Mel, who was sitting with her head in her hands, curled up on the floor in the corridor on level four of her building.

'I had nothing to do with it,' she started, her words tumbling over each other as she tried to stand up.

'Whoa there. You've got yourself into a state, have you?' Hart's face softened a little. Mel rubbed her hands over her face and realised she had started crying at some point. 'My colleague is going to go into the apartment and have a look while I'll stay here with you, okay?'

Mel nodded and sniffed.

'Before they go inside, is there anyone in there?'

'Um, only the body, I think. I don't know her name, but I've seen her around. Mid-thirties maybe, petite, brunette, she's on the floor in the bedroom. But everything is covered in mud. Like, everything.'

'Alright. And you didn't see anyone else inside? No one waiting to jump out and scare me?' the other police officer said. Smith according to his name tag.

Mel shook her head. 'No, but I didn't like, do a proper search or anything. I came straight back out here when I realised it was . . . too late.'

Smith nodded to Hart, pulled on blue disposable gloves, pushed the front door of apartment 407 and stepped inside. Mel put her hand up to chew the fingernail on her left hand but realised it was the one she'd put into the mud on the wall, and quickly dropped her hand.

'Did you get some on you?' Hart asked.

'Yeah, when I was looking for the light.' She held her hand out for the police officer to inspect. Hart nodded but said nothing further.

Smith came out of the apartment a few minutes later. 'Just the one deceased inside. No one else. I'll call it in.'

Hart nodded, and both women waited silently as Smith spoke over the radio to the station.

'Now, tell me exactly what happened?' Hart's eyes were hard this time. Smith was making notes on a small pad of paper.

'After I got the note, like I told you earlier, I went to see Helen, she can access the CCTV, but she said the cameras don't cover the corridors, only the entrances, so there wouldn't be anything to see of someone putting the note under my door. I was worried there was someone in the building who wouldn't show up on the cameras and I decided to check.' Mel took a shaking breath, trying to stave off more tears that threatened.

'I started at the top and worked down. Then when I was here, I thought I heard something and I knocked but no one answered, so I tried the door which was unlocked and … and then I called you.'

'I see. And you said you don't know the name of the deceased?' Hart asked.

'No.'

'I see.'

Smith made more notes on his little pad, the silence stretched out punctuated only with the scratching of pen on paper.

'I'm going to have to ask you to come with us to the station.' Hart looked at Smith, who nodded subtly.

'Are you arresting me?' Mel asked.

'At this stage, no, you're a person of interest. But I it's not looking very good that you've discovered three bodies, all with the same uh . . . situation. We need to have a proper chat.'

Mel shuddered, her whole body shaking as she processed the idea. 'I didn't do this. What about the threatening note?'

'I didn't say you'd done anything, but it really is time we have a good sit down, no more taking statements in hallways,' Hart said, and Smith nodded. 'I'm going to leave my colleague here to mind the scene until the coroner and the forensics people arrive. If you'd like to come with me to the station, that would really be best.'

Hart put out her hand as though to nudge Mel away from the door, but Mel leaned away from the hand.

'Before you go, can you tell me what you touched inside? We want to make sure to isolate those areas,' Smith asked.

'The wall, on the left, I was trying to find the light switch, so I probably ran my hand down the wall. I don't think I touched anything else with my hands, and I tried not to step in anything.'

'Thanks.' He bent his head to scribble something on his pad.

'After you,' said Hart, her hand hovering in a shepherding motion, but at least she didn't try to touch Mel this time.

*

They drove to the police station in Hart's blue and white marked car. Mel was in the back seat, and although she wasn't handcuffed, she felt very vulnerable. As though she couldn't escape, especially given the car doors had no interior handles.

They were mostly silent for the ten-minute ride, punctuated by burbling over the radio that had been turned down low. Mel couldn't make out what they were saying but assumed Hart could still hear.

The police station was in a back street behind the town hall a couple of suburbs over. It looked very small, and the signage was subtle and easily missed. Mel thought it was closed at first, or not in use, but as soon as

Hart pulled open the dark green metal door Mel realised she was wrong.

The interior was a depressing shade of grey, with occasional splotches of colour where bare wood peeked through on the bump rails that lined the corridor. Mel was shown into a small interview room that smelled of body odour and instant coffee. It had no windows and the fluorescent light above buzzed loudly from inside a metal cage.

'Have a seat. I need to grab something from my desk. Can I get you a cup of tea?' Hart asked, indicating for Mel to take one of the maroon-coloured plastic bucket seats.

'White with one, please,' Mel replied, the tea might give her something to look at and do with her hands in the absence of anything else. She'd only taken her phone and keys with her to check the building, figuring she wasn't going far and wouldn't need her bag, or ID.

Hart nodded and stepped out of the room. The silence in the interview room seemed much heavier with the buzzing light, and occasional clank of a heavy door closing outside. Mel picked at her cuticles and tried not to think about how she'd ended up here. Or about the threat waiting for her when she got home. No doubt whoever was doing this knew she had found the latest body. She would probably be next.

Mel jumped when Hart pushed open the door and came in bottom first, her hands full with two steaming paper cups, and a selection of paperwork tucked under one arm. Another woman followed her in, dressed in a plain blue suit, white button-up shirt, and sensible shoes, Mel assumed she was a detective.

'Mel, this is my boss, Detective Sergeant Haley Morris. She'll be helping with the interview.'

Mel nodded robotically. It was all too surreal.

'Nice to meet you, Ms Green, I hope you don't mind if I call you Mel.'

Mel nodded again. Hart sat down, plonking a cup of milky tea in front of each of them. Morris didn't have a beverage, only a small notepad and pen.

'Senior Constable Hart has been telling me about the situation in your apartment building. Very grizzly by all accounts. And you found all the bodies so far, is that right?'

'Yes.' Mel's voice croaked, she took a sip from her tea, which was scalding and flavourless.

'Can you tell me a bit about that?' Morris prompted after a beat of silence.

'There's not much to tell. The first time, my neighbour Julia, she's in three-oh-seven, there was a blackout, and her door was open, so I went in to check she was alright—she wasn't. Then I—'

'You said you thought you heard a noise the second time,' Hart said.

Mel took a breath and another sip of tea. 'I did say that.'

'But?' Morris asked.

'The truth is, I . . . smelled the mud. After Julia, like later that day, I noticed muddy footprints outside the building, I followed them down to the river, and the smell of that mud was seared into my brain. So, a while later when I saw there were footprints outside again, I . . . went looking for the smell.'

'I see,' Morris said, her tone neutral, as she wrote something on her pad.

'It know it sounds mental, but it's the truth. Anyway, I smelled the mud in Darius's apartment, it's not like any other smell, and well, I was worried, so I knocked on the door, and when he didn't answer, I tried it. It wasn't locked so I went in.'

'And today?'

'I don't know if Senior Constable Hart has told you, but I got a threatening letter, so I went to speak to the woman who has access to the building CCTV—but there isn't any coverage of my apartment front door—and then I wanted to make sure there was no smell of mud in the building before I felt safe to go home again and . . . I found the recent body. I don't even know her name.' Mel's voice caught in her throat, and she fought a sob. Rubbing her suddenly sweaty hands over her thighs was soothing as she tried to get her emotions under control.

'I see,' Morris said again. Mel dared not look up from her lap, but in her peripheral vision the two women were still, waiting for her to go on.

'I had nothing to do with this. I was trying to work out how to stop it, but I couldn't even get my head around what was happening. Why did the footsteps stop outside the building? Why was there so much mud at each scene? Why these people? I mean they were all in the oh-seven apartments, which sit on top of each other but why would someone kill people vertically? None of it makes any sense.'

'And you're sure you don't know the name of the woman you found earlier today?' Morris asked, after a lengthy pause.

'I mean, I think I've seen her around, maybe passed her in the corridors or taking out the bins but other than that I don't know her.'

'Her name is Jennifer Cabot. She moved in a few months ago. We'll have someone notify her next of kin. There is so much to be done when someone dies, not to mention the emotional toll it takes on people. Why would you be so stupid to start killing people in your apartment building?'

'I told you; I didn't do this.' Mel sat slumped forward in her chair, all her energy drained. Morris had no interest in hearing her theory about the mud person, or who was controlling it. 'I didn't send myself a threatening letter, why would I do that?'

'I've known people to do all sorts of devious things to try to divert the police gaze from them.'

Mel didn't say anything, she wanted to go home and had decided to only answer direct questions. 'Do I need legal representation?'

'Of course, you are entitled to have a lawyer present, we can put you in touch with legal aid if you don't know anyone, or can't afford a lawyer, but it will hold things up considerably. We can't let you go home until we've had our conversation, and who knows how long you'll have to wait for legal aid.' Morris said. There was a hint of a smug smile on her lips as she spoke, as though trying to convince Mel to waive her rights just because she said so.

'Am I being charged with something?'

'No, you haven't been arrested or charged at this time.'

Mel folded her sweaty hands in her lap and looked at the dull grey surface of the table between her and the two police officers.

'If you were us, Mel, what would you think about someone who keeps finding corpses? It's not normal.'

Mel shrugged.

'How many dead bodies do you think the average person finds a year?'

Mel stayed silent.

'It's zero. Most people will never come across a corpse, let alone one who has died violently, and here you are, having discovered three in your own building in a couple of months. You must see we're concerned by that?'

It felt like Morris was fishing, throwing out ideas, trying to get Mel to start talking, her questions were rhetorical, perhaps she expected Mel to spill her guts, though that's exactly what she'd done at first.

'Let's go through each one of the bodies you've reported in a bit more detail.'

Mel stayed in that room telling them again, in excruciating detail, the circumstances around each person she'd found dead. Her story didn't change, despite Morris coming back to each neighbour repeatedly over the couple of hours she was there.

Of course, Mel didn't tell them about the riverbank, or her suspicions of a wizard controlling a mindless killing machine for reasons as yet unclear, but she told them everything else.

'You said earlier you didn't really know Ms Cabot?'

'That's right,' Mel answered.

'When we go through your phone records, we won't see any calls to her? Or messages? You aren't friends on Facebook?'

'I didn't even know her name, why would I have been calling her?' Mel's patience was wearing thin.

'And we won't find any overlap in your lives?'

'I'm sure you will, we live in the same building. No doubt she's in the online group for the building, I've probably commented on something she's said, or vice versa, but we weren't friends.'

'What about Darius Todd?'

'He's been living there a while longer, I've probably had more interactions with him, but even so, we're neighbours, not friends.'

'And Julia McConnell?'

'We lived on the same floor, not far from each other, so I knew her better. We'd have conversations in passing, I'd seen her at the Christmas do and the general residents' meetings. I tried to keep an eye out for her since she was older and lived alone. I met her nephew, Tony, earlier today.'

I can't believe that was today, time seemed to have lost all meaning in this boxy, grey office.

'When did you meet him?' Hart sat up a little higher in her chair.

'I don't know, on the way to get coffee, maybe eleven?'

'And what was he doing?'

'He said he was clearing out her apartment, he's the next of kin.'

'Did you catch his last name?'

'No, but it might be McConnell as well, I guess.'

Morris leaned over to whisper into Hart's ear. Mel wasn't entirely following what was going on between the two cops, but it felt important. Hart stood and left the room without another word.

'Can I get you another cup of tea? Perhaps a bathroom break? Senior Constable Hart needs to check a couple of things before we continue our chat.' Morris put her notepad and pen face down on the desk, sitting forward as though about to stand.

'I'd really like to go home,' Mel replied.

'I understand. It would really help if you could stay a little longer.'

Mel wasn't sure if she was able to leave or not, but it didn't seem worth the argument. 'A bathroom break would be great. I need to stretch my legs.'

Morris collected her papers and stood up. Mel did the same realising only when she went to move how stiff she'd become after sitting for so long. The stress of the situation must have caused her to sit in an awkward position, her buttocks were numb, and her joints complained when she moved.

'Follow me, we'll go to bathroom then stop at the kitchen.' Morris strode off down the oppressive grey corridor as though having sat for so long didn't affect her at all. Mel trotted a little to catch up before falling into step behind the detective.

The bathrooms were the same grey with austere stainless steel sinks and toilets. Mel was relieved Morris didn't follow her in, and instead waited outside in the corridor. She wasn't sure how to feel, the situation was incredibly stressful, being questioned so thoroughly but not charged with anything had made Mel suspicious, they thought she was to blame somehow, but was it because she was the only lead they had?

Even when she was allowed home, the only thing Mel had to look forward to was that threatening letter. It might be better not to stay in her apartment, maybe her sister, Emma, would let her crash there for a couple of nights to let things calm down. The note writer would not be pleased she'd spent the afternoon finding the latest victim and being interrogated by police. How had she gotten herself into this mess? If only she hadn't been curious maybe she would have been safe, though maybe whoever was controlling the mud creature was planning to take out the whole building.

The pattern of the deaths didn't make sense yet. Why were they all in on top of one another? She didn't know who lived in 207 or 107, but if the magic was traveling up the building perhaps one of them was doing something nefarious.

Mel finished up her business and came out of the bathroom to find Morris waiting for her at the door.

Good thing she didn't need to go as well, Mel thought.

'Let's get you a cuppa, and we can go back for a bit more of a chat.'

It took all of Mel's strength not to groan at the idea of more questions, probably ones she didn't have good answers for. More circular conversations going over the same old ground.

Morris led her down a few more grey corridors, passing one or two uniformed officers on the way, to a staff kitchen area. It was as oppressing as the rest of the building, but there were a couple of uniforms hovering around the coffee machine chatting. They stopped talking as soon as Mel and Morris approached.

'Tea, is it?'

Mel looked at the coffee machine for a long moment wondering if it was worth drinking.

'It's not bad, but it's also not great,' Morris said, inclining her head to the machine. 'What do you want? Latte? Flat white? I mean, the buttons say they're not the same, but I'm not convinced there's any difference in the output.'

'Latte, I guess,' Mel replied. The two in uniforms dipped their heads towards Morris and wandered off without another word. In the absence of other people and idle chatter the staff kitchen felt exactly as the interrogation room had, only a little larger.

At least Morris didn't try to make conversation. She made herself a tea after putting a paper cup under the coffee machine's nozzles for Mel, who couldn't work out why they didn't have ceramic cups if this was supposed to be the staff room, perhaps it was a safety thing. Once they each had a drink, Morris ushered Mel back the way they had come to the small grey room. Hart was already waiting inside.

'I'll be right back,' Morris said, before retreating out of the room.

'I see you found the coffee machine then. It's not bad for an automatic machine.' Hart was trying to make small talk, but Mel was too tired to return the gesture.

When Morris came back into the room a few minutes later they resumed their questions.

'I was able to talk to Tony McConnell, said he saw you leave the building when you said you did, which

would probably eliminate you from the last death based
on timelines. And you phoned me a couple of hours later
when you found the note. Jennifer Cabot looked to have
been killed a couple of hours before you found her, given
rigor had started, but wasn't full at the time of discovery
so you might be out of the frame for that one.'

'It doesn't mean, of course, that you didn't have help
or hire someone—' Morris started to say.

'Now wait a minute. I came down here of my own
volition, you said I wasn't being charged with anything
and now you're working out where I was and whether I
could have killed Jennifer. Either you think I did it, and
you arrest me or charge me with something, or I am
going home.' Mel put down her half-empty coffee cup on
the table with a bit too much force and the contents
slopped over her hand. She slurped some of the liquid
into her mouth but the spill on the table would need a
paper towel or something.

'You're not being charged at this stage, and of course
you're welcome to leave at any point, but we really
would appreciate if you can answer a couple more
queries.' Morris frowned and leaned forward as though
trying to give weight to her words.

'Thank you for the coffee, but I'm going to go home
now. The possibility this person is still out there, and I've
had a threatening letter seem to be lost on you, so I'll
have to take care of myself. I'm not answering anything
else.'

Morris was sitting bolt upright; the angriest posture Mel has seen her in all day. 'If you plan on staying somewhere else, for safety, please let us know where we can reach you. We wouldn't want to lose touch.' Her smile was more like a grimace.

'I'll show you out,' Hart said, gathering up some papers and standing. Morris remained seated and didn't follow them.

'Thank you for coming down, I'm afraid we can't give you a lift home, you understand.' Hart lingered in the doorway between the main reception area and the private section behind the door.

'That's fine.' *If I'd known I'd be stranded in the cop shop I wouldn't have come,* Mel said to herself.

Stepping outside, the wind on her face helped to bring Mel back to reality. Despite wanting more than anything to be away from the police, she now faced the idea of going home, where whoever was killing her neighbours seemed to have it out for her.

I'll stop home and get some stuff and then stay with Mum or Emma, Mel thought as she started towards the train station. *I don't want to stay in that apartment alone right now.*

6.

Mel tried not to think about who, or what might be waiting for her when she arrived home. After walking back from the train station close to her building, she stood outside looking for fresh muddy footprints for ten minutes before she felt safe to go in.

The hallway was empty, she caught whiffs of cooking smells, maybe onions, and on the first floor a curry. On the third floor, her floor, there was an overpowering sweet scent of incense, she thought it was coming from Julia's place.

Maybe Tony wanted to get the smell out of the apartment, it probably reeked of decaying mud which would have been unpleasant, and off-putting for potential buyers who might come through.

Mel paused in front of her apartment for a moment, key in hand.

It's okay. There were no new footprints outside, there's no mud smell. Just grab a few things and head out.

She unlocked the door and stepped into the darkness inside. Flipping the light switch next to her, she relaxed a little; the apartment seemed less scary in the light. She packed up her toiletries, a few changes of underwear and a couple of outfits. She could come back if she needed to, she didn't want to impose on her mother too long. Plus she hadn't actually asked if it was cool to stay yet.

The packed overnight bag sat on her bed as she called Emma. The phone rang and rang before going to voicemail. Mel harrumphed and dialled her mother.

'Hi darling,' her mother's bright voice answered.

'Hey, Mum.'

'Are you alright? You sound funny.'

Mel took a deep breath and focused on relaxing her throat. 'I've had a bit of a day. I won't go into it now, but I wondered if I could stay with you for a while.'

'Of course, darling, you know you're always welcome but I'm not any less worried now you've said that.'

'I know.' Mel gave a hollow laugh under her breath. 'I'll tell you all about it when I get there—easier in person. I'm leaving now. I'll be about twenty minutes.'

'I expect the full story when you get here. I've got a lasagne in the oven so it should be ready by the time you arrive.'

'You're the best, thanks, Mum,' Mel said and hung up, the ball of worry in her belly slightly smaller.

She zipped up her bag, and slung it over her shoulder, grabbed her handbag and headed for the door. As she pulled it open, she saw a tall, gaunt man standing there, hand raised as though to knock.

'Can I help you?' Mel asked, the hairs on the back of her neck stood up. The man wore a slim-fitting dark suit, his hair was black, though it had a fair amount of grey through it, slicked back, and a little longer than jaw length around his skull-like face. He smiled, but his dark eyes remained hooded. It didn't alleviate any of the apprehension Mel felt.

'Mel, can I come in for a moment?'

'No, I'm about to leave.'

'It won't take long.'

'No, thanks. I don't know who you are.' Mel stepped forward hoping he would move back as she tried to pass him.

'As I say, it won't take long.' The man lifted his hand, his fingers facing Mel, and pushed her in the chest.

Electricity pulsed over Mel's skin where he touched her, and she stepped back and dropped her bags in surprise. The man stepped forward and she stumbled away from him, not wanting another shock, but her bag had fallen behind her, she flailed and fell down hard.

The man advanced without a sound as she scrabbled away from him across the floor. She wanted to yell, to scream, but she couldn't catch her breath, and her voice wouldn't work.

'You've been a great inconvenience to me, Melanie Green.' The man stood over her, the apartment door had closed behind him, and she would have to pass him to get out.

'Don't try to speak, I've taken care of that,' he said, with a half-smile. 'It was my note you received. I thought it would be enough to frighten you off, but of course I underestimated your desire to die.'

He reached into his trouser pocket and withdrew a small, maroon leather pouch. He held the bottom of the pouch and tipped it upside down, spilling pale brown dust onto the floor.

'I think you've met my helper. *Surge amicum,*' he said with a flourish of his hand. The dust drew together and formed a neat pile, before it began to pulse and ripple. The surface of the pile become wet, and the smell of decay and mud grew. As the blob swelled and writhed, Mel stared at it, unable to move, or think. She just looked on, knowing she was watching the formation of the golem creature that had killed the others.

Her mouth moved, working up and down in silence. She lay, half-sprawled over the floor watching this monstrous mud man rise from nothing, unable to defend herself. Soon its vast humanoid shape towered over her, and the gaunt man.

Mel recovered enough of her mind to turn away and crawl across the floor, but something wet and cold grabbed her ankle. The mud man pulled her back, her hands scraping uselessly over the floorboards. She was lifted up, and the wet, cold arms wrapped around her waist and neck.

She turned her head to see the gaunt man smiling that dead smile, watching her struggle against the golem. Mel grabbed the arm against her throat, but her fingers went straight through; she couldn't get a grip on it. The pressure on her throat increased; she couldn't breathe. Black spots floated in her vision, sparkles and bursts where the lack of oxygen and blood to her brain showed themselves.

'I can't have you interfering anymore Melanie. Relax, your death is inevitable.'

Time stood still as she struggled to breathe, to get away. Then her arms and legs stopped responding, her efforts to get free became smaller as her life ebbed out of her. And then everything was black.

The Gift

1.

Jessie was about to push open her door after a long day at work when her phone rang. After putting the keys in her mouth to fish her phone out of her pocket she answered.

'Mmm, hello?' Her words were muffled around the keys. She clamped the phone between her ear and her shoulder removing the keys from her mouth to enter the house.

'Jessie?' The voice on the phone seemed far away, wobbly; like they were under water.

She dropped her backpack, keys and shopping on the living room floor, pulling the phone away from her ear to check the call, she didn't recognise the number. 'I can barely hear you. Who is this?'

Shuffling came down the phone line, then the voice spoke again. 'It's Ben. You have to help me.'

'Ben?' Jessie frowned. She hadn't heard from Ben in over a year, not since they broke up and she deleted his contact from her phone. He sounded weak, gasping. 'Help with what? Are you okay?'

'I'm not doing so good. Can you come around? Now. It's urgent.'

'I . . . It's not a good time. I don't even know where you live anymore.'

'I know it's been a long time—' he paused to breathe heavily, 'I can explain when you get here. But please hurry.'

'Hang on.' Jessie looked up at the ceiling. She was tired and hungry. She and Ben hadn't split on the best of terms, but he wasn't a bad guy. 'What do you need help with?'

'It's easier if I show you. Please come.' He sounded desperate.

'Where are you?'

'I'm at home. Same place as before.' He sighed, as though the effort of talking was wearing him out.

'And you're sure it has to be right now? I'm half an hour away at least, and I need to get something to eat on the way.'

'Yes, please come. Hurry.'

'Alright, alright. I'll be there soon.' Jessie hung up the phone, annoyed at having to change her plans. She bent to pick up her keys and fished her wallet out of her backpack.

Wallet, phone, keys. I guess I'm off to Coburg. Her shopping would have to wait to be put away later, with a sigh she turned and headed back out the door.

*

She didn't need to put the address into her phone's GPS to get to Ben's house. She would have struggled to give someone else the address but the route there was hard wired into her brain. Jessie and Ben had dated for four years before he had started to withdraw. Eventually she sat him down for a chat, said he needed to tell her what was going on, or she would have to move on with her life. He couldn't tell her what it was; he'd shrugged and said it wasn't her. She told people he'd broken up with her, but it would have been more accurate to say he'd stopped participating in their relationship, and she walked away. They hadn't spoken since then. A couple of times she'd been curious how he was doing, and looked up his social media, but he had largely disappeared.

Jessie drove on auto-pilot, arriving at his place, stopping for Maccas in Bell Street on the way. She pushed the last bite of the squashed, soggy burger into her mouth, and regretted her decision to come.

This better be a proper emergency, she thought, balling up the rubbish from her meal and stepping out of the car.

The house looked different from the last time she was here. Plants were overgrown, and the grass was dry, yellow, and needed a mow. Ben lived in a two-bedroom brick veneer unit; he'd had a housemate for a while, but she wasn't sure if he still had one. Everything had an air of neglect, almost despair. Even the sensor light that should have come on as she approached the front door was busted, the only light came from the yellow-tinged streetlights.

The Gift

Jessie knocked and shook her head. Why had she come all the way out here? If this was a prank, or some weird ploy to get her back, she'd be livid. No sounds came from inside, she knocked again, harder.

'Ben? Are you in there?' she called out. Jessie stepped back and looked in the front window. The room was dark, and she couldn't make out any people. *He better be home.*

A minute passed, and she called out again, trying the doorknob. It turned in her hand and she pushed the front door open.

'Hello? Ben? It's Jessie. I'm coming in; you said it was urgent.'

A smell hit her as she walked in that she couldn't easily identify, an undercurrent of rotting food, body odour and maybe mildew. Her face scrunched up as though to stop it entering her nostrils, but it was too late.

'Are you here? What's going on?'

On the wall opposite the front door was the light switch for the lounge, she flicked it on. A dull light cast over the room. Ben hadn't exactly been house-proud, but he'd been neat in his own way. There was a basket filled with scrunched-up laundry sitting on the floor next to the couch, and where the other couch used to be, perhaps the housemate had taken that, were bits of paper, old take away containers, and dust bunnies. Everything was filthy, the kitchen sink was piled high with dishes. It was then she saw a wisp of hair over the back of the couch.

'Oi, are you asleep?' she asked, striding forward to come around to the front of the couch. Ben was sitting on the couch, his mouth hanging open, eyes staring. He was thin—much thinner than he had been when she last saw him. Her tummy fluttered; the scene didn't make sense.

'Ben? Are you okay?' She leaned forward to shake his shoulder. He slumped to the side, sliding down the couch, eyes open and mouth still slack.

'This isn't funny,' she said, hoping his face would spring back to life, and everything would make sense again. She waited, her heart beating loudly in her ears, and nothing happened. Ben didn't move, he just sat there, crumpled over to the left. He was so still he wasn't even breathing. A small drop of panic settled in her belly, and she started to breathe faster.

'Ben, seriously, stop it.' She kicked at his foot. No response. She reached out her hand, retreated, then reached out again, to place it on his neck. She felt no pulse. Jessie's hands were shaking, she took her phone out of her back pocket and dialled triple zero.

'Emergency, do you need police, fire or ambulance?' a calm voice answered.

'Uh—ambulance please.'

'Putting you through.'

'Ambulance service, can you tell me what seems to be the problem?' another calm voice, deeper this time, probably a man.

'My friend is umm . . . I can't find his pulse and he's like, not moving.' Her voice was shrill even to her own ears.

'Do you know how long he's been like that?'

'No. I mean, I spoke to him like forty minutes ago when he asked me to come by, but I got here and he's .. is he dead? That can't be right.'

'What's the address?'

'Umm…' She thought for a moment then gave the man the number and street name.

'Okay, I'm sending an ambulance to you. You need to do CPR while they're on the way. Do you know CPR?'

'I don't know.' Jessie couldn't remember the training she'd had.

'That's okay, I'll talk you through it. You need to lay him on something flat, and firm, like the floor, and start chest compressions. Put the phone on speaker and I'll stay here till the ambulance arrives.'

'Okay.' Jessie put the phone on speaker, laying it on the floor, then pulled Ben off the couch and spread him on the carpet too. He weighed very little, all skin and bones.

'Now you need to put both hands together over the centre of his chest, and push down quite firmly, I want you to count out loud to thirty, then two breaths into his mouth, okay?'

'Okay.' Jessie pushed down on Ben's chest and heard a great crunching crack. 'Oh God, I broke something, I broke something.'

'That's okay, just keep going, count out loud remember.'

'One, two, three…' she kept counting, thankful for something to think about that wasn't feeling of the lifeless chest of her ex-lover beneath her hands.

It felt like hours before the ambulance arrived, she was tiring quickly doing the CPR. The paramedics looked over Ben, checking for signs of life, but they didn't keep going with chest compressions.

'How long did you say it was between when you spoke to him and when you arrived?' the older of the two paramedics asked.

'About forty minutes.' Jessie's voice was robotic, hollow.

'I don't think we can revive him; looks like he's been gone for a while.'

Jessie was silent, she'd held onto hope that he would come back but looking at the greyish tone of his skin, it was clear he was dead.

'We'll have to wait for police now,' the younger paramedic said.

'What? Why?' Jessie was brought back into the present by their words.

'We need to determine whether it was a suspicious death. Could be natural causes, he's very frail-looking. Did he have a condition you were aware of?' the older paramedic asked, taking over the formalities.

'I don't think so. I hadn't seen him for over a year before tonight.'

'Do you know his next of kin?'

'Umm. I met his mum a couple of times, his dad's not with us anymore.'

'Okay. Are you feeling alright? Do you need to sit down?'

Jessie looked around the room, the only chair was the couch, where Ben had been, and it had an unpleasant-looking wet patch on it. She folded her legs under her and sat where she had been standing, landing on the carpet with a thud. From her position on the floor, she saw a neat stack of papers she hadn't noticed before. She reached forward to grab them; the two paramedics were busy and not paying attention to her.

It was a bundle of letters, tied together with a dark green ribbon. She untied the bundle; the top letter was addressed to her. It was Ben's handwriting but looked wobbly, as though he had been unsteady writing it. Opening the letter, she read it.

Dear Jessie

I'm sorry about how things went with us. I never intended to let you go, but I was in a bad place. You were, you are, the love of my life. I would have done anything in my power to keep you, but it was too much. I'd already started to fade away.

I wanted to reach out to you so many times, especially in the last few weeks.

**I've been getting weaker, I know I needed to
find something, find you, to hold on to, but it
kept slipping away. It's like I've been walking
through mud for months. My limbs have been
too heavy to lift to call you.
I knew it was coming, I tried to stop it, but I was
too weak.
I love you, I always will. Take care of yourself,
don't let it get to you like it did me.
Ben**

A drop of water fell onto the letter, and Jessie realised she'd started crying. Was this a suicide note? Had Ben killed himself? How did he die? Why was he so thin, and wasted? Where was all his stuff? He'd had posters on the walls, dumb car stuff, and some weird boho sculptures his sister had made, but there was nothing now. The room was bare, the entertainment unit where his huge TV had been housed was gone, the TV was gone too. The white expanse of wall was stained where the paint had faded around the cabinet. One lone pot plant sat on the carpet, the leaves brown, crispy, and withered.

With a shiver, Jessie put down the letter, and looked at the rest of the pile of papers. They were all addressed to Ben, in her handwriting. All the little notes she'd written to him when she'd been away or thinking of him.

I didn't know he'd kept these, she thought, shuffling through the envelopes, looking at postmarks for Sydney, Brisbane, those few from the weeks in Darwin.

The Gift

The police arrived without lights and sirens; Jessie only realised they were there when the paramedics started talking to them.

'Did you find the deceased?' a young, uniformed police officer asked her.

'Yes.'

'I'm Constable Nick Cleary, I need to ask you some questions, okay?'

Jessie nodded; her brain felt like it was full of fog. Cleary had come down on one knee next to her to talk to her, he looked awkward semi-hunched, trying to write down some notes. His colleague was looking around the rest of the house.

'Was he there on the floor when you arrived?'

'No, he was sitting on the couch. Triple-oh said I should put him on the floor to do CPR. I think I broke his ribs. I'm sorry.' Tears were streaming down her face, but she felt oddly calm.

'That's okay. It happens quite a lot with CPR. And you said you were on the phone with him before that?'

'Yes. Do you need to see?' she started to reach for her phone, but it wasn't in her pockets. 'It's over by the couch.'

'That's okay, we can look later. Is there anyone else in the house?'

'I don't know.'

'Okay, and what's this in your hand?'

'Ben left me a note.'

'Can I look at it?'

Jessie handed the note to Cleary, it had become a little more crumpled in her clammy hands. The officer stood to look over the note, motioning to his colleague to read it. They conferred in hushed voices, if her ears hadn't been ringing so loudly, she might have caught what they said.

The other officer started speaking into his radio. 'Suspected suicide. Not sure the method, but there's no signs of foul play, and left a note. Ma'am is this you? Jessie?'

She nodded.

'Yeah, the note addressed to the discoverer of the body. I need to keep this for evidence.'

'No, you can't.' Despite the fatigue and confusion that had washed over her since the ambulance arrived, she knew the letter was important.

'It's okay, we'll get it back to you as soon as we can okay.'

'You can keep the others for the moment.'

'Thank you.'

*

The police took her details, and Jessie stayed at Ben's waiting for someone to take away his body, occasionally getting up to pace around the kitchen when sitting on the floor was unbearable. At one point she fell asleep, the officers must have taken pity on her and left her that way.

In the morning, Cleary shook her shoulder. 'Jessie?'

'Have you been here all night?' she asked.

'Yeah, perks of the job. When you're the first on scene for a body you get stuck with minding it until they take it away. But he's all taken care of now, you should go home.'

'That's probably a good idea.' She wasn't sure why she'd stayed, they didn't need her, she'd given her statement, they had her number. Was it inertia or some morbid need to make sure Ben was really dead?

'Will you be okay to drive? We can call you a taxi if that's better.' Cleary had purple circles under his eyes, but otherwise seemed unaffected by the all-nighter and the corpse.

'I think I'll be okay.' She pushed herself into a seated position and her whole body complained. The carpet did not make a very good bed. 'Thank you.'

'You're welcome. We might need to be in touch later.'

'Will you let me know what, y' know, happened?'

'Sure, we'll be in touch.'

'Will you lock up then?'

Cleary smiled a tired smile, like he might have for a child. 'We'll make sure everything is in order.'

Jessie walked out to her car, still sitting in front of the house, as though nothing had happened. She clutched the bundle of letters in her hand, shuffling her feet, still stiff from the night before. The drive went by her without her notice, it wasn't until she had parked in her street, she realised she was home.

Fleur Blüm

The letters came inside with her, when she opened the front door, she remembered the shopping she'd forgotten last night—it was still sitting in an inelegant jumble on the living room floor. She put the letters on the table, picked up the shopping, and dragged it into the kitchen.

'Shit,' she said, as she realised her milk had sat out all night and would be no good. The vegies were a bit wilted, but everything else was salvageable. Standing over the sink, she poured out the milk, watching it swirl and gurgle down the plughole. She was so tired her eyelids felt like sandpaper.

If I want coffee today it'll have to be black, she thought. It was eight-thirty, she needed to be at work by nine, but it seemed an insurmountable hurdle to leave the house again. She wanted to sleep, and to cry, but she felt numb, unable to do anything much except stare at the milky residue in her sink.

Hi Maria, I won't be able to come to work today. I've had a sudden bereavement, it's quite a shock to be honest. Sorry.

She texted her boss, it was probably something she should have done with a phone call, but it was too difficult. Tomorrow was Saturday, the weekend, Jessie was sure after some sleep, and time to process Ben's death, she would be able to explain it to her boss on Monday. She filled the kettle and went to have a little lie-down while it boiled.

The Gift

When she woke, fully clothed, on top of her bed, she didn't know where she was. The light coming through the curtains was orange, twilight had come, she'd slept the whole day, yet didn't feel refreshed at all.

Her teeth were furry, and her belly rumbled—the last meal she'd had was Maccas on the way to Ben's. A full body shiver wracked her, making her cold all over, when she thought of Ben. Her phone, which was still in the kitchen, had gone flat. She plugged it in waiting for an angry reply from her boss.

It took a little while for the handset to start buzzing with missed notifications. Maria had replied.

My goodness, of course, take all the time you need. I'm sorry to hear about your loss. Please let me know if there's anything I can do to help.

Maria's kindness was overwhelming. All the emotions Jess had bottled up inside started to spill out of her, tears came in a rush, her face contorted, and she howled. A small part of her wondered if the neighbours would hear her, but the thought was pushed out by her sudden, enormous sadness. She curled into a ball on the couch, the cushion beside her face slowly becoming soaked with tears.

After some time, she hiccoughed to a stop, her eyes swollen, and her face smeared with tears and snot. If Ben could see her now, he'd be ashamed. The thought of Ben nearly set her off again, but she had no more tears left.

It was fully dark outside, her hunger had returned, and she forced herself to sit up, wiping her face on her sleeve, before dragging herself to the kitchen. She had some bread, which she toasted and reboiled the kettle for green tea.

Spreading peanut butter over the toast, she caught a whiff, reminding her of her childhood, when her mother would make her toast and canned soup if she was sick. She missed her mum, since she'd moved in with her new husband, they didn't see each other much.

How am I going to tell people? I shouldn't be this upset about an ex. Pull yourself together, Jessie berated herself, taking her tea and toast back to the couch, careful to sit on the non-wet side. She turned on the TV, found something mindless to watch, and spaced out.

Later, when the credits rolled for the second, or possibly third time, Jessie remembered her mother.

Do you remember Ben? I dated him for a while, you met him that Christmas down at Phillip Island, I think. Well … I have some bad news. He died. Yesterday. And I found him. I've been sleeping and bawling all day. What a mess. I hope you're well.

As soon as she put the phone down on the coffee table it started to buzz and light up.

'Mum? I thought you'd be asleep.'

'My God, darling, I was just getting ready to turn in for the night when your message came through. What happened? Why were you there? You didn't get back together, did you?'

Jessie choked a little, stifling a laugh. 'No. I—he called me out of the blue, and said he needed help, and could I come right now. I stopped on the way for a burger, and by the time I got to his house he'd died.'

'What did he die of? Was it very gruesome? I don't think I've ever seen a corpse.'

'I don't know. The cops think it might be suicide. He was so thin, Mum, barely looked like himself. And he was grey.'

'His hair had gone grey? That's early, wasn't he your age?'

'No, I mean his skin . . . but his whole, I dunno, energy was grey. Like he'd faded.' Jessie shook her head. Her throat was tight with unshed tears, the toast in her belly felt like lead.

'I'm so sorry darling. It must have been awful.'

'It was. I know we weren't speaking but like, I didn't want him to be dead.'

'No one should be dead at thirty-five.' Her mother yawned noisily, her jaw cracking a little through the phone line.

'Do you need to get to bed?' Jessie asked.

'I can stay and chat if you need to, darling.'

'It's okay. I don't really have anything to say, I . . . thought someone should know.'

'If you're sure you're alright. I'll go and you can call me whenever you need to, okay? Did you have the day off today?'

'Yeah, I couldn't face work.'

'Of course not. Very sensible. Try to take it easy—you'll be delicate for a while yet.'

'Thanks, Mum. Love you.' Jessie smiled a little, her mum could be thoughtless, but this time she was glad she'd made the effort to reach out.

'Love you too, I'll come to see you soon, okay?'

'Okay, bye.' Jessie's head felt heavy, the wet spot on the couch was almost dry, so she lay down again, the burbling of the TV keeping her company through the night.

2.

Saturday and Sunday blurred together, Jessie's sleep schedule was all over the place, and when her alarm went off on Monday at seven, she considered calling in sick again.

No use doing that, I'll just stay here moping, at least at work I'll be distracted, she thought, as she struggled out of the bed clothes into the cool morning air.

Jessie worked in the office of a high school, she was the Executive Assistant to the Vice Principal, which sounded important but was more like a glorified dogsbody and resource for the heads of department to use. She needed to keep a lot of information straight in her mind; what projects were due when, who needed to be reminded about what deadline. It would have been mind-boggling if she stepped into the job today, but she'd been there seven years, and over that time the role had grown and changed.

Jessie drove the twenty minutes to the campus, parked in her usual spot and sighed. If she could get through the day without crying, she would call that a win.

'Morning, I'm glad to see you, I'm sorry for your loss.' Maria's words tumbled over one another as Jessie walked into the office.

'Thanks. It's . . . it's good to be back. I should probably warn you; I'm not firing on all cylinders today, you'll have to forgive me if things are not up to their usual standard.'

Maria stood, hovering on her toes, and Jessie worried she was going to be swept up in an awkward hug. She hoped by staying still Maria would think better of it and leave her to get settled. She was holding her emotions in check, but anyone who was too compassionate would set her off.

'Of course, you've had a terrible thing happen. It's natural to be a bit shaken.' Maria rocked back on her heels. 'Were you close to the, uh, deceased?'

Jessie squeezed past Maria to her desk and plopped her backpack down on the desk chair. 'It's hard to explain. He was an ex-partner, so in some ways yes, we were very close, but we also hadn't seen each other for over a year, so no.'

'Death is funny.' Maria perched on the edge of her desk. 'You might not have seen someone for years and years, but knowing they're not in the world anymore still hits you. How did you find out?'

Jessie opened her mouth to reply but no words came out. She swallowed and tried again. 'I found him.'

'No! The body? You found the body?'

'Yeah.' Jessie's throat started to tighten; she could feel the tears prickling in her eyes.

'How awful. I'm sorry, darling, that's really tragic.' Maria pushed herself off the desk, closed the distance between them in two powerful strides and hugged Jessie. She wanted to push her boss away, but the firm arms wrapped around her were comforting, so she stood there, until Maria moved back. 'If you need anything, need to step out for a breather, or to take time off to do… I don't know, whatever, you say the word. Alright?'

Jessie nodded, the tears welling in her eyes threatened to spill over if she spoke.

'I'll leave you to get started, and I'll see you at eleven for the heads of department meeting.'

Jessie nodded again, she'd forgotten the meeting, had done no preparation or it, but it would probably be okay. *I hope I don't have to tell everyone the whole story again at the meeting*, she thought, it felt okay to be a bit emotional in front of her boss, but the whole leadership group? It would be humiliating if she started bawling in the middle of that.

Her inbox wasn't too full after her unscheduled absence last week, but as soon as she sat down the phone started ringing and the emails came pouring in. She watched the unread number climb, and knew that even if she read them, they would all need her to action something. Her grip on her emotions faltered and she thought about hiding in the bathrooms until the end of the day. Then she saw the time, she was supposed to be in that meeting.

'Maria, can you, um, tell everyone that I've had some bad news, and that I would appreciate everyone being a bit patient with me, but that I also don't want to talk about it? I don't think I can say anything to all the heads.'

Maria patted her upper arm. 'Of course, I'll make a little announcement, nothing excessive, and we'll leave it at that. Are you sure you'll be okay in the meeting? You look quite pale.'

'I'll be okay, y' know, don't want too many people asking questions about why it looks like I've been crying.'

Nodding, Maria strode into the meeting room with an air of calm confidence, something Jessie had always admired and envied about her boss. She held herself together so well, she couldn't think of a single instance when her boss had lost it at work, unlike her.

Jessie shook her head, trying to dispel the negative thoughts, and followed. The meeting was the same combination of boring and officious it always was, she had to fight to remain focused on the topic at hand, as much of her work for the next month until the next meeting would come from projects the people in the room were running, or other assorted jobs that needed to be done yesterday and no one else had the time or skills to do.

Normally, it would have made Jessie feel accomplished and important to be handed so many vital tasks, but today it was as though every expectation was another brick added to the load she was already trying to carry.

The Gift

'I nearly forgot to mention, before we wrap up, a comment on Jessie's capacity at the moment. I'm asking for patience from the group, perhaps even asking for a few of those odd-job tasks to be directed to another resource for the next—' she paused to glance at Jessie, as though looking for confirmation, 'until the end of the term as she'd had some bad news over the weekend. Nothing for anyone to be worried about, and Jessie has asked that you don't grill her about the details. Just a heads up for some empathy at this time.'

Jessie's cheeks burned hot and flushed. She had asked her boss to say something, but it still stung her pride that it was necessary.

If only Ben hadn't gone and... no, stop it. Jessie looked at her notebook, avoiding the gaze of the others, pretending she wasn't there, as Maria and the principal, John, wrapped up the meeting.

Afterwards, Jessie was worried she would be bombarded with well-meaning but intrusive questions, but no one tried to offer their sympathies and she returned to her desk uninterrupted. Despite the relief of not having to answer a bunch of questions, Jessie felt let down that no one had said anything to her. It felt foolish to wish for two contradictory things; to be left alone, but also not to be left alone, but that's how she felt.

The tears she'd pushed down at the start of the day welled in her eyes again, her throat was tight, and her breathing short and loud.

Hold it together, she told herself, dashing away the single tear that escaped over her cheek.

'Do you need anything from the canteen?' Maria asked in a loud voice as she walked into the office. 'Oh, I'm sorry, hun, did I catch you at a bad moment?'

Jessie sniffed. 'No, I'm okay. I'm not hungry, but thanks.'

'Suit yourself.' Maria patted her shoulder in an awkward maternal gesture before turning and sweeping back out of the room. Jessie pushed down the feelings, telling herself she would deal with them later, and thinking of who she might be able to talk to who would understand.

Her best friend, Aurora, was her go to for anything and everything that happened, but since last Thursday, Jessie had been avoiding her. Aurora had never been keen on Ben, and the idea of telling her filled Jessie with dread. Jessie sent her a text message.

How was your weekend?

Maybe a chat with her bestie would boost her spirits even if she couldn't say what was going on.

The email inbox was still crammed with items she hadn't read or actioned, so Jessie took a deep breath and started to sort them into a priority list. By the time Maria came back from lunch she had managed to settle into something of a groove, though it felt like everything was taking longer, and required more effort than usual.

OMG, you will never believe my weekend. I went to this bush doof with Kelly, you know the chick I met at the gig a few months ago? She's a mad raver, even had a few party favours going around, though I declined. I am beginning to think that raves are only good if you're off your face.

Jessie sent an immediate reply.
I didn't realise you were out of town. Did you pull up okay for work today?

Aurora replied a couple of hours later as Jessie was packing up to leave.

No way. I only just got back into the city. I took the day off annual leave, knew I'd have no hope of working today. That being said I'm not looking forward to tomorrow. Haha! What did you get up to?

Jessie was at home, sitting on the couch and thinking about making something for dinner when her friend messaged again. There wasn't much food in the fridge, and she had no energy to make anything. She looked over options on the food delivery app on her phone but she couldn't decide. Her belly growled, perhaps she should have had something at lunchtime. Her mind felt full of fog, it shouldn't be hard to choose something for dinner, but her fingers wouldn't make a choice. Jessie replied to the text instead of choosing a meal, then set her phone down and closed her eyes.

I didn't get up to much, hung around at home.

She woke up, hours later, television still playing a reality fashion show she'd put on earlier. Her hunger seemed to have faded, but she was cold, and her neck was stiff from the position she'd been in. She dragged herself from the couch and went to bed, turning off the TV and lights, but not bothering with cleaning her teeth.

*

The rest of the week went by in a blur; get up, go to work, go home, fall asleep. Her usual evening activities, exercise, hanging out with friends, weren't of interest to Jessie. She scrolled through her social media in bed on Saturday morning becoming more and more annoyed with how little she'd done in the last week. Other people seemed to be having such a good time; dinner and drinks, trips to the beach now the weather was starting to warm up.

Her house was a mess. Her lack of energy had meant her usual tidiness had gone out the window. And the fridge was still empty.

I'm going to get on top of this, she said to herself. She had two slices of pizza, cold, from last night's order, before starting on a cleaning spree. She vacuumed, mopped the kitchen and bathroom floors, took out the bins, including the multiple takeaway food containers. She stripped the sheets from the bed and put on fresh ones. Two loads of laundry later, she took everything to a laundrette where she could use the dryer while she did a grocery shop.

Things are going to be better this week. She would occasionally think about Ben, he would pop into her thoughts at the most inopportune times. At work her breath would catch in her throat, and it would be all she could do to stop herself crying, but it seemed like those times were fewer and fewer as time went by.

She arrived home in the late afternoon, her arms laden with shopping and clean washing, exhausted. It was the most activity she'd done in days. Jessie dropped the washing basket on the lounge room floor and unpacked the groceries—leaving out the bread so she could make some toast and a cup of tea.

Then she walked back into the lounge with her tea and toast and sat on the couch. Her first bite of toast was a shock, looking down she saw she'd put Vegemite on it, but was sure she'd spread jam instead.

I must be more tired than I realise, she thought, and finished off her toast, now that she knew it was Vegemite, it tasted fine. The evening slipped away from her, the unfolded washing sat there on the floor, but it was more than she could handle to put it away. Tomorrow would be fine.

She woke to her phone ringing. The sound pulsed through her sleep, though it took her a while to realise what the sound was. At some point during the night, she must have put herself to bed, though she had no memory of doing it, she rolled over to grab her phone from the nightstand, frowning to see Aurora's name.

'Hey?' she mumbled.

'How far away are you?' Aurora sounded annoyed.

'What?'

'I said, how far away are you?' She paused for a loud sigh. 'We set this brunch date weeks ago. What's going on with you?'

'Shit. Shit. I . . .' Panic started to flood Jessie's system, the skin on her throat prickled. Deep in her memories a vague recollection of the arrangement floated to the surface. 'I'm still in bed. I must have slept through my alarm,' Jessie lied.

Aurora was quiet for a moment; Jessie could almost hear the internal debate with herself. 'I'm going to order a coffee. You have half an hour to get up and come here, otherwise I'm leaving.'

'Okay yep. I'll get up now. Where are you again?'

'I'm at Grumpy's—the same place we always go. I swear you've left your brain somewhere, hurry up, would you?' Aurora hung up the phone. It wasn't like her to be so cranky, but waiting was a pet hate. Jessie felt queasy, the thought of having completely forgotten her best friend's brunch date was mortifying, but she would think about that later. She levered herself out of bed, she was nude but at least she hadn't slept in her clothes. No time for a shower, she peed and splashed water on her face. She pulled on a pair of jeans and a T-shirt from the pile of clean laundry that was still in the basket, shoved her feet into her runners and ran out the door.

Grumpy's was a ten-minute drive from her place, though sometimes getting a park was a nightmare in Richmond. She would just about make it on time.

Leaving now. Be there ASAP.

It wouldn't hurt to text Aurora to make sure she didn't watch the clock too closely.

'Wow. You weren't kidding when you said you were still in bed.' Aurora stood to hug Jessie when she finally walked into the café.

'I—no I wasn't. It totally slipped my mind; I must have forgotten to put it in the calendar. I'm sorry you had to wait.' Jessie sat opposite her friend and glanced at the menu.

'I felt a bit less mad after my coffee arrived. You know how I can be pre-caffeine.'

Jessie nodded. 'I'm the same sometimes. Thanks for waiting.'

'You said that already, it's forgotten, let's order.' Aurora clicked her fingers to attract the waiter's attention, a habit Jessie hated. As an ex-hospitality worker, clicking fingers were a sign of rudeness, so perhaps Aurora was more annoyed about the delay than she let on.

'How's work?' Jessie asked.

'Oh, you know, the same old thing.' Her friend was always ready to talk about herself and required little prompting. Jessie took a moment, trying to clear her head of the cotton wool feeling she'd woken up with. She hoped the forgetfulness and weird sleeping pattern would settle down, she'd had a shock finding Ben, but this was an over-reaction. They ordered food part-way through Aurora's report on how her boss was starting an Air BnB in an investment property in the city; the waiter looked less than impressed about being summoned with clicks, Jessie felt for him, mouthing the word 'sorry' as he left.

'He's the Executive Director of Finance, like, how many income streams does he really need? And using the apartment as an Air BnB, that smacks of wanting to get more money out of it that he could renting it.'

'That does sound a bit . . . . much.'

'Greedy is the word you're looking for.'

'But isn't he, y' know, hustling? Getting a good return on his investment.'

'He's hoarding property. And no one in their right mind will want to pay the rates he's asking for more than a few days. I bet it's going to be a huge amount of effort to keep it clean and turned over between guests, although maybe his partner will do that with all her spare time.'

Jessie mumbled agreement, though she wasn't sure. It might be a strange choice, but Aurora seemed genuinely outraged.

'I'm still annoyed about being stood up.'

'I know, I'm sorry. I . . . haven't been feeling myself lately.'

'It feels like you don't care about me when you forget stuff like that.'

'I know. I don't mean it that way.'

'What do you mean you haven't been yourself lately?' Aurora frowned, perhaps she was listening after all.

'It's no big deal, I had some unhappy news.'

'You know you can tell me anything babe, I might be a bit of a grouch sometimes, but I care about you.'

Jessie took a breath, and waited as their coffees were set between them. 'Do you remember Ben?'

Aurora laughed. 'Your ex? Yeah, what's that ratbag up to these days?'

'He's—' Jessie hesitated, it was hard to say out loud even after a week, 'he's dead.'

'Good one. No really, has he asked you for money or something? He was such a drainer.'

Jessie was quiet, waiting for her friend to catch her eye, to show she was serious. 'No, he's really dead. I found out last week.'

'God. He was only our age, what did he die of?'

'Not sure, it looks like he, uh, killed himself.'

'Fark. Even for a dude I didn't like, that's sad.'

Jessie nodded, sipping her café latte.

'How'd you find out? You're not listed as his next of kin are you,' Aurora asked.

'No, I found him.'

'I didn't think you were in touch with him.'

'I'm not . . . I wasn't. He called me, said he had to see me urgently, I thought he was taking the piss, I mean really, it had been over a year, but something in his voice was like, chilling. And by the time I got to his place—dead.'

'Oh, my God. What did you do?' Aurora's eyes sparkled in what could have been mistaken for glee if Jessie hadn't known any better.

'I called the ambos, and had to do CPR, but he was too far gone. Then the police showed up and I had to give them the note—' she regretted telling her best friend that part, but it was too late to take back now.

'How did he do it?'

'I don't know. I mean, he was slumped over.'

'Wild. I've never seen a real dead body. What was it like?' Aurora's interest was starting to feel ghoulish.

'Awful. It was like he was there but not there. It's hard to describe. I don't really want to talk about it anymore.'

'No, of course. What a terrible thing to discover right after he called you out of the blue. Do you think he planned it, so you'd find him? Horrible.' Her grin belied her words.

Jessie had been trying not to think about it, but the evidence was clear; Ben knew he was close to something serious, and he called her to come to see him right before he died. He must have known what he was planning to do. Jessie wouldn't wish finding her body on anyone, let alone from self-harm. Her thoughts strayed to the pile of letters, since that night, she hadn't read them, they'd been sitting on the coffee table since she'd thrown them there, as though they were radioactive. She didn't want to look at, let alone read, love letters to her dead ex.

'Earth to Jessie?' Aurora prompted. She'd been speaking while Jessie had been ruminating.

'Sorry.'

'I get that you've had a shock, but that was a week ago. You're such a space cadet. I was so close to storming off when you weren't here earlier. It's really rude, you know?'

'I know.' Jessie stared at the table, instead of cheering her, time with Aurora had the opposite effect; she wanted desperately to go back to bed. The coffee hadn't made any difference, and she barely tasted the food though it was no doubt excellent.

'Freddie wants me to go Margaret River with him, he's got a client there with a vineyard. I'm dying to get out of Melbourne, have a little romantic retreat.'

'That sounds nice.'

'I'd invite you, but it's not the sort of thing you bring your sad-sack friend along to. And it's Freddie's work trip, I shouldn't even be going. He's going to pay for my plane ticket, because he's a darling like that, his work is paying for his, so that seems fair.'

'Very generous of him.' Jessie thought it was a bit much having her boyfriend pay her airfares when he was supplying the accommodation, but saying so would only annoy Aurora further, and given how many times she'd brought up being late, it was more than Jessie could handle to be told off about something else.

'You'll have to bring me back a fridge magnet or something,' she said, attempting a smile.

'Of course. Maybe I'll have room for a couple of cheeky bottles, no doubt Freddie's supplier is going to be swimming in delicious wines.'

Now she was able to show off about her amazing boyfriend, the sommelier and wine importer, Aurora was back in her regular stride. The creepy grin she had when they were talking about Ben's death had disappeared and was replaced with her usual self-satisfied expression. Aurora had been Jessie's best friend since high school, but since then they had grown apart. Aurora went into advertising, was concerned with her appearance, and how she could show her wealth with it, while Jessie was much more concerned about whether the kids in her school were doing well, and in stretching her moderate budget far enough to live on her own.

'I better get going, Freddie's out golfing and I have an appointment to get my nails redone.'

Jessie looked at the time, it was after midday. Despite feeling like time was dragging, they had been at the café over an hour since she arrived, granted it was half an hour late. 'We'll do it again soon.'

'When I get back, I'll hit you up. But don't forget me again this time, okay?'

'I won't.' Jessie didn't believe it, the way she'd been going lately it was just as likely she would sleep through her alarm even if she did manage to put the entry in her calendar. They split the bill, Aurora was tight as well as rich, perhaps that was how she managed have money for nails, hair, bags, clothes, and the rest.

They hugged goodbye and Jessie walked back to her car feeling ashamed. How could she have forgotten their brunch date? Aurora must have been really hurt to mention it so many times. Jessie sat behind the steering wheel and tried to psyche herself up for the short drive home, fighting the waves of yawns that seemed impossible to stop.

3.

Jessie got home without falling asleep at the wheel, though she wasn't sure exactly how. As soon as she returned home, she flopped onto her bed, still clothed, and fell asleep.

She woke in the late afternoon, her neck stiff from having slept at a strange angle.

What happened? Why did I sleep like that? she wondered. Pushing off the bed, she went into the kitchen, and looked into the depths of the fridge for a very long time before realising she wasn't hungry. The ingredients in the fridge from her shopping trip yesterday sat there, as though accusing her of wasting them. It was too much for her to think about cooking and despite having spent much of the day sleeping, her eyes ached and stung with fatigue, and her teeth were covered in furry plaque from skipping brushing them last night and this morning. Jessie brushed her teeth; the smooth clean feeling was a relief after the fur. After washing her face, she shuffled back to her bedroom, changed into her PJs and climbed into bed.

For the second day in a row, Jessie woke to the sound of her phone ringing. It was the school, probably Maria.

It was almost half past nine, well after she was supposed to have been there.

'Hello?' Jessie's voice was weak and scratchy in her throat.

'Where are you? Are you alright? Are you coming in?' Maria, didn't wait for her answer between questions.

'Sorry, sorry. I didn't realise what time it was. I must have slept through my alarm. I'll be there as soon as I can.'

'That's not like you, are you sure you're not coming down with something?'

Jessie hesitated, she had been feeling awful for days, waves of fatigue that overwhelmed her, but it didn't feel like a virus. 'I'm okay, tired.'

'Alright, if you're sure. See you soon.' Maria sounded harried. No wonder if she'd been waiting for Jessie to turn up for nearly an hour already. Looking at her phone, Jessie saw four text messages from Maria before the call. She'd gotten into a real tizzy. Though she was awake now, getting out of bed proved to be a bigger barrier than usual. It was as though her limbs were weighed down with lead, or perhaps all the strength in her body had left her.

It was almost an hour before Jessie arrived at school, Maria looked up from her desk as she walked in but was on the phone. Her mouth was pinched, and her brows drawn, perhaps unrelated to Jessie's lateness though it seemed unlikely.

'My goodness, what happened? You look like something the cat dragged in.' Maria had finished her phone call and came over to Jessie's desk about ten minutes later.

'Thanks.'

'I don't mean to be rude, but you don't look well. Are you sure you should be here?'

'Yes, I'm sure I'll perk up soon.' Jessie tried to smile, the effort made her jaw and cheeks sting. The rest of the day, shortened though it was, dragged on. Every task was more difficult than she remembered it being, she would get halfway through something and forget what she was doing, she had started composing an email at least three times only to forget who they were for and what they related to.

This isn't normal, Jessie thought when she packed up her desk and computer for the day.

'I'm going to take my laptop home tonight, in case I feel worse tomorrow, I can do a bit of work from home,' she said to Maria when she was leaving.

'I appreciate the effort, but really if you're too sick to come in, then you shouldn't be working from home.' Her boss gave her a short pat on the upper arm. 'See you tomorrow, I hope you feel better than you did this morning.'

Jessie nodded, slipping the laptop and charger into her bag.

At home, she slumped onto the couch, and her eye landed on the pile of letters from Ben's house. She felt compelled to open them and read through the first three. Love letters between the two of them, though Ben only had the ones she's sent. Somewhere in her storage tubs she had the ones he'd sent. It had been so tempting to throw them out, or burn them, when they split up, but for some reason she'd put it off.

Reading the letters, she was struck by how happy and energetic she'd been; out to trivia, or drinks or a meal after work every day. Ben had been the same, with the gym, and running, and his motorcycle buddies. What happened to the motorcycle she couldn't remember, but it hadn't been at his place when she visited that last time. He'd been so thin. When they got together, Ben had been a strapping muscular man, broad-shouldered, and stout, with short dirty blond hair and a neat beard.

He'd been strong, much stronger than he appeared. Ben was the sort of person who would store fat over his muscles, but could lift enormous weights at the gym a several times a week. Though he had never been part of an outlaw motorcycle club he would have fit in on looks alone.

By the time they broke up, that man was fading. His hair and beard were shaggier, his muscles had started to atrophy. The vibrancy was disappearing, but Jessie had thought it was a symptom of their dying relationship— they weren't suited and staying together was destroying both of them. What if what had killed him, depression or whatever it was, had started even before they broke up.

She had thought letting him go would allow him the space to get back on track, but maybe she'd abandoned him to whatever internal demons were sapping his strength.

What if I killed him by leaving? She shook her head; he'd started changing after he went to visit his family for the funeral of his grandfather. It made sense he'd re-evaluated his relationship after a death in the family. He'd come back different, distant, surly, because he had decided they were over.

Jessie put the letters back on the coffee table. She felt drained, though she felt that way most of the time. Her head had started to ache, and she felt nauseated.

Maybe I am coming down with something, she thought.

*

In the morning, she slept through her alarm again. She woke up to her second alarm, the one that told her it was time to leave the house.

'Shit,' she said aloud. Her options were to get to work late, again, or call in sick. Given how she felt last night, and how tired she was lately it might be time to admit she had some sort of low-level virus.

Hi Maria, I'm not up to coming in today. I'll try for tomorrow.

Jessie lay back and fell asleep. Her dreams were filled with stress. In one she remembered being at a party of some sort with Aurora, but her friend was being nasty to her. Ben was there, alive this time, but he started kissing Aurora. Jessie felt unwell and tried to look away, but her eyes were stuck on the couple.

Another dream followed, in this one Jessie had lost a baby. As was the way in dreams she knew it was her baby, and it was vital she recover it before something tragic happened. She ran through the shopping centre looking for the baby, stopping people to ask them, but they only looked at her with vacant eyes full of incomprehension.

She woke a little after noon feeling less rested than before she went to sleep. Her body felt heavy and weak but she didn't have symptoms of a cold or virus—no sore throat or runny nose.

Then her bladder reminded her she hadn't relieved herself since last night and she struggled out of the bed clothes to go to the bathroom. Washing her hands, Jessie looked at herself in the mirror. She did look terrible; skin turned a pasty shade of grey, deep purple circles under her eyes, her hair lank and tangled, perhaps from tossing and turning through her nightmares.

Now that she was up, she went to make coffee only to discover the coffee machine wasn't where it usually was on the kitchen bench. Jessie frowned, there was no reason for the machine to be anywhere else—she'd used it once or twice a day since she got it. Ben had given it to her their second Christmas together. She'd always thought he really wanted it for himself, but she'd been determined to master it, and insisted on taking it with her after the split.

Where the fuck is it? she thought, her mind struggling to comprehend why it wasn't there. She opened all the kitchen cupboards, but it wasn't in any of them. She looked in the linen cupboard, though why it would have been there she couldn't imagine. She was at a loss; it had disappeared completely. Perplexed, she went back into the bedroom, considering whether she had the energy to walk to the shop for coffee, and whether she could afford to get a replacement. She opened her wardrobe door, and there it was sitting under her dresses on the bottom of the wardrobe.

I definitely didn't put that there, she thought grabbing the machine, which was much heavier than she remembered, and taking it back to the kitchen. At least she didn't need to go out now.

With her coffee brewed, and a couple of pieces of vegemite toast, Jessie sat in front of the TV and tried to get her head to stop pounding. If coffee and food didn't help, she would have a painkiller, but most of the time it wasn't necessary.

Somehow the day slipped away, it was getting dark and she hadn't done anything except sit on the couch watching whatever came on the TV. Jessie still felt awful, had no energy, and a nagging sense of unease that hadn't let up since she realised the coffee machine had moved.

The Gift

She didn't even know if Ben was going to have a
funeral, or whether it had passed. Who would she ask
about that? She'd had his mother's phone number once
upon a time but had deleted it in a fit of anger after their
breakup.

What was her name? Mrs Ben's Mum would not be
useful in a telephone directory or internet search. She
opened Facebook and looked for Ben, he had a few
members of his family linked; none of the names seemed
to belong to his mum, though Laura Jenkins was his
younger sister.

Jessie opened a direct message window to Laura.

**Hey, you might not remember me, but I dated
Ben for a while, we separated about a year ago. I
wanted to extend my condolences; I know he's
passed away. I wondered if there will be a
funeral? I hope I'm not too late. Please let me
know if there's anything I can do to help in these
difficult times.**
Jessie.

It seemed entirely inadequate, but what else could she
do? Jessie sent the message, then she leaned her head
back against the arm of the couch and fell asleep.

On Wednesday morning Jessie felt no better but also
no worse, so she dragged herself to work. Concentrating
on work was a struggle all day. She drank three coffees

which made her shaky and anxious, but still sleepy and vague.

That evening as she sat on the couch trying to get up the energy to make herself dinner Laura replied.

> **Jessie – of course I remember you. You were at that Christmas up in the Grampians where Ben gave himself a funny tummy for the whole trip by eating too much pineapple and pavlova. We're having the funeral this Friday, at a place in Camberwell. I'll forward you the details. It's been a difficult time for everyone, thanks for reaching out. I hope to see you there.**

A trace of a smile crossed Jessie's lips as she read the message. At least she hadn't missed the funeral.

Yet. Her inner voice piped up. The way she'd been going it was possible she'd miss the funeral because she couldn't drag herself out of bed, but she was determined not to let this, grief hangover, or whatever it was, stop her.

*

Camberwell, where the funeral was to be held, is a well-to-do suburb in the inner east—full of rich families, and private schools. It started at ten in the morning, so Jessie had taken the day off work. Her ability to do her job had been so compromised lately it would hardly make a difference if she wasn't there. And she figured the funeral would aggravate whatever was happening.

The Gift

Her alarm was set for seven o'clock, as usual, but she had added seven-thirty, eight o'clock and nine o'clock alarms to make sure she was awake in time. Before going to bed on Thursday she set out her clothes; the smart black trousers she wore to work, a button-up blouse in dark maroon, and her black suit jacket. She wanted to make sure nothing went wrong.

The alarm blared its abrasive tune, and Jessie rolled over to turn it off. The time was already nine o'clock, somehow, she had missed the other three alarms. Her gut clenched, and her mind filled with panic.

How did I sleep through all of those? she thought as she pushed herself out of bed with an enormous effort. She skipped the shower, but washed her face. She was still pale, her skin seemed to hang loosely from her skull in a way that made her look older than her twenty-nine years.

She set the coffee machine going and went back to her bedroom to change into her funeral outfit. The pants and jacket were still hanging on the back of the door, but her blouse wasn't with them. The panic in her belly intensified, her empty stomach gurgled with stress. The blouse wasn't in her cupboard, and she found it scrunched in the laundry basket.

I can't wear that now. There were other blouses in the wardrobe but they were all more colourful; not suitable for a funeral, but there was nothing for it—she was already running late. A glance at the clock showed quarter to ten already, time was not behaving today.

Jessie threw her clothes on, shoved her feet into some neat black flats, and headed out the door. With traffic it would take her half an hour to get to the venue.

Better late than never, she told herself.

Her hair was a mess, and her outfit seemed to have grown so it sat awkwardly on her body. The funeral home was a slick-looking building, all tones of beige and light grey.

My face matches the décor, she thought walking in. The proceedings were already underway, and Jessie snuck into the back of the hall, hoping no one would see her.

The family were taking turns to talk about their experiences with Ben. His coffin was at the front of the room, closed casket, perhaps he had deteriorated since she found him a couple of weeks ago, or perhaps his vacant, gaunt face was too distressing. Laura was the last to speak.

'I never knew a world where Ben wasn't in it,' she began, her voice high and tight with emotion. 'I was, I am, Ben's little sister. He looked after me, in his way, since I was born. Most of the time he was kind, generous, caring, but sometimes he was a little shit.

'I remember once when we were kids, he took one of my dolls, gave it a haircut and told me she liked it better like that, since she was a lesbian.' She laughed a little. 'Neither of us knew what a lesbian was, really, but every time Dad saw a woman with a short haircut, he would tell us that meant she was gay. Thanks for that, Dad.'

The Gift

Their dad wasn't present, having moved away to Brisbane to be with a much younger lover. Jessie had met him only a couple of times and he had been a blokey bigot every time.

'I will miss you, Ben, more than you'll ever know, because you're dead.' A half-smile crossed her face. 'We didn't agree on much, you don't believe in an afterlife, so I probably won't see you there. We loved you, and—' she paused to compose herself, her face had contorted in grief for a moment before she schooled it back to neutrality. 'I love you. I hope you are at peace now. I know the last year or so was really hard.' Laura stepped back from the podium and hiccoughed, silent tears streamed from her eyes, her grief escaping in soundless pain now her speech was over. Their mother came up from the crowd, took Laura's arm and ushered her back to her seat.

A woman Jessie didn't recognise, wearing a very sombre expression and a neat all black suit, came to the podium.

'Thank you all for coming, the family will be having a short morning tea, at which you are all welcome, while the body is transported to the crematorium. There will be no internment ceremony at this time.'

Jessie waited as a semi-transparent curtain closed in front of the coffin, and the other mourners started to file out of the room. Laura was still shaky and crying a little, though she'd calmed down. The morning tea was in another room in the funeral home, a bleak beige-walled, grey carpeted room that could have been any anonymous hotel conference room. Hot water urns were set up on a long trestle table at the back, with small white cups and saucers and a selection of teas. The food looked small and lonely sitting on the enormous table, lemon slice, hedgehog, and caramel slice in tiny single serving portions.

Ben had been popular before they broke up, before he'd become strange and unsociable. Jessie had expected more people to be there, but the dozen or so mourners all looked like family.

'Jessie, we thought you weren't going to make it,' Laura said, touching Jessie's arm.

'I . . . haven't been well. I'm sorry I was late.'

'It wasn't a criticism.' Laura smiled, though her eyes were still tight, red, and swollen from tears.

'I know.' Jessie swallowed, she wanted to pull away from Laura's touch, but it seemed she needed the contact. 'I thought there would be more people.'

Laura sighed. 'After you broke up, Ben changed. He stopped seeing people, he slept all day, wouldn't eat, we were all really worried about him, but whenever I asked how he was he would pull away even more, so I stopped asking. He lost his job a couple of months before he died.'

'What happened?'

'He was chronically late, and sometimes wouldn't show up at all. They tried everything but he was, I dunno, too sick I guess.'

Jessie nodded, if she kept up the way she was going she'd end up like Ben.

I will not let it get that bad, she promised herself.

'That's so sad. I'm really sorry for your loss.'

'I need a drink, come with me?' Laura's expression was pinched, as Jessie walked with her to the meagre buffet.

Once they each had a tiny cup of weak coffee and a minute piece of the slice, Laura sipped hers and scrunched her nose slightly, before returning the cup to the saucer.

'We don't really know what happened. The coroner said it was indeterminate, not enough evidence to say whether it was natural causes somehow, he was very thin and unwell, or if he'd taken his own life. You were the one who found him, is that right?'

The memory of Ben's house jolted as it sprang back into her mind. 'Yes.'

'Must have been awful. The police said there was a note.'

'Yeah, I saw it. It could have been a suicide note, I guess, but it didn't seem like one. I don't know.'

'I wouldn't have ever thought he was capable of it, y' know, offing himself, but the last year, he was so different.' She shook her head and sipped her coffee again. Jessie didn't want to talk about it anymore, Laura seemed callous, matter-of-fact, about the death of her only sibling. Perhaps she hadn't really come to terms with it, but then again, maybe she'd seen Ben's decline and wasn't surprised.

'I'd better mingle,' Laura said. 'Thanks for coming, sorry you missed the start.' She walked away towards a group of women who all looked very similar, perhaps they were aunts. Jessie felt alone, despite being surrounded by people. They didn't know what she knew, that something was trying to kill Ben. Though maybe they were right, he'd changed, and his death was self-inflicted.

Since that phone call, nothing had been right in Jessie's life; things were moving around her house, she slept all the time, barely ate, and felt drained and exhausted constantly. She grabbed another couple of pieces of lemon slice before slowly retreating towards the exit.

I doubt anyone will even notice I've gone, if anyone knew I was here in the first place, she thought. The whole thing had taken a little over an hour. She was drained and wanted to get away from the pall of death over everyone, though it wasn't much better at home, she would prefer to be sad on her own than in company.

4.

No matter how much she rested, Jessie didn't feel any better. Her daily tasks, her work, even socialising was overwhelming. She had stopped going out after work, hoping that would help, but after a few months of cancellations her friends had stopped inviting her to things.

Maria was concerned about her at first—showing up late and looking like she was going to keel over at any moment, but as the months dragged on her tolerance for Jessie's continuous lateness and sloppy work lessened.

'Jessie, have you done that report for the end of year report?' Maria asked one day in late November. The Year Twelve students had mostly finished their exams, and the other classes were coasting in the lead up to Christmas holidays. It should have been a time for getting some more done, tackling the backlog of things, but Jessie couldn't keep her mind on the task.

'Um . . . no, I've been working on getting all the information together, but it's not finalised yet.'

'What's the hold-up? Are people not getting you the stuff you need, or are you just getting through it all slowly, like everything else since June.' Maria's hands were waving around the air between them to punctuate her words, the bigger the gestures the more agitated she was.

Jessie hated being bad at her job. She hated spending her life catching up to where she was supposed to be a week ago instead of being able to anticipate, to keep track of multiple things at once, like she used to.

It was as though Maria heard her interior voice.

'I know you're trying, and we've had conversations about your performance over the months, but you must know you're making it very difficult for us to keep employing you.' She shook her head. 'You've been with us a while, and you've been an excellent worker in previous years, but something's changed. It may not be feasible for us to give you a contract for next year.'

Though she had been employed on a constantly renewing contract, Jessie knew it wouldn't be easy for Maria to recommend dropping her. They were good friends, at least as far as work friends went, Jessie had been a whiz at keeping all the balls in the air until the night with Ben. It was as though she left her brain, and her joy, back at his house.

She was giving it her all, but everything was much harder than it used to be; getting up in the morning, choosing what to wear or what to eat, even remembering to eat was too difficult sometimes. Her clothes looked baggy and sack-like on her body as she lost more and more weight. The missed meals probably had an effect on her energy levels too.

The Gift

Aurora had kept in touch for a while but seemed to
have abandoned her now. Perhaps too busy with her new
boyfriend—whoever it happened to be at the time, they
never lasted much longer than a couple of months. The
activities she had been interested in before, trivia nights,
swimming, jazzercize for a laugh every so often; none of
them held any joy for Jessie. Slowly she stopped doing
all of them, and her friends from each activity stopped
asking if she was coming.

Christmas was in less than a month, the year had
passed in a flash, yet each moment had felt stretched out
to the point of pain. Jessie sighed, her desk was a mess,
she'd let so many things fall off her radar that Maria was
considering letting her go. There was no way she could
cope with a new job on top of feeling like shit all the
time. She closed her eyes and wished it would all stop.

*

That night at home her mother called.

'Hi, Mum,' Jessie answered, trying to sound pleased
to hear from her mum.

'Hi sweetheart, are you alright? Did I wake you?'

'No, I was watching TV.' At least Jessie was sitting
on the couch and the TV was on, though what the show
was about she couldn't have said.

'I'm calling about Christmas. I thought we could all
come to your place for a change. You know I usually like
to have everyone here, but I feel like it was so much
work last time, it would be nice for someone else to have
the responsibility.'

Jessie's throat tightened. 'Uh,' she managed to croak.

'Your brother isn't going to do it, as much as I love him and his partner, they've just had a baby and it's not fair to ask them to host this year. Maybe next year, we could do a rotating roster or something—'

'I don't think I can.' Jessie swallowed.

'Don't be silly, you're great at organising. I'll bring a few things. Your aunt will bring something. Most of it can be done the day before and put in the oven on the day.'

'No, really—'

'I know what you're going to say, your place is quite small, that's okay, we understand it will be a little bit more compact than we're used to. It might even work in your favour; people won't want to hang around as much if we make the environment less inviting.' Her mother chuckled softly, it would have been comforting if the last six months hadn't been such a battle and all of this on top of the news her job was probably going to disappear.

'Listen to what I'm saying, I can't host. I'm not up to it.'

'I'm sure it's the end of the year fatigue.'

Jessie sighed, her mother hadn't seen her in person since before Ben had passed away, they spoke on the phone sometimes but only when Jessie called, and her withdrawal from the world had included her mother, not that she'd noticed. 'I've been having a hard time lately.'

'Really? You never said anything. What's been happening?'

'I . . . nothing really, I haven't been right since Ben died.'

'That was months ago love, surely you're not still in a funk about that.'

'I know it was months ago.' Jessie clenched her teeth, if she hadn't been so tired, she would have been furious. 'I'm not sure I'll keep my job next year either.'

'What?' Her mother was incredulous. 'That's ridiculous, you're fantastic at your job, they're lucky to have you.'

'If you'd asked me this time last year, I would have agreed with you. But now, I'm barely getting by, I'm constantly late because I sleep through my alarm, I haven't been well for months, I look terrible, I keep expecting someone to ask if I have cancer.'

'You look fine.'

'You haven't seen me.'

'I don't like your tone. If you had taken the time to call me a little more often, maybe we would have spent more time together. But I don't hear from you, and when I do make the effort to call you, you tell me I don't know anything, and I should shove my ideas.'

A tear rolled down Jessie's cheek. It was more than she could take to have her mother yelling at her the same day she found out she might be losing her job. It had been fine to ignore the decline, Jessie had been able to pretend it would all sort itself out, give it a little more time. Not anymore.

'I can't host Christmas, maybe ask Vera to host instead? I have to go.'

'We've only been on the phone a few minutes.'

'I have to go. Bye, I love you.' Jessie hung up the phone and laid her head back on the couch, silent tears rolling over her cheeks. The weight of being alive was so heavy, she knew why her mother was upset she couldn't take the burden of Christmas lunch off her shoulders, but at the same time, she hadn't heard anything Jessie had tried to tell her.

She didn't know how, but her life had shrunk to the bare essentials; work, sleep, repeat. Now her job was being taken away, was there anything left after that? Maybe if she closed her eyes she would be swallowed up by the earth and wouldn't have to worry about any of it anymore.

*

The next morning, she woke up late, again. Her limbs were full of lead, so she called in sick instead of struggling through another day. She had no more sick leave, she'd used it all up over the last few months, it would be unpaid.

Jessie lay back on the pillow, too exhausted to cry.

I wonder when the last time I changed the sheets was, she thought. It had been a while, all the housework kept being pushed back because she was too tired or too sad to do it. Now the house looked like she did—tired, grey, untidy. The bins were full because she couldn't face taking them out. The floor was gritty because she hadn't vacuumed for a long time. She did her dishes one at a time when she needed them, so they were all dirty all the time. At least she hadn't been eating much so that was less of a problem.

That day she didn't get out of bed, except to pee. The next morning was a Friday, she woke in time to get to work, but her body was weak, and no amount of internally yelling at herself could make her get up.

It wasn't the first time she'd had to have two days off in a row, but it felt worse this time. Maria had said she was losing her job anyway, there didn't seem any point in pushing herself to get to work. Why not let it go, like everything else?

There were text messages from Maria asking if she was alright, but Jessie ignored them too. What good was it trying to explain how she felt to her boss when they were going to fire her anyway? Everything was pointless.

On Saturday she was hungry enough to want to eat, so she hauled herself out of bed, and managed to eat some toast, and have a cup of tea; black because her milk had turned sour. Everything around her seemed to be decaying more and more rapidly.

When Jessie caught sight of herself in the mirror, she was gaunt. Her eyes sunken and purple-grey, eyelids half-closed, skin tight. She wasn't surprised by the person staring back at her. She had no energy left to fight, no survival instinct. If she went to bed and never woke up that would have suited her fine.

Fleur Blüm

The letters she'd collected from Ben's were on her nightstand when she went back to bed. She had no memory of putting them there, and in sudden burst of anger, she threw them into the wardrobe, out of sight. This was all Ben's fault. If he hadn't called her, she wouldn't have found his body, if she hadn't found his body, she wouldn't have been so haunted by it. Jessie didn't know what was wrong with her, but it had started with Ben.

Her phone showed a missed call from her mother, no doubt wanting to yell at her some more for all the ways she was failing. There was a voicemail, but Jessie didn't check it. Even recorded, she didn't want to hear her mother's bitter disappointment.

On Sunday, Jessie felt a little bit of hope. She got up, showered, and dressed for the first time in several days. Her clothes stunk of sickness and sweat. Her bed did too. The clothes went into the washing machine, and she pulled the sheets off the bed for the next load. It was sunny enough they might even dry before she ran out of steam.

When the clothes were done, she put the sheets in, and hung the clothes over the tiny line outside. Back inside the floors were caked with dust and toast crumbs, the only thing she was interested in eating. The floors would have to wait, the effort of hanging out the washing had drained the hopeful energy from Jessie's body, and she wanted to go back to bed, but realised there were no sheets so even that was impossible.

The Gift

Jessie lay her head down on the arm of the couch, listening to the rumble and whine of the washing machine. *I'll put sheets out in a little bit,* she thought.

A loud knocking woke Jessie some time later, someone was at the door.

If I don't answer, they'll go away.

'Jessie? I know you're in there. Open the door,' her mother, shouted from outside. More knocking, though it sounded more like banging this time. 'Let me in, Jessie. Your boss is worried about you. I'm worried about you.'

Jessie squeezed her eyes shut and wished her mother would go away. She didn't care that Maria was worried.

Then there was a scratching, jangling sound as her mother tried to open the door. Jessie had forgotten her mother had a key.

'I'm coming in,' her mother said, pushing the front door open. 'Oh! What is that smell?'

Jessie remained in her position, lying awkwardly on the couch, waiting for her mother to come into the house.

'My God, you look terrible.'

'Thanks.' Jessie's voice croaked after so long without speaking.

'Why didn't you tell me you were this sick? What's wrong with you?'

Jessie shrugged. 'I don't know.'

'You're so thin. I know I've been critical of your weight in the past, but this is too much. No wonder you don't feel good if you've been starving yourself. We need to get you something to eat.'

'I'm not hungry.'

'Nonsense. I'll have a look in the kitchen.'

Don't, Jessie thought, her mouth incapable of forming the word.

'Christ on a stick. What the hell happened in here? There's mould on your dishes. How long have they been like this?' her mother called from the kitchen.

'I dunno.' Jessie wanted her mother to leave more than anything, but she just lay there. She looked at her watch, after four, the day had disappeared again. She forced herself into a seated position, feeling only a little bit dizzy in the process.

Her mum stood in the doorway between the lounge and the kitchen, a disapproving frown on her face. 'How did you let yourself get into this state? Haven't I taught you better than that?'

Jessie didn't answer, she closed her eyes and wished her mother wasn't there.

'Maria called me when you didn't show up to work today or answer your phone?'

'What? It's not a workday.'

'It's Monday. Maria was worried because, as you told me the other day, they're going to have to let you go, and when you didn't come in, she thought . . . well, she wasn't sure if you had hurt yourself.'

Jessie rolled her eyes. 'I haven't offed myself; can you go now?' Her mother's presence was sucking what little energy she had left. When had it gotten to Monday?

The Gift

She must have slept all through Sunday night and into Monday morning without knowing it.

Often her bladder or belly would wake her when she'd slept that long, but nowadays she didn't eat or drink enough for those alarms to work. Her phone must have been in the bedroom too far away to hear, or else she was too deep in sleep to notice.

'I'm not going to leave you in this state. Are you sick? You're terribly thin and your house is a shambles. Maria said you've been going downhill for months, that's why they can't keep you—on the days you do manage to show up you're unwell, careless, forgetful. I had no idea. Why didn't you tell me?'

'What would I have said? I'm grieving Ben. I can't do by job; I don't want to eat; I don't want to go out. I sleep all the time and never feel refreshed. What could you have done to help, mother? You never asked me how I was going in the few times we've spoken since you last saw me, why would I think you gave a shit?'

Her mother's face fell, the frown melting into pinched sadness, her lower lip quivering. 'How dare you? I love you. I'm your mother, I birthed you, cared for you.' Her mum dashed away a tear that had spilled over her lower eyelid. 'You made it quite clear the level of involvement I was allowed to have in your life years ago. I didn't like the way things ended with Ben, and when I told you that, you said unless I had something supportive to say I should stay out of your business. So, excuse me for wanting to have a relationship with you, on your terms.

One where I don't pry, and I don't ask how things are because you bite my head off. I thought that's what you wanted?' Tears were streaming down her mother's face unheeded now. Jessie rubbed her hands over her eyes and forehead.

Of course she's making this about her, she thought. 'I don't know what you want me to do.'

'Let me help you. Or at least tell me what wrong?'

'I don't know what's wrong. I just . . . since Ben died, I haven't been the same.'

'Grief is a funny beast. But that was months ago, are you sure there isn't something else? You don't have cancer, do you?'

'No, I don't have cancer.' *As far as I know.* 'I'll be fine, let me have a couple of weeks without the stress of work and I'll be right. I'll get another job in the new year, and everything will be back to normal, you'll see.'

It always worked out she ended up comforting her mother, never the other way around. Since her teens, her mother had been needy, interfering, and had tried to sabotage when things were going well by having some manufactured drama or another. This was no different, Jessie was the one falling into a black hole, but here she was reassuring Heather everything would be alright. Too bad it didn't feel like that.

'Maybe. Here's what we'll do, I'll do some tidying, that way you won't have to fix everything up, just maintain it. And I'll make you some food… on second thought, I'll order something in, we can have dinner together. I'm happy to help with your résumé or job stuff later, but you have a little holiday, you deserve it.' Her mother backed out into the kitchen and started banging around. There was much tsking and exclamation of horror at the state of things, but Jessie was too tired to care, let alone help.

A deep-seated sense of shame started burning in her belly, where before she had felt nothing now all her failures seemed so much more real. Her mother was cleaning up after her, her job had gone down the tubes along with her health.

After a while, the vacuum cleaner started up. Jessie had no idea how her mother had found it amongst all the piles of detritus she'd left around the place, too overwhelmed and tired to put anything away. When she dragged the machine into the loungeroom Jessie found the energy to get up and walk into the bedroom. It was too much to bear watching her mother clean her house.

Maria had called her phone seven times that day, each time with a text to follow up.

9:30am Hi Jessie, are you coming in to work today?
10:30am I hope you're doing okay, please check in with me.
11:55am I'm starting to worry, please call me back.
12:30pm I'm sorry about the contract news. I hope you're not too upset. Call me?

3:30pm The kids have just been let out, I still haven't heard from you so I'm going to call you mother. I'm really worried something terrible has happened. Let me know you're okay.

Part of her was annoyed Maria couldn't leave well enough alone, but perhaps if Jessie were in her shoes, with an employee who's mental and physical health were declining and who had been given bad news she would panic too. Another part of her wanted to let Maria stew for a while longer, as punishment for letting her go.

I'm fine. Mum came to check on me. If you're not going to renew my contract, maybe I'll take my final day as Friday last week. It's probably easier for everyone if I don't come back.

Jessie sent the reply off, her belly tossing with unexpressed anger and that same deep shame her mother had triggered earlier. She heard the vacuum coming down the hall towards the bedroom and wanted to hide, perhaps the bathroom would be safe for a little while.

*

For twenty minutes Jessie sat on the closed lid of the toilet hoping her mother would leave. She could hear her clanking around the house. There was quiet for a while and Jessie breathed a sigh of relief, perhaps she was alone again.

'Jessie? Are you alright in there?' Her mum's voice came through the pine door of the bathroom. When she didn't answer, her mother knocked on the door, loud enough to make Jessie jump, and she called out again. 'Jessie? I need to know you're okay. If you don't say anything I'm coming in.'

'Don't,' Jessie said.

'What, hunny?'

'Don't come in.'

'Are you alright?'

'I want to be left alone.'

'I can't do that right now. Please, come out here so I can talk to you.'

Jessie was silent, her head resting in her hands, elbows on her knees.

'I'm coming in,' she said, as she started to turn the handle of the door. Jessie did nothing. It didn't matter what she did, her mother was interfering now and wouldn't leave her alone until she felt reassured her baby was better. Jessie sighed loudly, if she hadn't been so exhausted, she would have wept.

'You aren't well. You need to let me help you. Why don't you have a nice shower while I keep on with cleaning up?'

'Can you go home? I don't want you here.' Jessie's voice was so weak and hollow it barely sounded like she'd spoken at all.

'Why would you say that? I'm trying to help, you've clearly lost the plot, or you're sick, or something. I know

I shouldn't take what you say too seriously but I'm very hurt by that. I'm your mother, and I'm trying to do the right thing.'

Have you ever done the right thing when it didn't suit you? You have been unreliable and absent my whole life, and now you want to waltz in and play saviour. Jessie's thoughts were venomous towards her mother, though she did not say any of it aloud.

'Have you got any clean clothes to change into?'

Jessie shrugged.

'I'll find something for you to wear. You really do smell awful you know. Have a shower. I'll have a nice clean outfit ready for you when you're done.' Heather turned on the shower taps and started trying to pull Jessie's shirt off over her head.

'I can do it myself. Just get out.' With an uncharacteristic burst of energy Jessie stood up and pushed her mother out of the bathroom. *You're not going to undress me like a child. If I can't get you to leave, I'll be damned if I let you watch me shower.*

The room filled with steam, thankfully she didn't have to see herself in the mirror as she undressed. It had become one the reasons she didn't like to wash, the sight of herself naked—a thin, pale, jumble of bones, her skin covered in weird purple blotches. She saw it if she looked down at herself, but that view was easier to ignore. The energy she had found to push her mother out disappeared as quickly as it had come, she rested her head against the cold tiles as the hot water ran over her back.

Jessie did the most cursory of washes, she soaped her armpits and groin, then stood under the hot water for a while. When she became lightheaded, she turned off the water and stepped out. The towel she used to dry herself smelled funny; she couldn't remember the last time she'd washed them.

I hope it doesn't transfer to me, she thought, wrapping it around her to walk back to her room, maybe she could curl up in bed and her mother would leave when she got bored of doing housework.

'My God. Look at you. When did you get so skinny?' her mother's voice was full of shock as she stepped out.

'Don't.'

'I know I go on about diet all the time, but I didn't mean for you to waste yourself away like this.'

Jessie put her head down and walked past her mother towards the bedroom.

'I found you some clothes, they seemed less dirty than the rest, the stuff on the line wasn't dry,' her mother said, trailing along behind her.

Jessie stopped and looked back; her mum was holding out a pile of clothing that looked like it had seen better days. She couldn't remember the last time she'd washed her clothes either. Not that it meant much, her memory was terrible lately. Jessie held out her left hand, her right held the towel close to her body, until her mother passed the pile of clothes over. Then Jessie turned, went into the bedroom and closed the door before her mum could try to come in there as well.

Now cold and shivering, Jessie pulled on the clothes and got into bed. She'd washed the old sheets, which were probably still in the machine but hadn't had the energy to put clean ones on. She lay her head on the uncovered pillow. It felt dirty, allowing herself to be surrounded by filth because she was too tired and sad to do anything about it. Even when she had a burst of energy, she would only half finish things, which was almost worse than not doing them at all.

For a moment she was sure she saw something move in the corner of the room, but when she looked, there was nothing there except the afternoon sun and a couple of socks.

'Are you decent?' her Mum said, coming into the bedroom. Jessie said nothing. 'I'm still very worried about you, but I can see you want me to go. I'm going to check in with you again later in the week. I've ordered some food, I can wait here until it arrives, I want to make sure you eat.'

'Please don't. I can feed myself.'

Her mum looked away, chewing her lip. 'Alright, I'll go, but I'll check in with you soon.

Jessie tried to say something in response, but she didn't have the strength.

'I love you.'

The Gift

'Okay.' Jessie's eyes were closed. There was a short pause, then she heard the bedroom door close, and then her mother leaving the house.

Maybe this is what Ben felt like at the end; drained, exhausted, wishing for death so she didn't have to struggle with it all anymore. If she stayed in bed, she would fade away like he did, she wasn't far off the condition he'd been in when she found his body.

How did this happen? She thought to herself as she slipped into sleep.

*

Heather had called Jessie once each day since Monday, she had looked so unwell but after cleaning up that filthy house for a couple of hours she was sick of fighting and gave up.

On Friday she went around, convinced Jessie needed to be hospitalised, despite whatever protest she might put up. When she arrived, there was a package on the doorstep; it was covered in ants and as she approached she realised it was the Italian takeaway she'd ordered on Monday.

'Oh God,' she said aloud. She banged on the door, yelling Jessie's name. Her heart was beating hard in her chest, and she wished she'd come around sooner when Jessie didn't answer the phone calls or texts.

'Open the door, or I'll come in . . . Jessie? Please.'

She walked along the front veranda, trying to see into Jessie's bedroom, but the curtains were still drawn.

After several minutes of distressed pacing, Heather turned the front door handle and found it was open. She walked in and the smell which had been bad on Monday was infinitely worse.

The bedroom was the first on the right, and when she opened the door, she discovered the reason for the foul odour—Jessie was curled into the foetal position, clearly dead.

A pile of letters lay on her bedside table, Heather wanted to open them, to see if they held any information on what had happened to her only child, but as she stepped forward the stench was overwhelming, and she retreated outside without touching anything.

Ouija Board

1.

The day of Sunday's fourteenth birthday dawned cold and misty, despite being early autumn. She woke to the sound of her alarm—her favourite song—but had snoozed it at least twice so far.

'Get up, you have school,' her mother, Polly, yelled from outside Sunday's room. She would shout through the door the first time, but the second time she'd barge in and drag Sunday out of bed even if she was still sleeping. This was their tried-and-true morning routine.

'I'm not going to school today,' Sunday yelled back.

'Yes, you are.' The door opened. 'We've had this conversation, and we agreed you would go to school like you have every other birthday, like every other child at school, and you can celebrate on the weekend.'

'We didn't agree. You stated.' Sunday frowned, and tried hard to pull her mouth out of the pout it was forming. 'And don't call me a child. I'm not a kid anymore.'

'When you can get yourself out of bed and to school on time without me having to come in and drag you, you can be considered an adult. Until that time, you're still a kid, now get up, we're late. Again.' Polly turned her back and walked away down the corridor leaving Sunday's bedroom door wide open. Sunday pulled the doona over her head and let out a stifled scream.

There was no use trying to change her mother's mind, there would be no special treatment, even on her birthday. She flipped the bedclothes off and shuddered at the sudden cold of the floor beneath her feet and the frigid air on her skin. *I hate mornings,* she thought.

Martin, her mother's new husband, was sitting in the kitchen, one hand on his coffee cup, and the other holding his phone close to his face.

'Morning,' he said, without looking. Sunday sometimes wondered how he knew she was there, he never glanced in her direction, must be some weird step-dad power, although she was wearing her big green boots which clumped in a satisfying way when she walked, so he probably heard her. She grunted in response before pulling open the fridge to stare into it hoping for inspiration.

'The muesli is in the cupboard. Can we skip the long deliberation and just eat this morning?' he said. The hairs on Sunday's neck stood up, it was way too early for him to be getting on her case, especially on her birthday, but she grabbed the milk and slammed the fridge door shut anyway.

Muesli was fine, but she had hoped for a special weekend type breakfast on her special day. Scrambled eggs, sourdough toast and maybe a sausage. Instead,

Sunday had to make do with the slightly dust-flavoured cereal her mother insisted was good for her. At least they weren't being stingy about buying orange juice anymore. The argument it was too much sugar had been resolved when Sunday said she would give up juice if she was allowed to have coffee with her breakfast like they did, after which orange juice was deemed a suitable breakfast beverage.

'Dressed, check—though I wish you wouldn't wear those awful shoes—breakfast, check. Have you got everything packed in your school bag?' her mother asked, trotting into kitchen in the burgundy stilettos she wore when she wanted to impress. Paired with a form-fitting grey power suit and black silk shirt, Sunday dreaded being anyone in a boardroom where her mother wanted something they didn't want to give her. "Mergers and acquisitions" was what she told people, but Sunday thought Polly's job would be better described as taking businesses apart and stripping them for cash, starting with the owners.

'Yes. I've got all my shit ready.'

'Language,' both adults said at once.

Sunday rolled her eyes and sighed. As if they didn't use the same words constantly. She shoved another spoonful of breakfast into her mouth and chewed, before dumping her mostly empty bowl in the sink and collecting her school bag from the loungeroom where it had been left at some point yesterday afternoon.

'Lunch.' Polly held out a mini-cooler bag which no doubt held a dreary selection. Sunday took the bag and pushed it on top of her schoolbooks. It wasn't cool to take a packed lunch, but she never had enough pocket money to get lunch from the canteen either. Despite her mother and Martin both having excellent jobs that paid the big bucks, they were total tightarses.

Polly dropped her daughter at school and drove away in her silent electric car. Sunday couldn't get her head around why they were so creepy but maybe it was their ability to sneak up on you while you weren't looking— not even doing anything wrong but still.

*

On Saturday, three long days later, Sunday had asked a couple of her school friends over for a pizza-movie-sleepover party. Polly and Martin had made faces like they would rather be dead than host half a dozen teenagers, but Sunday's other option had been laser tag, which was much more expensive and much more effort on their part.

'Better they're under our roof and we can keep an eye on them,' Martin had said. Polly had pinched the bridge of her nose, then nodded.

The guests were due to arrive about six o'clock, and from three that afternoon Sunday was stressing out.

'What snacks did you get?' she asked her mother, bouncing on her toes.

'You were there; corn chips, dip, popcorn, lots of chocolate and salted caramel ice-cream, though I suggest we keep that for another time, you'll have had plenty of empty calories without it.'

'No potato chips? Only corn chips? What if someone doesn't like corn chips?'

'They can have popcorn. Or they can suffer with corn chips. No one has allergies, I asked their parents, so if they're being fussy, it's for appearances, and not a medical thing.'

Sunday huffed. 'You're unbelievable, you don't care if I'm the worst host in the year. If this party is a flop everyone at school will know in milliseconds, they'll all be snapping their friends to complain about the shit food.'

'Language.'

'You have to get potato chips.'

'I'm not going out again, there's plenty to eat. Much more than needed for seven people.'

'I'm asking Martin.'

Polly rolled her eyes, and Sunday stormed past her towards her step-dad.

'Can you go to the shop and get more snacks? It's completely mortifying that we don't have any potato chips.'

'I heard you—and I agree with your mother, we don't need anything else.'

'I hate you both!' Sunday yelled, throwing up her hands in exasperation and rushing back upstairs to her bedroom. She lay face down on her bed, teeth and fists clenched as she waited for her rage to subside. After a few minutes it was too hard to breathe with her mouth full of the discarded clothes she'd thrown out of her wardrobe while trying to decide on an outfit.

She looked up at the clock, two hours until her friends arrived, and she needed to sort out her clothes and do her makeup, it was cutting it fine. Sunday hoped no one else noticed the embarrassing dearth of snacks, but she pushed herself up and hurried to dress before pushing all her unwanted clothes back into the wardrobe in a massive ball. That was tomorrow's problem, or possibly next week's problem.

Sunday's school had a uniform, so she was saved from the tyranny of having to choose an outfit each day, but it also meant that the days she saw her friends outside of school were at least five times as important. The choice had come down to dark blue skin-tight denim jeans, and a dusty-pink checked shirt over a tiny black singlet top. Sunday stared at herself in the bathroom mirror tying the front shirt tails into a knot, then untying them for several minutes, waiting for her hair straightener to heat up.

Her mother refused to let her dye her hideous mousy brown hair any cool colours, so the best she could do was to straighten it sleek and flat before arranging it in a complicated series of small braids like people in those Viking shows.

Sunday's makeup inspirations were incredibly talented social media influencers who made the most complicated looks seem easy. With an hour left, she started on a complex smoky eye cut crease look, but when one eye took her nearly half an hour, she despaired that she would never get the other one done in time.

'Mum, help,' she called out.

'What? Have you hurt yourself?'

'No, why would you think that?'

'You sounded like you were in pain,' Polly said putting her head around the door into the bathroom.

'I have to get the other eye to look like this before everyone comes.'

'Ah.' Polly frowned, taking Sunday's chin and looking intently at the eye that was already done. 'I think I can help. Do you have the tutorial there?'

Sunday tried to nod, but only managed an affirmative grunt in the vice like grip of her mother. For all Polly's faults, she was more skilled at makeup application than her daughter and they got the look done with a couple of minutes to spare.

'Right, go and start putting the snacks out, and I'll . . . hide the evidence,' Polly said, eyes travelling over the sprawling array of cosmetics covering the bathroom counter. Sunday hurried out to the kitchen just as the doorbell rang.

'I've got it.' Sunday ran to open the front door and saw her best friend, Megan, standing there, grinning her biggest grin, with her mother beside her, cheeks flushed and hair askew. 'Hey!'

'We made it.' Megan's mother pushed her daughter forward before turning around and hurrying back to the car. Sunday raised her eyebrows in curiosity.

'You will not believe the shit we had to go through to get here.' Megan walked into the house, and Sunday trailed behind her friend.

'Tell me everything.'

Megan was a little taller than Sunday, stockier and broader in the hips, with shoulder length auburn-brown hair that was constantly falling in her face. She wore skinny black jeans, a black T-shirt and a cropped pastel pink denim jacket. 'Mum forgot that your party was tonight so when I asked her if she was ready to bring me over, she nearly had a heart attack.'

'No! Didn't you remind her like, yesterday?'

'Obviously, but that was like a day ago. Mum can be a real space case sometimes.' Megan's mum ran a small business from home, a single mum with four kids, and was constantly running around doing things at the last moment. 'Anyway, we got you a present but . . . it's not wrapped. Can I borrow some paper or whatever to wrap it up?'

'Hi Megan,' Polly said entering the kitchen. 'Put your bag down in the corner there. I'll get you some paper and sticky tape.'

'Thanks, Mrs Vernon.'

'You're welcome. I know how hard your mum works. Even with my one I feel like I'm run ragged.'

Sunday's other friends arrived over the next half hour, and soon there were seven teen girls loitering in the kitchen talking over one another.

'Everyone's here now,' Polly said to Sunday. 'Do you want to move into the loungeroom and choose a movie?'

'Uh, yeah sure.' Sunday felt her mother was trying to shoo her out of the kitchen. 'Can we take some food?'

'Of course.' Polly collected a few bags of corn chips and some chocolate and led the way to the lounge. They had set it up earlier with cushions and air mattresses on the floor so they could all fall asleep later.

'Sit wherever you like, girls, make yourselves comfortable. I don't mind if you eat everything, we have plenty more in the kitchen and we'll get pizzas later, but please don't waste food, and be careful where you put your drinks. I don't want to be washing sugary beverages out of the cushions or carpet.'

'Yes, Mum, God you're so embarrassing,' Sunday said loudly.

'It's true.' Polly winked and retreated out of the lounge, sliding the doors closed.

The group of girls spent at least half an hour giggling and flicking through available movies before selecting their first feature—a romantic comedy with a very attractive lead actor, that they were all sure they knew from somewhere but couldn't remember where.

A while later Polly came back into the room. 'Pizzas are here. You'll have to come to the table to eat though, no pizza on the couch please.'

Sunday paused the film, they had another forty-five minutes to go, so they agreed to break for pizza and come back. After pizza, they resumed the film, and then took another break for cake and birthday presents at the end.

'I don't know if I have room,' Megan said, looking at the enormous Toblerone cheesecake in the centre of the dining table.

'I'm sure we can save you some cake for later, if you can't manage it,' Sunday said, winking at her best friend.

'I can probably find some room in the dessert stomach.'

'That's the spirit,' Martin said from the back of the room. Polly cut the cake, and handed out the pieces, Sunday thought they looked a bit small, but struggled to finish her piece nonetheless.

'Alright, I promised presents after cake, I hope you've got energy for that after all that food.' Polly cleared away the plates and Martin wiped the cake crumbs off the dining table while the guests went to collect their presents.

'Open mine first,' Emily said. She was Sunday's third best friend, they had known each other since they were babies; her mother was good friends with Polly. She had a tendency to demand things and want to be the centre of attention which annoyed Sunday, but she couldn't not invite her to things.

'Okay, what did you get me?' Sunday put her hands out to take the small brightly wrapped cylinder. She ripped the paper off and threw it onto the ground, Polly frowned slightly, but said nothing. 'Oh cool, candles.'

'They smell amazing. I have some the same.'

'Thank you.' Sunday hugged her friend, sure that her mother had picked the gift without input from Emily.

Grace had bought a silk hair wrap, which was supposed to be great for keeping hair from going frizzy overnight. Sunday thanked her but wasn't sure that her dead straight hair would benefit from it.

Abby gave her a terrarium; a small glass globe with tiny succulent plants in it. 'I made it, Dad and I did a class.'

Jade's gift was an envelope containing a voucher for a facial. 'I got one too, we can go together.'

Sunday appreciated it more than the terrarium, especially since spending time with her second-best friend was much more fun than some plants, no matter how cute they looked.

Rylee was a little shy to give her present, her family was usually tight for money, and she would often need to make up excuses to miss expensive group outings. The gift was a small round tin, Sunday lifted it up to shake it, but Rylee put her hand out to stop her. 'It's fragile.'

'Oh, sorry.' Sunday opened the tin to find it chock full of tiny sugar cookies, each decorated with multi coloured royal icing. 'They're gorgeous.'

'Mum and I made them, sorry it's not very exciting.'

'I love them.' Sunday hugged her friend. 'When I might not explode, I'm going to really enjoy these. And no, Martin, you can't have any.'

'You wound me,' Martin said, pretending to have been shot and staggering back.

'Okay, now me, now me.' Megan was bouncing in her seat, handed over a large rectangular package.

'This better be good, you're really hyping it up.'

'You're going to love it. I found it online and I knew you would absolutely die.'

Sunday peeled the paper off, carefully this time since she recognised it was from Polly's stash of "nice bits of wrapping paper that we need to keep for things". Inside was a large black box, the size and shape of a board game, but it was completely black with white writing.

'Holy shit—'

'Language,' Martin said.

'It's a Ouija board?' Sunday squealed.

'I knew you'd love it.'

'I've wanted one of these for ages. Ever since your sister, Hayley, had one at her sixteenth and they all freaked themselves out.'

'I know right?' Megan was beaming, her face lit up with the genius of her gift.

'Thank you, you're amazing.' Sunday hugged her best friend tightly. Polly would never have agreed to buy one, and the superstition said you couldn't buy one for yourself, it was bad luck.

Ouija Board

After cake and presents, the girls started another movie. Sunday tried to concentrate, but she was thinking about the Ouija board. She'd brought it in from the kitchen and could see the box on the floor near the TV. She crept over to it, trying not to block anyone's view, to read the instructions. In the flickering low light cast by the screen, only a few words were decipherable.

'Get out of the way!' Abby shout-whispered.

'Sorry.' Sunday backed herself into the nest of blankets and cushions she'd made and went back to pretending to watch the movie. Cheesy string music swelled and the two lead actors kissed in the rain. Their undying love was declared, and the credits rolled.

Sunday jumped up and turned on the one of the lamps, leading to indignant squawks from her guests.

'Turn it off, it's too bright,' Megan said.

'I want to read the box. I wanna do a séance.'

'No way. Absolutely not.' Rylee was wide-eyed, her cheeks paler than their usual fair red-headed complexion would make them.

'Come on, it'll be fun,' Megan replied.

'What's a séance?' Abby asked.

'Oh my God, you don't know?' Megan asked.

'No.' Abby looked down at the ground.

'It's like a ritual, or a magic spell, where you try to contact the dead. They're super cool.' Sunday said.

'Do you need the Ouija board for that?' Jade asked.

'It's not like, essential, but if you want to talk to the spirits, it's the best way,' Megan said.

'Okay.' Sunday was holding the box. 'Okay,' Sunday said again, eyes darting over the text. 'We need to sit in a circle around the board, then we rest two fingers on the planchette . . .' she frowned.

'The little triangle pointer thing,' Megan said.

'Oh. And take it in turns to ask a question. It says to wait up to five minutes for an answer before moving on. If the board doesn't answer, try another question.'

'Are we really contacting spirits?' Rylee asked.

'Who knows?' Jade said, her eyes sparkling, grinning.

'Okay, get the coffee table and put it in the middle. We'll have to move the mattresses, so we have a stable surface,' Sunday said. The girls scrambled around to rearrange the room so that they were all seated around the square coffee table. The Ouija board and planchette were in the centre of the table. To make sure they could all reach the board, they had to jam themselves together.

'This is horrendous. Let's take it in turns,' Rylee said, though Sunday suspected she wanted an excuse not to be involved.

'Okay, you and Emily and Grace sit out and we'll go first,' Megan said, shuffling closer.

'Wait—do we need candles or something?' Abby said, pulling her hand off the planchette.

'Stop stalling.' Megan yanked her hand back to the table. 'Unless you're chicken?'

'I'm not chicken.' Abby was frowning, but Sunday thought she was scared, even if she was pretending not to be.

'Okay, you're the only one who's done this before, so you're up,' Sunday said, nodding to Megan.

'Right, everyone needs to be quiet unless you're asking a question. I'm looking at you Rylee, no squealing or whatever, got it?'

Rylee nodded, shuffling a little further back on the couch.

'We're gathered here today to contact those who have crossed over. If there are any spirits here, we welcome you, and ask that you make your presence known,' Megan said in a solemn tone. Her eyes were closed, and everyone was silent, waiting for something to happen. After about a minute, Megan opened her eyes and looked around the room. Sunday shrugged.

'Is anyone here with us? We invite you to use the board to talk to us.'

More silence, the sound of seven excited teenagers breathing filled the room, along with the occasional sound from Sunday's parents upstairs.

'This isn't working,' Abby said.

'Don't move the planchette,' Sunday said, feeling it pull towards the top left, and stop over the word YES.

'Oh my God. Oh my God, did you do that?' Abby asked, her face pale even in the low light.

'I didn't move it,' Jade said.

'It wasn't me,' Sunday said at the same time.

'Who is here with us? Tell us your name,' Megan said.

The planchette shook, and sort of shimmied in a wobbly line around the board. It halted briefly on H, the girls all said the letter aloud.

H... E... L... L... O

'Hello to you too,' Sunday said, her blood pumping in her ears, and her fingers trembling where they rested on the planchette.

'What's your name?' Megan asked again.

DANA

'Dana? Hello Dana, thank you for speaking to us,' Megan said. 'What are we gonna ask?'

'Are there any boys at school who have a crush on me?' Abby asked.

The planchette jiggled, before dashing to the 'No' position.

'Oh, my God, what a loser,' Megan said with a laugh.

'Like some random ghost would know that—he's not a psychic,' Jade said.

'Okay, Dana, do you have a message for us?' Megan asked.

Yes

'Is it for all of us? Or just one person?'

SUNDAY

'It's a message for Sunday?'

Yes

'No way.' Sunday swallowed; how did it know her name? She didn't know anyone called Dana, although if one of her friends was moving the planchette of course they would know her name.

'What's the message?' Megan asked.

KILL

'Kill? That can't be right. Who's moving the thing? You're doing it aren't you, Megan?' Jade's voice was high pitched and choked.

KILL

'Don't spell it again, Jesus!' Abby said.

'Fine, I'll take my hand off.' Megan took her fingers off the planchette, while the other three held on.

MARTIN

'Martin? You mean Mum's husband?' Sunday asked.

Yes

'What about Martin?'

KILL

Sunday took her hand off the planchette as though it was burning hot, pushed herself away from the coffee table and stood up.

'This isn't funny. Whoever's moving it like that just stop it.' Sunday tried to breathe, but her lungs weren't working, it sounded like she was panting in her ears, and her vision was all blurry. She backed up into the wall and stopped, grateful for its solidity to lean against.

'Come back,' Megan said, her voice soft. 'I'm sure he's joking.'

'It's not funny. He can't mean to kill my stepdad, that's insane.' Sunday took a shaky step forward and hesitated.

'Let's ask. Maybe he's a malicious spirit, and we can ignore it, but maybe there's a reason.' Abby looked very pale, but her fingers where still on the planchette. Sunday approached the coffee table, cautious that touching it would make her lose it completely.

'Why do you want to kill Martin?' Megan asked, when Sunday's fingers were back on the board.

DANGER

'What does that mean?' Abby looked at Sunday, her eyes full of concern.

'I don't know. He's nice enough, like obviously a total pain in the arse, but like, so are all the adults I know. He doesn't seem dangerous,' Sunday said.

DANGER

The planchette was moving faster now, dragging their hands around the board.

KILL

MARTIN

'I don't think I want to play this anymore,' Rylee said from the couch.

'Yeah, how do we turn it off? Make Dana leave us alone?' Sunday asked Megan.

'You're right. This isn't what happened last time,' Megan said. 'Okay Dana. You've told us the message. Thank you for coming to visit us, we release you. Your business is finished.' Megan took her hand off the planchette and rested them in her lap. 'Let go now.'

Abby, Jade and Sunday all took their hands off the board and Sunday felt a chill pass through the room.

'That was super creepy,' Abby said.

'Let's not tell anyone we did that, yeah?' Sunday said.

'Agreed,' Megan said. 'I guess you three don't want to try it? We don't really want to risk contacting Dana again; he seems a bit hostile.'

'Just a touch,' Jade said, laughing nervously.

'I'm sorry, I didn't think it would be, y' know, that intense.' Megan's face was pale.

'It's not your fault. I'm going to put it in the garage though, I don't really want to sleep in the same room as it,' Sunday said, packing the board and planchette back into the box.

'Agreed,' said Rylee.

'You wanna find something light or funny to watch while we go to sleep while I'm out. I don't want to lie in the silence and dark.'

'I'll look, maybe a kids movie, they're nice and bright.' Megan grabbed the remote from where it sat in front of Grace. At least they would have something to do while Sunday went to the garage and would maybe be less likely to stew on the creepiness that had occurred.

The rest of her house was quiet and dark, Polly and Martin had done a preliminary clean up of the dining room and retreated upstairs. They would have no idea that the girls had done a séance and scared themselves silly. Sunday shook her head as she stepped into the dark, silent garage. The light switch wasn't working, so she used the torch on her phone to shine a light around the room. Along the opposite wall, Martin had an anally-organised set of shelves where his tools and bits and pieces were housed. Like many men of a certain age, he liked to have power tools and nails and whatever that he might need should a home repair be needed, though getting him to actually do the repair was worse than trying to bathe a cat. Polly and Sunday had a few plastic containers where assorted items were stored; winter coats, other seasonal clothing, games and toys Sunday no longer used, and leftovers from various old craft projects. She pulled out the plastic container that held board games and Halloween costumes, why they were in the same box Sunday couldn't have told you, and shoved the Ouija board into it.

The lid didn't close properly, but after a bit of shuffling and squishing of contents, Sunday managed to get the large plastic container closed and back into the shelf. Now the game, if that's what it was, was no longer in her line of sight, Sunday felt a weight of anxiety lift from her.

Back in the loungeroom, the other girls were having a whisper fight over which of the high school musical movies to watch.

'Just pick one. They're all ancient anyway,' Sunday said, flopping onto the middle of the air mattresses.

'What do you mean?' Abby said.

'They were made before we were born. That makes them ancient.'

'No way.' Megan stared at the screen. 'You're right, they're older than we are. So embarrassing.'

In the end they went for the original, always the best one in any series of films or books. Sunday thought about the Ouija board out in the garage and wondered if she had really gotten the lid on properly or not. It was no good going out there again tonight, with the light switch broken and her nerves frayed enough as they were. Sunday lay on her bouncy, noisy bed, her face turned away from the screen, and listened to the ridiculous, perky music as her eyes drifted closed.

2.

In the morning, Sunday's first thought, as soon as she woke up was of the Ouija board, packed in its carboard box, inside a plastic storage container a couple of rooms away. Secure as could be. But even knowing there was all of that separating her, her skin crawled with anxiety. Who was Dana and why did she want her to kill Martin? Was it some weird prank by one of the other girls moving the planchette? Megan was the only one devious enough to make it happen, and she had been the one to bring the Ouija board. She wouldn't sabotage her own gift, plus she wasn't touching it for some of the time.

On the other hand, why would a ghost, or spirit, or whatever want her to kill Martin? He was a bit of a pain, but more by being gross and romantic with her mum, not in an abusive way. Sunday didn't have much to complain about really, although if they managed to get pregnant, as they were trying to, Sunday might rethink how secure her place in the family was.

She lay looking at the lumps of her friends, sleeping peacefully, scattered around the room. Rylee had fallen part-way off the air mattresses during the night; her head and torso on the floor, her legs on the mattress. Jade and Abby were embracing, while Megan had her foot in

320

Grace's face. There was nothing weird about the night except for Dana and the message she couldn't get out of her mind.

Sunday had been friends with these girls for years, they'd all gone to the same primary school and then moved up to the high school at the start of last year. They were best friends, although Megan was her first best friend, and the others were not as important. Where had the Ouija board come from? Maybe if she asked Megan would tell her and Sunday could return it and get something else. Having it in the room was too much to bear. If anyone had asked her a day ago what she most wanted in the world for her birthday, a Ouija board was in her top three, along with a hot boyfriend and an unlimited shopping spree at Chadstone.

Trying not to disturb the others, Sunday eased herself up from the air mattress and walked into the kitchen. It was chilly; the tile floor spread cold up her legs and she shivered.

'You're up early,' Polly said, looking up from her seat at the head of the dining table. She had a coffee in her hand and her tablet in front of her, probably reading the paper because that's fun to do on a weekend according to her.

'Yeah, I didn't sleep much.'

'I'm not surprised, with all the sugar and excitement and those blow-up beds. It's the sort of thing you can do when you're a kid and bounce back pretty easily, but when you get old like me, you value a supportive mattress and a good night's sleep.'

Sunday rolled her eyes. 'Is there any coffee left?'

'Not for you, young lady, have some juice. There's plenty of pizza left over if you want to eat that.'

'Cornflakes?'

'My God, turning down pizza for breakfast? Who are you and what have you done with my daughter?' Polly smiled. 'Of course, there's always cornflakes.'

Sunday tried to smile, though it probably wasn't very reassuring. She made herself a large bowl of cornflakes and a glass of orange juice. She tried to be quiet, worried her friends would all rush out. The Ouija board was still lurking in the back of her mind, a malignant presence that she couldn't forget. She wanted to go out to the garage, see if it would tell her the same message now that it was daylight, but she was also scared that it would.

I guess I could do a tarot reading or something, ask if I should get rid of the board, she thought, chewing a mouthful of cornflakes.

'Did you play with the Ouija board?' her mother asked.

'What?' Sunday said, much louder than she had intended.

'I asked if you used Megan's gift, I assumed you had a go, it would have been a perfect evening for it.'

Sunday shrugged and looked away.

'I thought you loved all that occult stuff.'

'I do.'

'So, what did you think?'

Sunday continued to stare at the table, unsure what to say, or if she should say anything.

'I see. I'll stop prying, I remember important secret teenage business from when I was your age.' Polly shook her head and stood up, taking her cup and tablet with her.

You didn't have to leave, Sunday thought, as she watched her mother head back upstairs to the bedrooms. Her teeth were furry after all the chocolate and chips last night. Sunday followed her mother upstairs to the bathroom to freshen up a bit.

'Sunday and her friends used the Ouija board,' Polly said to Martin in the bedroom, Sunday heard them as she approached the top of the stairs.

'I'm not surprised. Did you get any details?' Martin replied. Sunday stopped on the third step from the top and listened.

'No, when I asked, I got the silent treatment.'

'They probably gave themselves a fright and she doesn't want to talk about it. Typical.'

'She'd not that bad.'

'I think her brain is rotting now she's into crystals and witchcraft and tarot stuff.'

'That's not nice, honey.'

'But it's true. Witchy girls are total morons, and if she believes any of it, she is too.'

'Ssh, you know I don't like it when you talk like that,' Polly said in a hushed tone.

They must talk about me like that all the time, and I've never noticed. Sure, Mum is defending me, kind of, but clearly Martin hates me.

Sunday walked back down the stairs being careful not to make any sound, then returned to the lounge, her teeth still felt gross, but she didn't want to overhear anything else. At first, she thought the Ouija board wanted her to kill Martin for no reason, but maybe there were things she didn't know. How could she live with a man who thought so little of her?

'How long have you been up?' Megan asked softly as Sunday shuffled past her to get to the air mattress she'd been sleeping on.

'I'm not up.'

'Well, you were until about five seconds ago.'

'I couldn't sleep, so I had some cornflakes.'

'I'm having left over pizza, that's the best part of having pizza if you ask me.'

'Who's having pizza?' Rylee asked, pushing herself back onto the mattress.

'You can have as much as you like, but you'll have to go get it yourself,' Megan said.

'And eat it in the kitchen,' Rylee added. 'Just one more minute.' She put her head back down and closed her eyes.

*

Sunday's friends were picked up by their parents in the early afternoon, Meg was the last one to be collected.

'Did you have a nice time, Meg?' her mother asked.

'Yeah, it was great, thank you for having me, Mrs Vernon.'

'You're welcome, as always,' Polly replied.

'Did Sunday like her gift?' Megan's mum asked.

'Yeah, it was sick—' Megan started.

Sunday frowned and gave a tiny shake of her head.

'I'll tell you about it later, we'd better let them get on with their day,' Megan added.

'You're right. Thank you again, Polly, and I hope you had a lovely birthday Sunday.'

'See you at school tomorrow.' Sunday waved as Megan and her mother got into their car and drove away. She wondered if her mother knew that Megan had bought her a Ouija board, though they probably bought it together they were all too young to have money for birthday presents.

'We'd better clean up that lounge room,' Polly said.

Sunday sighed.

'There's still some lollies and stuff left over; you can have some before dinner if we get the house looking back in order. Deal?'

'Okay.'

Martin had gone out to play golf after lunch, a sport that Sunday thought was a complete waste of time, and had managed to avoid cleaning up. When he arrived home, they were trying to fit the air mattresses back into the marked plastic tub in the garage.

'All packed up then?' Martin asked, as he stepped out of his car.

'Mostly, I'll run the vacuum around in a bit, there's corn chip crumbs all over the place,' Polly said.

'You could do it,' Sunday said to him.

'I could ask you to do it Sunday, given it was your friends who made such a mess.'

'It's my birthday, I shouldn't have to do all the cleaning up. That's not fair.'

'Are you volunteering to clean up when it's Martin's birthday then?'

'No, I don't have to clean up after him.' Sunday crossed her arms over her chest. This wasn't going the way she had hoped.

'You can't have it both ways, either you don't clean up after your own birthday, and then you will have to help for Martin's, or you clean up the mess your friends made when you had visitors.'

'Fine. I'll vacuum. God.' Sunday shoved the air mattress she'd been holding into her mother's hands and stomped away into the house.

Unbelievable. She could never understand why her mother constantly took Martin's side when it came to arguments about chores. As a man, he seemed to get away with doing the outside chores, which only needed to be done once every week or two, while Polly was constantly cleaning and cooking. Sunday tried to avoid it when she could, but gave in if it meant her mother would have to pick up the slack.

Men have it so easy, she thought as she pulled out the vacuum. They'd had the same one, a little round machine

326

on wheels that trailed behind, for as long as she could remember. It used to be painted to look vaguely like a ladybug, which amused Sunday, but the eyes and spots were wearing off, and the ladybug looked a bit drunk now. Sunday vacuumed the lounge room carpet much harder than necessary; she imagined Martin's face on it, getting pushed and pulled and sucked up into the handle.

For a moment she imagined what it would be like without him. Just her and her mum, like it used to be. It was nice when it was the two of them. Her real dad lived in Sydney and hardly ever saw her, which was fine with her. He was a car salesman, always chasing the next big sale, or the next scam he could pull over the punters, and neither Polly nor Sunday were keen to see him. On the other hand, Sunday admitted they were a lot better off moneywise with Martin in the picture. They'd moved into his house, and they had money for stuff like going to the movies and pizza now.

If Martin died, her mother would probably inherit the house, and whatever money he had. They'd been married for a little over a year now, and while Sunday had rolled her eyes, and dragged her feet through the wedding ceremony, they loved each other.

But Sunday never trusted Martin. He was rich, older than her mother, and had been married once before Polly. And she'd never met any of his family, no parents or siblings, and Martin had no kids of his own. It's probably why he didn't like Sunday. Still, she hadn't given him much to like, she resented the time he took away from her mother-daughter bonding, and all the extra stuff Polly had to do to look after him.

She'd been vacuuming the same spot over and over while thinking about how much she hated Martin. Sunday packed the vacuum back in the garage, sidling past Martin's massive SUV to get to the spot where the vacuum lived.

The Ouija board had been put into the games box, which wasn't far from the cleaning box. It wouldn't be hard to get it out and see what happened on her own. All that clean up time had made the idea of getting rid of Martin seem appealing. Sunday reached for the games box, and a shiver ran along her arm. She pulled her hand away suddenly.

No, leave it alone, she thought to herself. She shook her head, rubbed her hands up and down the sides of her jeans trying to bring herself back to the real world, it sort of worked. The chill passed, and Sunday went up to her bedroom to lie down.

*

The Ouija board was the talk of the school all Monday. Everyone who had been at the party had talked to the others in their class and it spread from there. But by the end of the day, the game of whispers had distorted the story completely.

'Do you wanna hear something truly wild?' Megan said to Sunday as they walked to small convenience store on the way home from school.

'Is it about me?'

'Yeah, but you'll love it. Promise.'

Sunday sighed. 'Okay.'

'Darcy told me that there was a murder at your party. Apparently, you killed Martin!'

Sunday stopped dead, Megan kept walking a few steps before turning around, her head tilted as though to ask a question. 'How would I be at school if I'd killed Martin?'

'Umm.' Megan frowned. 'I hadn't thought about that.'

'It's ridiculous. Darcy knows you're my best friend, why did he tell you that? Doesn't he know you were at the party?' Sunday resumed walking, her hands gripping the strap of her school bag tightly.

'Maybe he was joking.'

'It's not funny. I really wish you'd all kept your mouths shut about the stupid Ouija board.'

'Hey, don't diss my gift. I thought you liked it.' Megan's eyes looked moist, as though she might start to cry at any moment.

'I do. I just . . . wish people weren't going around saying I was a murderer. It's super not cool.'

'Yeah. I'll tell Darcy next time I see him that he's a douchebag and he better take it back or I'll smash him.'

'Don't smash him.' Sunday approached the doorway of the convenience store, the opening was covered in the long, thin, clear plastic strips to keep flies out, and she flung them aside rather more aggressively than was necessary.

'Are you gonna smash him?' Megan looked at her friend sideways.

'No.' Sunday sighed. 'Let's talk about something else.'

'Okay.'

The two girls went to the slushie machine in the back of the store. It was the only thing worth buying, and they were cheap. Megan stood in front of the machine, quietly considering, and Sunday was almost too angry for a slushie today, although maybe it would get her mind off what the kids at school were saying.

'I'm not a murderer,' she said mostly to herself.

'I know. I'm sorry I didn't tell Darcy to pull his head out of his arse.' Megan patted her arm, then stepped forward to pour herself a raspberry slushie, her decision paralysis apparently broken by Sunday's statement.

She wasn't a murderer, and she wondered if part of the reason she was so annoyed about it was that she was considering it. If they thought she was capable of it there was no way she'd get away with it if Martin dropped dead. Sunday wasn't sure what annoyed her more; the idea she couldn't murder her stepfather because she would be the number one suspect, or the suggestion she should do it in the first place.

She got herself the frozen cola flavour and walked the rest of the way to her place in silence. Megan was quiet too, maybe not sure what to say, or maybe she had nothing to add after the subject was off the table. Either way, Sunday was glad to say goodbye when she reached her house; Megan's was a little way further up the road.

'How was school?' Polly asked as she walked in, then saw the drink in her hand. 'I really wish you wouldn't waste your money on sugary drinks like that. They're empty calories, and you'll grow up to be fat and diabetic if you're not careful.'

'What the hell? You were never this mean before you met Martin. Just because he said you've put on weight doesn't mean you can take it out on me.' As soon as she'd said it, Sunday knew she'd gone too far. Polly went pale, her eyes wide and startled like a deer. Sunday opened her mouth to apologise but her mother put up her hand to quiet her.

'You can go to your room after that comment. I thought you were a better person than that.'

Sunday opened her mouth again.

'I don't want to hear anything else from you today. I'll call you when dinner is ready, until then I need you to not be near me.'

Sunday made a noise of frustration, somewhere between a grunt and a moan, before turning to stomp up the stairs. She slammed the door of her bedroom behind her, and face-planted onto her bed.

Why is she being such a bitch today? she thought, before rolling over so she could breathe again. Her mum was always going on about weight and she heard Martin telling her not to wear certain outfits because they were unflattering, not that he had any taste. But her mum took his criticism to heart, more so lately. As long as Polly wasn't pregnant, it would all sort itself out sooner or later.

The more she thought about it, the more reasons she found to resent Martin. Despite giving her the creeps initially, maybe the Ouija board was right, she needed to get him out of their lives, so things could go back to the way they were. Maybe Polly would be able to pull another husband in a couple of years, so she didn't have to die alone; and with any luck they wouldn't get together until after Sunday had moved out.

The board was still in the garage, she could slip down and get it. There no harm having another go when no one was looking. It probably wouldn't work anyway, but the idea had been bubbling in the back of her mind since the party. Sunday slipped off her school shoes and went back downstairs trying not to make any sound. The TV was on in the lounge room, maybe a cooking show. Sunday crept from the stairs through the kitchen to the door into the garage.

Please don't squeak, she thought as she gave the door a little shove where it stuck. Half the time the door would squeal in protest when opened, while other times it would be silent. Sunday hadn't figured out what made the difference, despite Martin trying to fix it on at least four occasions.

Martin wouldn't be home from work for another hour, the path to the games box was unobstructed. Sunday pulled out the storage tub, stifling a grunt as she lifted it to the ground. The Ouija board was on top of the other games, right where she'd left it, but a chill still ran down her spine as she picked it up.

Stop it, you're being dramatic, she scolded herself. Sunday put the storage tub back on the shelf, grabbed the box and went to make the trip back to her room. The garage door was silent again as she closed it, a small miracle, and as she was turning the corner on the stair landing, she heard her mother walk past to the kitchen.

If you had asked her why she didn't want her mother to see her retrieve her birthday present from the garage, Sunday wouldn't have been able to articulate it, though she would probably have come up with something about privacy and told her mum to keep her nose out of it.

Polly had laughed off her discomfort on the weekend, it wouldn't have been very hospitable to be freaked out by one of the gifts brought by her daughter's friends, but the fit she'd thrown when Sunday had brought home tarot cards didn't leave much to the imagination. Saying and doing were not very well aligned in her mother's case.

Sunday on the floor sat with her back to the bedroom door, that way if Polly tried to come in there would be a moment of difficulty and warning. She had started knocking but Sunday hadn't managed to get her to pause before entering the room.

The board seemed smaller in the late afternoon light, the beige background and black text were much less ominous, though she was probably imagining it.

'Alright board, it's you and me this time. What do you have to say?' she asked softly. Sunday put her fingers on the planchette and was only a little surprised to see they were trembling. 'I'm here to make contact with the spirits. Is there anyone here who would like to make contact?'

She waited, her fingers resting on the planchette, for something to happen. She tried to breathe normally, in and out, so as not to rush any spirits that might be around, but it didn't feel like anything was happening.

'Dana? It's me, Sunday, are you there?'

Again, nothing happened. She sat there listening to her mother clanging and chopping downstairs, her belly grumbled a little, the slushie she'd had earlier was indeed low in nutrition.

She was about to give up when the planchette vibrated under her fingertips. Not enough to move it, but Sunday had to fight her urge to pull her hands away and hoot with glee.

'Dana? I want to talk to you. About Martin.'

YES, the planchette pulled to the left, stopping on the word.

'Good, you're here.' Sunday paused. 'I'm sorry I wussed out on Saturday. I'm not used to speaking to ghosts.'

The planchette didn't move, it sat over the *YES* response.

'Do you remember what you said last time?'

The planchette shook for a moment, but stayed put, clearly another *YES*.

'Why did you? I mean . . . tell me more.'

KILL MARTIN.

'Okay, I got that.' Sunday chewed her lower lip. 'I mean, he's a scumbag and I wish he was dead, but like, I can't just kill him. That's insane.'

POISON.

'Poison? I could probably slip him something, but I don't know anything about poisons. Can't I . . . I dunno, break them up or something?'

KILL.

'Yeah, okay, kill Martin . . . but why? He doesn't deserve to die.'

YES

'That's not an answer, yes. Why?'

BAD MAN.

'What does that mean?' Sunday was frustrated by how long the planchette took to answer her, moving from one letter to the next felt as though it was taking hours.

KILLER.

'Martin's a killer? Yeah right.'

YES

'Martin killed someone?'

YES

'Martin Vernon, office drone, shitty golfer, is a killer?'

YES

'I don't believe it. No way.' Sunday took her fingers away from the planchette and pushed the board away. 'You're being stupid,' she said to herself.

There was a loud knock on the door, above where her head was resting against it.

'Dinner's ready,' Polly announced though the door, apparently not interested in pushing her way in today.

'Coming.' Sunday packed the Ouija board away and slid it under her bed. She didn't understand how the planchette had moved without someone to push it, unless Dana was really there in the spirit world. There was no way Martin was a killer, absolutely no way on earth.

Sunday sat next to her mother at the dining table, Martin came in a couple of minutes later and sat opposite them both. Sunday looked down at her lasagne and salad and tried not to imagine him killing her. It was ridiculous, the Ouija board must be broken, there was no spirit, just her own hands. Either that or the spirit was lying to her, maybe as a weird ghost prank.

'Martin,' Sunday said without looking up. 'How did your first wife die?'

'Sunday, that's not appropriate,' her mother said, her voice full of shock and disapproval.

'It's okay. I knew the question would come up eventually. Really, I had thought it would be before now. I've told your Mum all of this, of course, there are no secrets between us.'

Sunday flicked her eyes to her stepdad for a moment, his face seemed sincere; a small furrow between his brows, eyes hooded, mouth turned down in sadness, but she didn't trust it, and looked back to her food.

'We were married about five years, DeeDee and I—'

'I know that part.'

'Let him tell you the story Sunday,' Polly said.

'As I was saying, DeeDee was a wonderful woman, warm and kind, and she had a fierce temper if you did wrong by someone. I loved her. When we met, she was so full of energy, and life, and as the years went on, she started to fade. She was tired all the time, she kept losing weight, no matter what she ate. We saw doctors, all the specialists said they couldn't find any cancer, or anything else wrong with her. And then one day I woke up for work and when I turned to kiss her good morning, she was cold, and stiff. They did an autopsy, but the only thing they could find that was wrong with her was an enlarged heart.' Martin made a small choking sound and Sunday looked back at him. He squeezed his eyes shut and was breathing erratically, like he was trying to imitate crying and doing a terrible job of it.

'I'm so sorry, babe.' Polly put her hand on top of his and rubbed her thumb across his skin. He sniffled and wiped his dry eyes.

'It's still hard to talk about. I worry all the time that something bad is going to happen to you or your mum, I guess I can't trust a good thing after losing the woman I loved like that.'

'I doubt it would happen to you twice,' Sunday said. *Unless you killed her, that is.*

'You're sweet to say so. I guess my fears aren't quite as sensible as that.' Martin gave a watery smile, his eyes stayed cold and emotionless.

'I'm sorry she died like that. It sounds really hard.' Sunday stared at him, hoping to catch him out.

'It was awful. I didn't function for a year, my friends and family would bring me food, and help me clean. I was so inside my own head I would forget to eat and live in filth without their prompting. But after a while, things started to make sense again. I met Polly almost three years later, and you know the rest.'

'Yeah.' She had never noticed how dead Martin's eyes were most of the time. Since she'd lived with him, and since her mum had been with him, she'd generally avoided spending time with her stepdad but maybe that needed to change. If the Ouija board was right, she needed to study him, and the story about his wife's death was stretched credibility to say the least.

3.

Over the next few weeks, Sunday watched Martin; with her mother and on his own. She researched serial killers on the internet, watched documentaries interviewing them, and trained herself to see their dead-eyed expressions. The more she watched, the more convinced she became there was something wrong with Martin.

Nearly six weeks after her birthday, Sunday pulled the Ouija board out from under her bed. She'd left it there, having told herself she needed more proof before she consulted Dana again, and now that she'd seen how flimsy his story was, how easily his crocodile tears came, or didn't come despite him pretending to cry, along with his empty eyes, she was ready.

It was late June. Winter was in full swing, and she sat on her floor bundled in a massive hoodie, leggings, and favourite sheepskin boots. Like before, Sunday sat with her back against her bedroom door, it was dark, though only a little after five in the afternoon. She lit candles, low lighting for contacting spirits.

Sunday's fingertips resting on the planchette in the middle of the board.

'I'm here to contact the spirit of Dana. If you're there, make yourself known.'

For a long time, nothing happened. Sunday closed her eyes, occasionally opening them a crack to look at the board, to make sure the planchette hadn't moved, and to see how long she'd been waiting. The minutes crawled by and by eight minutes she was sure she wasn't coming.

'I'm here to make contact with the spirit world. If there is anyone here who wants to talk, now is the time.'

A shiver ran along her back, probably just a draft, but the planchette started to move.

YES

'Dana? Are you here?'

The planchette remained on *YES*.

'I'm sorry it's been so long. I was . . .' Sunday wasn't sure why she was trying to explain herself to a spirit. 'I was looking for evidence.'

AND

'I think he killed his wife.'

YES

'How did you know?'

The planchette didn't move. Sunday allowed a full two minutes to go by before deciding he wasn't going to answer that.

'What do I do now?'

KILL HIM.

Sunday took a shaky breath in before whispering 'I don't know how.'

POISON.

'How?'

Belladonna.

'What's that?'

PLANT.

'What do I do with it?'

TEA.

'Put it in his tea. Okay. What if he tastes it?'

The planchette didn't move.

'Where do I get belladonna?'

Still the planchette didn't move. Dana, or whoever was moving the little wooden pointer around, was gone. She sighed and waited another three minutes in empty silence.

'I guess that's all I get.' She leaned back on the door and ran her hands over her face and through her hair. *I hope this is a good idea.*

Sunday put the Ouija board back into the box and slid it under her bed before grabbing her laptop and opening a search window. Her fingers hovered over the keys.

What if someone finds my search history? I'll do it in incognito mode, she thought before opening up a second window.

She searched for belladonna, which turned out to be all one word.

'*Atropa belladonna* or deadly nightshade,' she read aloud. A toxic plant in the same family as tomatoes, eggplant, capsicum, and potatoes. 'The berries, which are sweet and more toxic, and the leaves which have a bitter flavour.'

Fleur Blüm

She searched through some other pages, trying
belladonna tea, which seemed to cause hallucinations and
found out there who took it on purpose for that reason.

*I could mix it in with his green tea, that's always
bitter. Maybe if I grind it up finely in the spice grinder
and put it with the matcha powder but it's brown. And it
looks like people take the powder as medicine I'd have to
give him a lot for it to kill him. The berries might be
better, I could make a smoothie and he'd never know.*

The berries were harder to buy online, maybe because
they were dangerous, so she looked for plant nurseries
that would have the plant. This was going to take longer
than she initially thought.

*I guess it gives me time to make sure he's really a
killer,* she thought, although she had already decided that
he was guilty of poisoning his wife. It was fitting she was
planning to do the same to him.

*

Sunday found a nursery near her which stocked
atropa belladonna in a small pot she could take home
and put in her bedroom. She got a couple of other plants
at the same time so as not to appear suspicious; a spider
plant that was mainly greenery, and a maiden hair fern
because it looked cute. She had a small window seat in
her bedroom, and she arranged the three pots along the
inside of the windowsill.

The belladonna plant wasn't in flower when she
bought it, apparently it flowered in early summer and
would produce fruit in late summer and early autumn, so

Sunday kept an eye on it, watered it, but not too much, and waited.

In the months until the belladonna berries were ready Sunday tried to be normal; went to school, hung out with her friends. The relationship with Megan had cooled somewhat since her birthday; she'd been demoted to second-best friend. Some days, Sunday wished she'd never got the damn Ouija board; it would have been easier to never have known about Martin. He was a downer, and a jackass to her mother on occasion but he wasn't a monster. It would never have occurred to Sunday that he'd killed his previous wife. Blissful ignorance was preferable to all this waiting, knowing he was capable of killing his wife, who he claimed to love.

If it was true, it was only a matter of time before Polly or Sunday pissed him off enough, he'd kill them too. She needed to take him out first. A couple of months shouldn't make much difference, she hoped.

*

One day in late October when Sunday was preparing to go to school, she noticed her mother wasn't up when she was getting ready.

'Mum, are you taking me to school or what?' Sunday called out as she approached her mother's closed bedroom door. There was no reply, so Sunday knocked and opened the door, not waiting to hear Polly say to come in.

'Mum? Are you up?' Sunday addressed the lump in her mother's bed.

'Hmm?' the lump said.

'It's nearly eight, are you taking me to school?'

'I'm sick. You'll have to get the bus or call Megan's mum.' Polly's face had a pale green tint to it, and she didn't open her eyes to talk.

'What sort of sick? You were fine last night.' Sunday frowned and put the back of her hand on Polly's forehead. 'Jesus, you're really hot. Do you have a fever? Do I need to call the doctor or something?

Polly brushed her daughter's hand away. 'No, Martin took my temperature before he left for work. I've probably got a virus; I'll stay here and I'll be good as gold tomorrow.'

Sunday hesitated, on one hand, she would be late to school if she didn't leave now, but on the other hand, she'd never seen her mother look so ill. She didn't trust Martin to look after her, not now she knew he was a wife-killer, especially since she didn't know if the symptoms Polly was displaying were normal illness, or signs of poisoning.

'I think I should check your temperature again. You might be dying.'

Polly sighed. 'The thermometer is on the bedside table somewhere,' she said, her voice raspy. Sunday picked up the electronic thermometer, and slipped it into her mother's mouth, keeping hold of the end to make sure her not-entirely-conscious mother didn't swallow it or drop it. After a few minutes it beeped and she looked at the numbers.

'Thirty-nine point five. Is that high?'

Polly's eyes opened a crack. 'What? Show me.'

Sunday turned the thermometer to her mother.

'That's too high.' Polly sighed and closed her eyes again.

'Mum? Mum!' Sunday shook her mother and she lay there without response.

Shit. Shit shit. She pulled out her phone and typed high fever into Google. It said anything over thirty-nine was cause for concern.

What do I do? She's too sick to stay here, if she's poisoned she might die, and if she's got some virus, she still might die. She flipped her phone over and over in her hand for a few seconds trying to decide if it was urgent enough to call the emergency number.

'Hello, triple-0, what service do you need?' a calm man's voice on the other end of the phone said.

'Ambulance I think.'

'Connecting you now.'

'Ambulance, what seems to be the problem.' This voice was another man, but seemed younger.

'My mum has a fever, and she was talking to me before and now she's asleep and I can't wake her. Is she going to die?'

'Okay, slow down. How old are you?'

'Fourteen.'

'What's your name?'

'Sunday. Can you send someone?'

'What's the address?'

Sunday gave her address. 'Are they coming?'

'Yes, someone is on the way. I'm going to get some more information from you while we wait, okay. How old is your mum?'

'Umm. Like forty-three, I think.'

'And what are her symptoms?'

'She was fine last night when I went to bed, and when I came in to check on her, she was all pale and sweaty and her fever is thirty-nine point five.'

'Okay, that's quite high, but she'll be alright when we get help to you. Did she say anything else? Headache? Sore neck?'

'She didn't really open her eyes. She was super sleepy.'

'And now she's not responding?'

'I told you that.'

'Sunday, I need you to take a deep breath with me okay,' the operator said. 'In and out, with me.' He took a loud breath into the phone and Sunday tried to do it with him. Her throat felt tight and dry, and her hands were shaking.

'My step-dad's poisoned her,' she blurted.

The operator paused. 'Why do you say that?'

Sunday hesitated, she had no evidence except Dana's word and Martin being a bit of a dick sometimes. 'Sorry. I worry he's trying to hurt Mum.'

'That sounds stressful, and now your mum is sick and that's the worst thing. The ambulance is a couple of minutes away, I'm going to hang up now. They'll be there soon, okay?'

'Okay.' Sunday didn't want to hang up.

The house was silent after she pulled the phone away from her ear, she strained to hear the sirens, but maybe they wouldn't use sirens. Polly's breath was shallow and fast, but at least while she was breathing, she wasn't dead.

Sunday looked out her mother's bedroom window, searching for the ambulance. She would have to run down and let them in.

It must have only been two or three minutes, but they were the longest minutes Sunday had ever experienced. She went from the window to her mother's side, back and forth, making sure she didn't stop breathing while she was watching the street.

The ambulance didn't have its siren on, which she thought was a mistake given how urgent it was, but they had the lights going. She started down the stairs to meet them as soon as they pulled up in front of the house.

'Help, please, you have to hurry.' Sunday was out of breath, bouncing on her toes.

'Are you Sunday? Is it your mum that's having trouble?' one of the paramedic's asked, a fit-looking man of about thirty.

'Yes, she won't wake up. I don't know what's happened.'

'It's okay, we're here now, can you show us where she is?' the other paramedic said, a woman a little younger than the man. They were wearing neat, dark blue uniforms and were in no particular hurry, despite the panic Sunday felt.

She led them up the stairs into her mother's bedroom, which now seemed very stuffy and cramped. They asked her the same questions as the operator on the phone and Sunday stifled her irritation.

'Can you take her to hospital?' Sunday interrupted, her voice louder than she expected.

'I know it's stressful, but we have to make sure we won't make her worse by moving her. We're doing our best, I promise,' the male paramedic said, his voice still infuriatingly calm.

They took Polly's temperature again, tried to wake her, took her blood pressure, and looked in her eyes with a little pen light.

'Bloodshot eyes, that's not good,' the woman said.

'Sunday,' the male paramedic addressed her again. 'We're going to take your mum with us to hospital. Do you want to come in the ambulance with us? Or will you be okay here?'

Sunday didn't know what to say, what was the right answer?

'Can you call someone to come look after you? Maybe your dad?' the woman suggested as she started to push the blankets off the bed.

'I want to come with you.'

The paramedics both nodded and went back to attending to Polly. They had brought a spine board with them up the stairs, Sunday wasn't sure how they were going to get her mother down to the ambulance.

After a bit of manoeuvring, they managed to get Polly down to the trolley and wheel her into the back of the ambulance. With Sunday and the woman paramedic in the back the van felt crowded, but she was glad she hadn't stayed behind.

'Do you want to call someone to meet you? We're headed to Saint Vincents.'

Sunday looked at the phone clutched in her hand. She'd left the house without even thinking about it, her house keys were in her other hand. She'd left her school bag inside the house. 'I'll call my stepdad.'

Martin might have poisoned Polly, but if she was sick, or something else was wrong, she had to call him. It would have been weird if she didn't call him.

'What is it, Sunday? I'm at work.' Martin answered the phone with anger in his voice.

'Mum's sick. We're on the way to Saint Vincents.'

'What do you mean sick? She seemed fine when I left.'

'I don't know what's wrong, she had a fever and then she wouldn't wake up. I called triple-zero.'

Martin was silent on the end of the line.

'I didn't know what else to do.'

'It's okay, you did the right thing. If there wasn't anything wrong the paramedics wouldn't have taken her. I'll be there as soon as I can, okay?'

'Okay.'

'You'll be fine. Just keep your head and I'll be there before you know it.'

Sunday swallowed hard, Martin was being weird, even for him. Time would tell if it was weird because he was worried about Polly, or because he thought he would get caught.

Once they arrived at the hospital everyone was rushing around—if the paramedics were cool and collected, the emergency department staff seemed to be losing their heads trying to get things happening as quickly as possible. They took some blood, set Polly up in a little screened-off cubicle, and gave her a drip, into which they injected several substances.

No one seemed interested in talking to her, not that she blamed them, she didn't know anything useful. Her mother's medical history was not very interesting, she didn't have any allergies as far as Sunday knew and hadn't been sick last night. The idea of poison wouldn't leave Sunday's mind, the beep of the heart rate monitor and the constant babble and ruckus of the hospital made her want to scream.

Martin arrived at some point later, Sunday's sense of time had completely slipped out of sync, but when she looked at the clock it was just after ten o'clock.

'Do they know anything?'

'No. They're running around. I don't think I helped very much.'

Martin took her hand and squeezed it. 'Honey, you got her here, that's the most helpful thing you could have done. She's in safe hands now.'

'Are you the husband?' A man in aqua-coloured scrubs came into the cubicle.

'Yes. Martin Vernon. What's happening?'

'I'm Doctor Shah, we're still not clear what's happening, but we've started your wife on some IV antibiotics, seems to be an infection from a wound that we found on her lower left leg. Do you know how she might have injured herself?'

Martin's eyes were wide. 'I hadn't noticed. Maybe in the garden? She was pruning roses in her dad's place a week or so ago.'

'Do you know if she was using potting mix?'

Martin frowned. 'I don't know. She might have been.'

'Alright, we'll add that to the possibilities. The wound is infected, but it may not be the whole story. We'll keep running tests and we'll let you know what we find.'

*

Polly stayed in hospital for days. She was given antibiotics and her leg infection started to heal.

'Now, we've done a few tests, and we think we've worked out the issues,' Doctor Shah addressed Polly, Sunday, and Martin. 'The infection of the lower leg was part of it, but you've also returned positive results for Legionnaires' disease, which is a respiratory infection. Thankfully the antibiotics we used on your leg will have helped with that but we're sending you home with some other medication to take for the next week.'

'Where the hell did she get Legionnaires from?' Martin asked, his hand squeezing Polly's so hard her fingers were turning red.

'It's likely to have come from the potting mix, it's quite common.'

'She nearly died.'

'You're right, she was quite unwell for a moment there. Thankfully your daughter was sensible enough to call the ambulance, and we were able to get her symptoms under control. After you're discharged, you'll need to keep an eye out for any changes—' the doctor continued to explain the symptoms they should look for and to bring Polly back in if anything went wrong. 'I don't expect there's anything to worry about, but we need to tell you all the possibilities.'

'Thank you.' Polly smiled, her face was still a little pale, but she seemed stronger and more alert.

'You should be right to leave, sign some papers at the nurses' station and you're all set.' Doctor Shah bobbed his head, somewhere between a nod and a bow, and stepped out.

Sunday had been watching Martin closely through the days Polly was in the hospital. She had been there most of the time she wasn't at school, and Martin had come in after he finished work. Sunday wanted to make sure he didn't have any time alone with her, in case he wanted to finish the job, but the doctor said it was potting mix, and not poison.

Could Dana have been wrong? Or worse, been lying about Martin? What if she had been suspicious of a man who hadn't done anything wrong? His wife could have died of natural causes. It was pretty extreme to believe he'd killed her, but the Ouija board had been so insistent.

They took Polly home and settled her in the bed upstairs. The trip from the hospital back home was enough to tire her out.

'I'll be downstairs if you need me. Your phone is just there, so call or text, don't try to shout, okay hunny?' Martin said, leaning over to kiss Polly's forehead. Sunday's stomach turned, as it did every time they showed physical affection, but even more so since her birthday.

Back in Sunday's bedroom, the belladonna plant was looking a little wilted. She had been neglecting it while she'd been worrying about her mum, but now she needed to make sure it survived long enough to produce berries.

Just because Martin didn't poison her mother this time didn't mean he wasn't a murderer. Sunday needed more evidence on his wife's death. If he'd done it once, he could do it again. She shuddered. If Martin was going to get rid of anyone, surely it would be her, as the usurper in the relationship; a child who was not his blood and who was suspicious of him.

She made a mental note not to eat anything he prepared as she watered the belladonna and trimmed off the brown leaves. The flowers were due in the next month or so, and the berries to appear by the end of summer. Sunday just had to make it till then, and she would be able to get rid of Martin and feel safe again all before her next birthday.

4.

The belladonna started to flower a couple of weeks later; beautiful deep purple flowers, with yellow towards the centre. Sunday understood why they were named after a beautiful woman, she hoped they would live up to their other name as well: deadly nightshade.

As the end of the school year approached, Sunday was thinking about how to get the berries into Martin's system without him being suspicious.

'I think I want to have smoothies for breakfast for a while mum, can you get some berries?'

'Sure hun, I'll get the frozen ones, they're better for smoothies. And some bananas and maybe oats? What do you think?' Polly said, adding the items to the shopping list in her hand.

'Yeah, sounds good.'

'Do you want to come to the supermarket with me?'

'Nah, I'll be in my room.'

Polly nodded and turned her attention back to the list. Sunday spent a lot of her time up in her room, more now that she wanted to keep an eye on her plants. Martin had commented a couple of times that she was anti-social, and she'd rolled her eyes at him. The moody teenager card was proving to be quite useful for getting time away from her stepdad, though she kept her ear out for any raised voices or signs that he was planning to get rid of her or Polly. Since the trip to hospital, it had been quiet.

For the next few weeks, whenever Sunday made a smoothie, she would offer to make one for Martin and Polly. Her mother didn't like them, and it was rare that she would accept the offer, but Martin was a bit of a health nut, and since Sunday would clean the blender afterwards, and he didn't have to do anything, he would almost always say yes. Sunday made sure to make his first, then her own, before she washed out the single serve blender and left it on the sink to dry.

She wondered if she would need to have of the belladonna berries some too, not enough to kill her, but enough that when she said she didn't know they were poisonous it would sound plausible. It sounded unpleasant, but necessary to help stay out of prison.

Sunday kept a very close eye on the plant. As the flowers drooped, and fell off, and berries swelled and grew where they had been she tried to hide her excitement. Being free of Martin would be the best thing that had ever happened to her. Her mother was so busy being a good wife she hardly had any time to be a mum. It was time Sunday was back at the top of her priorities.

At first, the berries were tiny, black, and glistening. Sunday was tempted to try one, but she knew they were powerful, deadly in large enough doses, and psychotropic in smaller doses. She'd found forums online where people discussed using the plant as a recreational drug, though it sounded very unpleasant to her. Sunday had made sure to use the incognito mode when she was doing her research; it would be no good to say she didn't know they were deadly if she had a vast browser history of research.

*

One Friday, she came home from school feeling anxious. Should she go through with this plan? Killing someone was an extreme way to get them out of your life, but then again, Dana said he was dangerous, and she would be protecting her mum, and herself, by getting rid of him.

Sunday decided to do one more session with the Ouija board. It had sat, untouched, under her bed for months as she cultivated her poisonous plant. Sessions with Dana were kind of fun, but mostly scary, and Sunday had avoided it for a long time.

'Alright, Dana. One last check in, I need to know the plan is solid.' She pulled the Ouija board between her legs, her back against the door, as she did every time, and took a deep breath. Her fingers rested on the planchette.

'Dana, I'm here to make contact. If you're around, give me a sign.'

Sunday's breathing was shallow, her heartbeat loud in her ears and she closed her eyes trying to calm herself. She was torn between wanting her life back just her and her mum and the possibility of being convicted of murder. She was nearly fifteen, they would put her in an adult prison.

Nothing happened. She counted her breaths, waiting. Forty-five breaths, and she opened her eyes a little. Everything was normal.

'Dana. Please, I need to speak to you,' Sunday's voice was small, tremulous. What if Dana had disappeared? Could she go through with the plan without Dana's encouragement? Then as she was about to give up, the planchette vibrated. Then the planchette slowly drifted up.

YES

'Oh my God, you're here. I'm so relived.'

The planchette remained on YES.

'I . . . I'm scared. What if I get caught?'

DON'T.

'But how? I'm only a kid. This plan is really elaborate. I don't think it's a good idea.'

MUST KILL HIM. DANGEROUS.

'I know you said he was dangerous, but like, I don't see it. He's a pain in my butt, obviously, but like—' Sunday stopped midsentence as the planchette zoomed around the board.

KILLER. KILLER.

'Okay he's a killer. You said that. Who did he kill?'

ME

'Oh shit. Oh shit.' Sunday pulled her hands away and leaned her head back against the door.

I thought he'd killed his wife, but if he killed Dana too, that makes him a serial killer. I can't let him kill

Mum too. Sunday's hands were shaking, and she realised she was crying a little.

'Dana? Are you still there?

YES.

'He killed you too?'

YES.

'Who were you to him?'

WIFE.

'Two wives? Holy shit.' Sunday tried to think straight but her brain wouldn't work. Polly was in danger, the berries were ripe, it was now or never. What if she waited too long and he killed her mother, his third wife? It would be Sunday's fault; she could have stopped him and she chickened out.

'Thanks, Dana. I know what I have to do.'

Sunday shivered, as though a cold wind rushed over the back of her neck, but it could have been her imagination.

The next morning when Sunday woke up, the belladonna berries were plump and glossy. She went downstairs for a bowl to collect them and picked all the berries on the plant; twenty-five. Some were bigger, some were smaller, but she figured they would be enough.

She hadn't thought about what would happen if she didn't kill him on the first try. If the berries weren't potent enough, he might not die and then he would know what she'd done. Sunday shook her head; it was too late to think about that now. She had to press on and sort out the consequences later.

Polly was in the kitchen when she came in. 'I'm off to play golf with Yvette, will you be okay here?'

'Sure. Is Martin going with you?'

'No, he wanted to come but… just between you, me and the gatepost, Yvette's got husband trouble and she needs someone to talk to. I know she won't open up with Martin hovering around.' Polly grabbed her keys and leaned forward to kiss Sunday's cheek. 'I'll see you later, you and Martin might need to do dinner for yourselves if we wind up on the wine at the clubhouse afterwards. I'll text you.'

'Okay, have fun.' Sunday smiled, trying to block the contents of the bowl from her mother's view. When the front door clicked shut after Polly, Sunday relaxed a little. Martin wasn't up, she'd seen his feet sticking out of the bed covers as she came down. The blender would wake him if he had managed to sleep through her mother's preparations to leave, but she suspected he was pretending to sleep.

Sunday put the small bullet blender on the bench, filled one cup with milk, oats, a banana, most of the belladonna berries and a couple of frozen raspberries, then attached the lid and turned it on. The little device was incredibly loud, Sunday winced a little every time she used it, but this time she hoped Martin would come down to investigate.

Ouija Board

She jiggled the blender and gave it a couple of pulses to finish off, before pouring the smoothie into a large glass. Without washing the blender container, she filled it again; milk, oats, banana, raspberries and the remaining belladonna berries, only four. As soon as she started to blend again, she heard Martin's footsteps at the top of the stairs. Her heart was pounding and felt as though it was trying to escape through her throat. She thought he wasn't going to come down and then she would have wasted her whole crop of berries.

'Morning. That looks good.' Martin stepped into the kitchen rubbing his hand across his left eye. His hair was standing up at strange angles and his pyjama pants were slung dangerously low around his hips, leaving a strip of skin exposed below his ratty T-shirt.

'I made that one already, you can have it. I'll have this one.' Sunday nodded to the smoothie still spinning in the blender under her hands.

'Thanks kiddo.'

Sunday kept her face still, despite hating it when he used the word kiddo to refer to her. 'You're welcome.' She poured her smoothie into a matching glass and leaned against the kitchen counter to drink it. Martin had taken a seat at the dining table and was browsing his tablet, reading the news probably. He was so boring and predictable.

'Your mum told me about golf, I don't know if I trust that story about Yvette's husband. Sometimes I think she's trying to get away from me on the weekends.' He was smiling at her, clearly finding his joke amusing. Sunday smiled back.

'Yeah.'

'How come your smoothie is a different colour?'

'Different packet of the berries.' She shrugged.

'Interesting, it tastes like… something, I can't quite put my finger on it.'

'You don't like it?'

'No, it's great, but—' he looked off into middle distance for a moment. 'I feel like it's on the tip of my tongue, but I can't think of it. Never mind, must be going senile.'

'Definitely.'

Sunday finished her smoothie first, having drunk it quickly so she could clean up the evidence and get out of Martin's presence. She washed the blender, and her glass, with much more care than she would have usually, leaving them both to drain on the rack next to the sink. Martin was engrossed in reading on the tablet and paid her no attention when she took his glass from the table and washed it as well.

Retreating upstairs, Sunday put on her large headphones and started playing a medieval adventure video game she'd been trying to get to the end of. She didn't know how long the poison might take to kick in, and she didn't want to hear Martin if he cried out or something.

Ouija Board

It's all about plausible deniability now, she thought to herself, though the voice in her mind sounded unlike her usual internal monologue.

About half an hour later, Sunday started to feel light-headed, and the images on her computer screen swayed and danced. She tried to keep playing, but the screen was glitching and melting and she started to think she might be sick. She closed her eyes, and tried to calm herself, but the glitching continued inside her eyelids.

Sunday turned off the game and put on some music before laying back on her bed. Having her eyes closed made it feel less gross, but she would have to ride out the feeling until her mother got home. She wondered how Martin was doing, he'd had a lot more berries than she did, hopefully he didn't vomit them all up and ruin everything.

As she lay on her back watching the dancing colours inside her head, she heard mumbling, as though someone was talking to her.

'Thank you, Sunday.' The voice was very quiet but sounded feminine.

Who are you? Sunday thought, her mind vaguely aware that other people don't usually talk inside your brain.

'It's me, Dana.'

After all that time with the stupid Ouija board, now I can hear you.

'Yes, you've done a great job. Well done giving yourself some too, it might help with the police.'

Might? Sunday frowned, or at least she thought she was frowning, her face didn't feel right.

'It doesn't matter now. You've done what I couldn't.'

You tried to kill Martin? Who ARE you?

'Martin's first wife. He killed me. That's why I had to stop him before he destroyed you and your mother too.' Her voice was stronger now, husky and deep as though she had been a heavy smoker. For a moment Sunday thought she could see Dana, hovering at the side of her inner vision, but as soon as she tried to look, there was only smoke. She didn't understand the rules of the hallucinations, assuming that's what she was experiencing.

He can't hurt us now, Sunday's thoughts started to feel far away, and the woman's voice in her head faded again. All sense of time started to blend and stretch, she couldn't tell if time was moving very fast, or it had stopped altogether, though it didn't seem to matter much either way.

*

'Sunday! Wake up!'

Sunday opened her eyes to see her mother's face over hers, she smiled and pulled off her headphones.

'Hey, how was golf?'

'I've been trying to call you, and Martin. Where is he?'

'Is he not here?' Sunday frowned. Thinking seemed quite hard. 'I don't feel so good.'

'What do you mean? What have you been doing all day?'

'Umm . . .I don't know. I was playing video games for a while, then I put on some music, and umm, I guess I fell asleep?'

'Shit. Shit.' Polly stood up, pacing around Sunday's room with one hand rubbing her forehead.

'Are you okay?'

'No. I'm bloody not. You can't not answer your phone. I've been worried sick. And now I can't find Martin.'

'He didn't say he was going anywhere. Last I saw him he was in the kitchen.'

Polly turned and hurried out of the room, Sunday struggled into a seated position, waited a moment for her head to stop pounding, then stood up. She moved gingerly around the first floor before realising her mother was downstairs. As she looked down the stairs blurred and stretched before going back to their normal shape.

I guess the hallucinations are still here then.

She ran her hands down the walls as she carefully descended. Her mother was in the courtyard at the back kneeling over something.

'What are you doing?' Sunday asked, standing in the doorway. Now that she was closer, she could see Martin was lying on his back on the fake grass. He was wearing only his boxer shorts. 'What's Martin doing?'

Polly looked up, eyes wide and wet. 'He's cold.'

'What?' Sunday's heart started to hammer in her chest. It had worked, but now he was dead. Properly, irreversibly dead.

'I tried to wake him but when I shook him, he was all limp and cool to the touch.'

'Can you . . . did you try his pulse?' Sunday asked, her cheeks heating.

'Uh.' Polly put her hand to Martin's neck, then leaned over to put her ear to his chest. 'I can't hear anything. Oh God, oh God, Martin.' She let out a long wail.

'I'll call an ambulance,' Sunday said, though her feet seemed rooted to the spot. With great effort she tore her eyes away from her mother and stepfather. For the second time that year, she called triple-oh.

'Ambulance please.' Her voice was surprisingly calm, at least it seemed like it from her end. There was no telling whether it was true, her brain was still all sorts of fuzzy.

'They're coming,' she said as the ambulance operator ended the call. Polly's face was wet with tears and snot, and her eyes were red; Sunday had never seen her look so upset. 'It'll be okay, Mum. It's okay.

I didn't mean for her to be this sad. I was protecting her, Sunday thought as she patted her mother's shoulder in an attempt to be comforting. They waited for the ambulance, Martin's body weirdly motionless on the fake grass, and it felt like time had stopped. Perhaps Sunday still had some of the poison clouding her mind, or maybe it was that thing when you're upset that everything feels like it's in slow motion.

Polly and Sunday both jumped at the banging of the door knocker.

'I'll go.' Sunday stood and ran to the front door, though it was far too late for that to make a difference.

'Did you call for paramedics?' the taller, older ambulance officer asked when Sunday swung open the door.

'Yes, come through.' Sunday turned to lead the two paramedics through the house.

'Didn't we come here a while ago?' the female officer asked. Now she thought about it, the woman looked familiar, though the man didn't seem like anyone she'd met before.

'Yeah. Mum had an infection a couple of weeks ago.'

'Is she the patient?'

'No, it's my stepdad, I think he's dead.'

'Alright, we'll see about that,' the older paramedic said.

The two ambulance officers set their kits down on the fake grass and set about their tasks; they were efficient and direct, though they both had kind tones.

'What happened?'

'I came home and found him like this.' Polly's eyes were glazed, she seemed not to be all there.

'How long has he been out here?'

'I got home about fifteen minutes ago, but he might have been here before that.'

'And you, young lady, do you know how long he's been on the ground like this?'

'I was asleep upstairs. The last time I saw him was like midday, I guess.'

'He's not breathing, pupils dilated and unresponsive.' The male paramedic was flashing a penlight into Martin's eyes, then he tried to put up his hand, but it was difficult as though he was resisting. 'Looks like we have partial rigor… is it possible he's been out for a couple of hours?'

Polly looked at Sunday, and back to the paramedic. 'I left before noon.' It was almost eight in the evening now.

'I didn't see him after lunch, I was in my room. I fell asleep,' Sunday said, looking at the ground.

'There's nothing we can do for him, I'm sorry but he's gone. We'll have to get the police here; they'll take him away and do their investigation.'

Polly wailed, a long hard cry of pain.

'What happened to him?' Sunday asked.

'It's hard to tell, there's no obvious marks, maybe a heart attack? Brain aneurism? Stroke? Overdose . . . it could be a lot of things. They'll do a post-mortem,' the woman replied. 'You'll have to stop touching him, and everything else, and wait for the cops to arrive.'

Sunday swallowed hard. A post-mortem would show the poison, though she had planned that. She thought she was anxious before, while she was planning the death— the murder—she told herself, but now it was three times as bad. Her hands were shaking, and she felt sick, though that could still be the belladonna in her system.

'I'm sorry for your loss.' The woman put her hand on Sunday's shoulder as she stood up. The world around her shimmered, and Sunday realised she was looking through a layer of unshed tears. She hadn't expected to feel anything when Martin died, and if she thought about it, she still didn't really feel anything—her body seemed very far away. It might have been the belladonna, but some small part of her brain that was still firing thought it might be shock. She sat down with a thump on the tiled floor of the kitchen.

The two ambulance officers pulled the sheet off their trolley and placed it over Martin's body, before taking Polly gently by the arms and helping her back into the house. Sunday watched, stunned, as they steered her mother into the loungeroom. They spoke in hushed tones for a while, then the woman came back into the kitchen.

'You wanna come into the front with your mum? She needs you to be there for her, and we need you to be away from the deceased.'

Sunday blinked slowly, trying to make her head work, but it was so hard. She stood up, swayed a little, braced her hand against the dining table for a moment, then looked back at the female paramedic.

'Come on, love, have a sit down on the couch. Much nicer than the hard old floor.'

Fleur Blüm

Sunday nodded, and shuffled into the lounge where her mother sat, eyes staring into middle distance while the other paramedic mumbled indistinct soothing words.

5.

Two police officers turned up a little while later, looked around the house taking pictures, and then they took Martin's body away in a black zip up bag.

Polly and Sunday answered a lot of questions, and then when the police and the crime scene people were all finished, Sunday got rid of all the plants on her windowsill. It would have looked suspicious to just toss the belladonna plant, so she took all of them down to the garden, shook the soil off their roots, and poured the earth into the garden beds, before putting the empty pots and the remnants of plants into the bin of one of the neighbours a few doors down. They left their bins in the street most of the time, so they may as well have been asking for it. Her mother was lying down in her room, maybe crying, maybe sleeping, though probably not.

A few days later they were asked to the police station to answer the same questions all over again. They spoke to Polly alone, but when it was Sunday's turn, her mum was there.

'Do you know what happened to him yet?' Sunday asked, as the two police detectives started to pack up his various pieces of paper and notes. One was a barrel-chested man with light blonde or grey hair, it was hard to tell, and thick, black-rimmed glasses, he seemed to be in charge, the other was a thin faced blonde woman with eyes that were permanently narrowed as though always suspicious.

'The results of the post-mortem indicate respiratory failure, at this stage it seems likely that he overdosed, though we haven't ruled anything out, it might have been an accident.'

'Overdosed on what?' Polly asked, her voice rising in pitch.

'Yet to be determined, but most cases like this it's opioids; oxy, heroin, that sort of thing.'

'He wasn't a junkie!'

'No-one is suggesting he was. As I say, the results are yet to be confirmed from the toxicology report. We'll let you know when we have a firm cause of death. Until then, try not to worry.'

Polly opened and closed her mouth a couple of times, as though trying to find the words to reply and failing. In the end she seemed to give up and look down at her hands instead.

'Thank you, detectives. We look forward to hearing from you.'

She and Sunday followed the detectives as they walked out of the room.

They drove home in silence, Polly's eyes set on the road. When they returned to the house, Polly sat on the couch in the lounge and wouldn't speak. Her face was wet with tears and her hands were shaking.

Ouija Board

'Mum? It's okay, it'll be okay.'

Polly said nothing, she didn't even wipe the tears away. She was somewhere locked inside her own mind, unaware of what was happening around her. Sunday dabbed her mother's cheeks and guided her to lean back into the couch.

Maybe she needs to let her feelings out, Sunday thought. *I'll keep an eye on her until she's ready to be back here again.*

As she sat waiting for her mother to return to herself, Sunday wondered if they would find the belladonna in Martin's blood. His death wasn't from natural causes, they had to figure out if it was accidental or not, and then whether it was suicide. Sunday took her mother's trembling hand in hers and rubbed her thumbs over the delicate skin on the inside of her wrist. When she'd been little her mother had done the same for her and it had always made her feel better, she hoped it would get through to her, wherever she was in there, and give her a little comfort.

It didn't seem fair to be soothing Polly for something she had done, and not for the first time, Sunday regretted going through with her plan. Dana had been so certain, so convincing, but now the deed was done, Sunday couldn't believe it. She thought of herself as a kind, loving person, and yes, Martin was a bit of a dick, but what evidence did she really have that he was plotting to kill them? The word of a ghost? A year ago, she wouldn't even had admitted she believed in ghosts, and now she'd killed a man on orders from one.

There must be something wrong with me, Sunday thought, before wiping away a tear from her own cheek.

'Are you okay, love?' Polly asked. Sunday turned to her and tried to smile through the tears.

'Are you? You've been sitting there for over an hour; you didn't answer when I spoke to you.'

'Have I?' Polly sniffed and rolled her shoulders back. 'I'm sorry to have worried you.'

'It's okay.'

They sat in silence for a moment before Polly patted Sunday's hand and stood up. 'I'd better start thinking about dinner.'

As Sunday lay in her bed later that night, she considered whether to confess. Her mother would be shocked, and angry, but not knowing must be weighing on her. If she thought her husband had killed himself, and didn't know why, that would be a terrible fate. Then again, if Sunday told her she'd killed him, would that be better? What reason could she possibly give that would make any sense? Saying he was threatening her, or abusing her, wouldn't spare her mother any pain, and the more Sunday thought about it, the more she believed he was innocent.

Dana, if she was even a real ghost and not some figment of Sunday's imagination, could be anyone. The things she said could as easily be lies as they could be truth. Sunday turned over and over in bed trying to quiet her thoughts, to get some sleep, but it evaded her.

As she lay there thinking, it occurred to Sunday that her fifteenth birthday was only a few weeks away, but she had no intention of having a party or celebration of any kind, given how the last one went, even if her mother wanted her to.

'Time to get up, love.' Polly's voice woke her from the other side of the bedroom door. Sunday must have fallen asleep, though she couldn't remember doing it, or dreaming for that matter. It was probably better since her dreams were scary and stressful ever since she'd had the belladonna.

'Coming,' she yelled back. Sunday went to school and tried to do everything she would normally have done.

*

Her teachers kept asking if she was okay, and though she said she was fine, sometimes she would burst into tears and the teacher would look concerned and pat her upper arm.

'You can take time off school, if you think that will help,' Mrs. Klein, the history teacher, said three weeks after the visit to the police station. 'You're only in year ten, we can catch you up if you miss some days.'

'I'm okay. I—' Sunday hesitated. 'I think it's better to be out of the house, I can pretend things are normal, at least while I'm at school. At home it feels so . . . empty, I keep expecting him to tell me to get my feet off the couch or clean my room, and he never does. I even miss him snoring in the other room. Is that weird?'

Mrs Klein smiled, though her eyes stayed sad. 'That sounds normal. We miss funny things about people when they're gone; their smell, their laugh, even things that used to annoy us can make us sad when they're not there anymore. Why don't you call it a day and we'll see you tomorrow?'

It was two in the afternoon, a little early to go home from school, but given she'd been crying in her history class and wasn't listening anyway, Sunday nodded and slipped out of the class.

She caught the bus home, as usual, and stopped to get a few jelly snakes from the corner shop on her way home. There was a car parked in front of their house she didn't recognise, she wondered if it was some well-wisher or more police.

Sunday opened the front door, and her mother called out from the kitchen.

'Hunny? Is that you?' Polly called Martin honey, not her. She walked into the kitchen and her mother's face was pale, as though she'd forgotten for a moment that her husband was dead.

'It's just me, sorry.'

Polly swallowed, her throat bobbing up and down, and her eyes fluttering, trying to process what was happening. 'Of course.' She cleared her throat. 'You're home early?'

'Yeah. Mrs Klein thought I should leave; I was crying in class. I think it was putting her off.'

'I'm sure that wasn't the only reason she thought you might need to go home. I'm sorry you've been having such a hard time with everything.'

'I shouldn't even be upset.'

'What do you mean?' Polly frowned.

'He was your husband; it wasn't like he was my dad. I don't know why I should be having a cry at school all these weeks later when he wasn't even related to me.'

'How can you say that? You had your differences, I know, but he was an important part of your life for years. It's natural that you would have some complicated feelings about that.'

Sunday made a non-committal sound. *Why should I be allowed to skip school for being sad when it was me who killed him?* She opened her mouth to tell her mother what she'd done, the guilt was too much, when there was a knock at the front door.

'Mum, I need to tell you something,' she said as Polly started walking to open the door.

'Okay sure, I'll see who this is first.'

Sunday put her hand out as though to stop her mother, but it was too late, she had already swept by, out of reach. Her moment to confess had passed and she didn't know if she would have the courage to do it again later. Dragging her feet, Sunday walked towards to front door of their townhouse to see her mother inviting in two police detectives. A huge ball of lead settled in her stomach, and she thought she might be sick—their faces were serious, and their stances vaguely defensive.

'Won't you come in?' Polly said.

'We have something to tell you Mrs Vernon, and—' the male detective looked up to see Sunday in the hallway. 'You're here too, Sunday. We should probably sit down before we start chatting.'

Polly's face, which was already pale, seemed to lose even more colour. She went back to the kitchen and sat down at the dining table in silence. Sunday sat at the far corner, the male detective took a seat next to Polly, and the younger female detective remained standing.

'Mrs Vernon,' he started.

'Polly, please.'

'Polly.' He swallowed and took a moment's pause. 'We have some news from the forensics lab. The toxicology report has come back, and I'm afraid it doesn't look like your husband's death was an accident.'

'What do you mean?' Polly said, her voice not much more than a whisper.

'The results indicate he was poisoned. *Atropa belladonna*, a common poison found in the belladonna plant, was found in his blood. It's the cause of death.'

Polly's mouth flapped up and down as though she was trying to speak but failing. 'What? How?'

'There are a couple of possibilities in poisoning cases, the first thing to figure out is whether it was self-administered or not.'

'Self-administered?'

'And the second,' the detective cut over Polly's question, 'the second thing we need to figure out, is whether it was accidental or intentional.'

'That's four possibilities,' Sunday said.

'Yes, you end up with four ways it might have happened. He took it himself, or someone gave it to him, either accidentally or on purpose,' the female detective said.

'Why would he have taken poison? What would have possessed him to take poison?' Polly said to no one in particular.

'The belladonna plant produces berries, they're small and black, and very tasty apparently. We found traces of berries and milk and a few other things in his stomach contents.'

'It was a smoothie,' Sunday said, she didn't know why she was telling them, but the weeks of guilt were getting too much to bear.

'A smoothie?' the male detective asked.

'Yeah. I made them for the two of us. We had a thing going, like a sort of daily ritual, were I made us both smoothies for breakfast.'

'I see.' He paused to look back at his colleague. 'What did you put in the smoothie that day Sunday?'

Sunday felt cold and hot at the same time, she'd started to sweat, and her heart was pounding in her ears so loudly she wasn't sure she heard him right. 'I had this plant in my bedroom. It had berries. There were only a few, but I picked them and put them in the smoothies.'

'Did you eat them too?'

'Yeah, some.' Sunday's vision blurred as tears formed and spilled from her eyes.

'Were you sick?' the female detective asked.

'I mean, I felt weird, and I fell asleep and had these epic trippy dreams, but then Martin was dead, and I didn't think it was important enough to mention.'

'I see.' The male detective wrote something in his notebook and waited, perhaps for Sunday to say more, but she didn't want to talk anymore. She'd hoped the confession would be a relief, but she felt empty, as though she wasn't really in her body anymore.

'Did you know what the plant was?' he asked after a pause that seemed to last forever.

'Yes.'

'What?' Polly asked, her face streaked with silent tears. She turned to Sunday; her red-rimmed eyes were boring into her in a way she hadn't ever felt before. 'What did you do?'

Sunday said nothing. Polly started to breathe heavily; her hands were gripping the table so hard her fingers were white.

'What did you do?' Polly screamed, as she did, she stood up suddenly and lunged towards her daughter, though the male detective was ready and blocked her move. He held her shoulders and pushed her back onto the chair.

'Sunday, did you know the berries were toxic?' he asked.

Sunday nodded. It was all happening in slow motion. She could see his body lying on the patio in front of her as though it was still happening.

'I think maybe we should all go to the police station and continue this in a more formal setting.'

'You tell me right now what you thought you were doing?' Polly said.

'I can see you're upset, let's not do anything rash. We'll have to take Sunday for questioning, I would normally want a parent there, but we might need to ask her father—'

'I did it. I killed him,' Sunday said.

'Don't say anything else,' the detective said.

'I killed him. I meant it, but then when he was dead, I wished I could take it back.'

'Why would you do that, Sunday?' Polly's face was contorted in grief.

'It doesn't matter. It was fucking stupid. I killed a person, and I can't take it back. You'd better arrest me.'

The two detectives stood up, the man took Sunday gently by the shoulder and looked into her eyes. 'I'm going to arrest you now for causing the death of Martin Vernon. I must inform you that you do not have to say or do anything but anything you say or do may be given in evidence in court. You'll need to come with us.'

He looked so sad, as though he'd lost faith in the world after hearing her confession. The two detectives escorted Sunday out of the house and into the back of their car.

'Why? What did he ever do to you?' Polly said through the open car door, having followed them out into the street.

'I thought he killed his wife. I thought he was going to kill you too. And maybe me.'

'What possessed you to think that?'

'You remember the Ouija board?'

Polly nodded.

'I was talking—I thought I was talking to a ghost and she said he'd killed his first wife.'

'DeeDee?'

'No, she said her name was Dana.'

'DeeDee was a nickname. Martin's first wife's name was Dana.'

Sunday stared at her mother; she had convinced herself that she'd hallucinated the whole thing or had convinced herself out of some repressed rage against Martin.

'She was very sick. He told me. She killed herself. She was poisoning herself to make it seem like she had cancer and one day she died. It all came out in the postmortem.'

'What does that mean? Was she real?'

'I don't know, but Martin certainly didn't kill DeeDee. She did that all on her own.'

'We should really get going. We'll have plenty of time to sort this out down at the station.'

The male detective closed the car door and stepped around to get into the driver's seat. There were no bars or grills in the back of the car, Sunday supposed they hadn't expected to be taking anyone in, but she was handcuffed. It was impossible to sit comfortably with her hands behind her back, but they'd put the seatbelt on for her before they left.

Not that it would matter if I died on the way there. I have nothing to live for now, Sunday thought. Her mind was working so slowly, and yet felt like it was running a hundred miles an hour. The cars slipped by outside in a haze, she heard the detectives talking but it was like they were underwater.

I'm so sorry Mum, she thought, and closed her eyes, hoping things would be better when she opened them.

Acknowledgements

My writing process is largely solitary, that is the typing, editing, staring off into space part. I take inspiration from everything around me, books, television, movies, and dreams, and mash it together to make new stories.

In this instance, I would like to formally acknowledge the contribution of Nigel Brookes as a content consultant for *The Gift*. The original concept of this story was his, and I have taken it and made my own version, with his gracious permission.

I would also like to acknowledge my writing colleagues, members of the Melbourne Romance Writers Guild, and Romance Writers of Australia, along with friends and family who have helped in my journey. I would have struggled to keep at this weird business of writing without their love, support, beta reading and handholding.